Tanner t...
Looking. Finding. Her.

Kathleen stood silhouetted in the doorway.

His chair thudded to the barroom floor in a teeth-jarring landing. No flight suit for her tonight. She'd changed.

Man, how she'd changed.

Leather pants molded themselves to her every curve. They sealed over her trimly muscled calves, up her thighs, to cup that bottom he'd been trying not to watch all day. Her hair flowed in a fiery curtain around her face, brushing the collar of her satin shirt. Scorching his eyes from across the smoky room.

She leaned over the bar to place her drink order. Her blouse inched up, baring a thin stripe of skin along her back.

Twelve years.

Twelve years hadn't dimmed the memory of how soft, how warm, that skin had felt beneath his hands....

Dear Reader,

Things are cooling down outside—at least here in the Northeast—but inside this month's six Silhouette Intimate Moments titles the heat is still on high. After too long an absence, bestselling author Dallas Schulze is back to complete her beloved miniseries A FAMILY CIRCLE with *Lovers and Other Strangers*. Shannon Deveraux has come home to Serenity and lost her heart to travelin' man Reece Morgan.

Our ROMANCING THE CROWN continuity is almost over, so join award winner Ingrid Weaver in *Under the King's Command*. I think you'll find Navy SEAL hero Sam Coburn irresistible. Ever-exciting Lindsay McKenna concludes her cross-line miniseries, MORGAN'S MERCENARIES: ULTIMATE RESCUE, with *Protecting His Own*. You'll be breathless from the first page to the last. Linda Castillo's *A Cry in the Night* features another of her "High Country Heroes," while relative newcomer Catherine Mann presents the second of her WINGMEN WARRIORS, in *Taking Cover*. Finally, welcome historical author Debra Lee Brown to the line with *On Thin Ice*, a romantic adventure set against an Alaskan background.

Enjoy them all, and come back again next month, when the roller-coaster ride of love and excitement continues right here in Silhouette Intimate Moments, home of the best romance reading around.

Yours,

Leslie J. Wainger
Executive Senior Editor

Please address questions and book requests to:
Silhouette Reader Service
U.S.: 3010 Walden Ave., P.O. Box 1325, Buffalo, NY 14269
Canadian: P.O. Box 609, Fort Erie, Ont. L2A 5X3

Taking Cover
CATHERINE MANN

INTIMATE MOMENTS™
Published by Silhouette Books
America's Publisher of Contemporary Romance

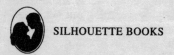

SILHOUETTE BOOKS

ISBN 0-373-27257-X

TAKING COVER

Visit Silhouette at www.eHarlequin.com

Printed in U.S.A.

Books by Catherine Mann

Silhouette Intimate Moments

Wedding at White Sands #1158
*Grayson's Surrender #1175
*Taking Cover #1187

*Wingmen Warriors

CATHERINE MANN

began her career writing romance at twelve and recently uncovered that first effort while cleaning out her grandmother's garage. After working for a small-town newspaper, teaching on the university level and serving as a theater school director, she has returned to her original dream of writing romance. Now an award-winning author, Catherine is especially pleased to add a nomination for the prestigious Maggie to her contest credits. Following her air force aviator husband around the United States with four children and a beagle in tow gives Catherine a wealth of experience from which to draw her plots. Catherine invites you to learn more about her work by visiting her Web site: http://catherinemann.com.

Endless thanks to my editor, Melissa Jeglinski,
and my agent, Barbara Collins Rosenberg.

Chapter 1

Captain Tanner "Bronco" Bennett gripped the cargo plane's stick and flew through hell, the underworld having risen to fire the night sky.

"Anything. Anywhere. Anytime," he chanted the combat mantra through locked teeth.

His C-17 squadron motto had gone into overtime today.

Neon-green tracer rounds arced over the jet's nose. Sweat sealed Tanner's helmet to his head. Adrenaline burned over him with more heat than any missile. He plowed ahead, chanted. Prayed.

Antiaircraft fire exploded into puffs of black smoke that momentarily masked the moon. The haze dispersed, leaving lethal flak glinting in the inky air. Shrapnel sprinkled the plane, *tink, tink, tinking* like hail on a tin roof.

Still, he flew, making no move for evasion or defense.

"Steady. Steady." He held his unwavering course, had to until the last paratrooper egressed out of the C-17 into the Eastern European forest below.

Off-loading those troopers into the drop zone was critical. Once they secured the nearby Sentavo airfield, supplies could be flown into the wartorn country by morning. Starving villagers burned out of their homes by renegade rebels needed relief. Now. The scattered uprisings of the prior summer had heated into an all-out civil war as the year's end approached.

Anything. Anywhere. Anytime. Tanner embraced it as more than a squadron motto. Those villagers might be just a mass of faceless humanity to other pilots, but to him each scared, hungry refugee had the same face—the face of his sister.

A flaming ball whipped past his windscreen.

Reality intruded explosively a few feet away. Near miss. Closer than the last. Time to haul out.

"Tag—" Tanner called over the headset to the loadmaster "—step it up back there. We gotta maneuver out of this crap. In case you haven't noticed, old man, they're shooting at us."

"Got it, Bronco," the loadmaster growled. "Our guys are piling out of this flying coffin as fast as they can."

"Start pushing. Just get 'em the hell off my airplane so we can maneuver." Urgency pulsed through Tanner, buzzed through the cockpit.

His hand clenched around the stick. No steering yoke for this new sleek cargo plane. And it damned well needed to perform up to its state of the art standards today.

He darted a glance at the sweat-soaked aircraft commander beside him. "Hey, Lancelot, how's it look left? Is there a way out on your side?"

Major Lance "Lancelot" Sinclair twisted in his seat toward the window, then pivoted back. A foreboding scowl creased the perspiration filming his too-perfect features. "Bronco, my man, we can't go left. It's a wall of flames. What's it like on your side?"

Tanner leaned forward, peering at the stars beyond the side window for a hole in the sparking bursts. Bad. But not impossible. "Fairly clear over here. Scattered fire. Isolated pockets I can see to weave through."

"Roger that, you've got the jet."

"Roger, I have the jet." He gave the stick a barely perceptible shake to indicate his control of the aircraft. Not that he'd ever lost control. Lance hadn't been up to speed for weeks, a fact that left Tanner more often than not running the missions, regardless of his copilot status. "Tag, waiting for your all-clear call."

"You got it, big guy." Tag's voice crackled over the headset. "Everybody's off. The door's closing.... Clear to turn."

Anticipation cranked Tanner's adrenaline up another notch. "Hold on to your flight pay, boys, we're breaking right."

He yanked the stick, simultaneously ramming the rudder pedal with his boot. The aircraft banked, hard and fast.

Gravity punched him. G-forces anchored him to his seat, pulled, strained, as he threaded the lumbering aircraft through exploding volleys in the starlit sky.

Pull back, adjust, weave right. Almost there.

A familiar numbing sensation melted down his back like an ice cube. Ignore it. Focus and fly.

Debris rattled, sliding sideways. His checklist thunked to the floor. Lance's cookies, airmailed from his wife, skittered across the glowing control panel. Tanner dipped the nose, embers streaming past outside.

The chilling tingle in his back detonated into white-hot pain. His torso screamed for release from the five-point harness. The vise-like constraints had never been adequate to accommodate his height or bulk. Who would have thought a simple pinched nerve just below his shoulder could bring him down faster than a missile?

Doc O'Connell had even grounded him for it once before. He knew she would again in a heartbeat. If he let her.

Which he wouldn't.

Tanner pulled a sharp turn left. The plane howled past a shower of light. He hurt like hell, but considered it a small price to pay. By tomorrow night, women and children would be fed because of his efforts, and he liked to think that was a worthwhile reason to risk his life.

Yeah, saving babies was a damn fine motivator for going to work every day. No way was he watching from the sidelines.

He accepted that none of it would bring his sister back. But each life saved, each wrong righted, soothed balm over a raw wound he knew would never completely heal.

Tanner's hand twitched on the stick, and he jerked his thoughts back to the cockpit. He couldn't think of his sister now. Distractions in combat were deadly.

He reined his thoughts in tight, instincts and training offering him forgetfulness until he flew out over the Adriatic Sea.

"Feet wet, crew." Tanner announced their position over the water. "We're in the clear all the way to land in Germany."

He relaxed his grip on the stick, the rest of his body following suit. The blanket of adrenaline fell away, unveiling a pain ready to knife him with clean precision. Tanner swallowed back bile. "Take the jet, Lance."

"Bronco, you okay?"

"Take the jet," he barked. Fresh beads of sweat traced along his helmet.

Lance waggled the stick. "Roger, I have the aircraft."

Tanner's hand fell into his lap, his arm throbbing, nearly useless. He clicked through his options. He couldn't avoid seeing a flight surgeon after they landed. But if he waited until morning and locked in an appointment with his pal

Cutter, he would be fine. Doc Grayson "Cutter" Clark understood flyers.

No way was Tanner letting Dr. Kathleen O'Connell get her hands on him again—

He halted the thought in midair. Her hands on him? That was definitely an image he didn't need.

Keep it PC, bud. Remember those soft hands are attached to a professional woman and a damned sharp officer.

All presented in a petite package with an iron will that matched her fiery red hair.

Forget reining in those thoughts. Tanner dumped them from his mind like an off-loaded trooper.

Lance pressed the radio call button on the throttle. "Control, this is COHO two zero. Negative known damage. Thirty point zero of gas. Requesting a flight surgeon to meet us when we land."

"What the—" Tanner whipped sideways, wrenching up short as a spasm knocked him back in his seat. "What do you think you're doing?"

"Calling for a flight surgeon to meet us on the ground."

In front of the crew? Tanner winced. "No need, Lance. I'll be fine until I can get to the clinic."

"Yeah, right." Lance swiped his arm across his damp brow as he flew. "I've seen you like this before. You'll be lucky to walk once we land. You need a flight surgeon waiting, man. I'm not backing off the call."

"Listen, Lance—" Tanner wanted to argue, fully intended to bluster through, but the spasm kinked like an overwound child's toy ready to snap.

He couldn't afford to be grounded from flying again, not now. He only had six weeks left until he returned to the states to begin his rescheduled upgrade from copilot to aircraft commander. Not only could he lose his slot, but he would also lose six weeks of flying time, of making a difference.

Why the hell couldn't he and O'Connell have pulled different rotations, leaving her back at Charleston Air Force Base with her perfectly annotated regulation book and haughty cat eyes?

The strain of ignoring the stabbing ache drizzled perspiration down Tanner's spine, plastering his flight suit to his skin. Options dwindled with each pang.

"Fine." Tanner bit out the word through his clenched teeth. What a time for Lance to resume control. "Just have them find Cutter to meet us. He'll give me a break."

Not like Doc O'Connell. She probably hadn't colored outside the lines since kindergarten.

"And, Lance, tell Cutter to keep it low-key. Would ya? No big show." Rules be damned, he wasn't going to end a combat mission publicly whining about a backache. Cutter would understand. Tanner was counting on it.

If by-the-book O'Connell ran the show, he would be flying a desk by sunrise.

Waiting on the tarmac, Captain Kathleen O'Connell braced her boot on the ambulance bumper and tugged down the leg of her flight suit. Lights blinked in the distant night sky, announcing the approaching aircraft carrying her patient. Time to report for duty.

Snow glistened as it drifted past the stadium-style lights casting a bubble of illumination over the airfield. She shivered inside her leather jacket and longed for her sunny Charleston town house rather than the American airfield in Germany. White Christmases were highly overrated.

Of course, the holiday season hadn't held much allure for her since her divorce.

Thank God she had her job. She loved working flight medicine, but dreaded calls like this one. Familiar with Captain Bennett's medical and personal history, she knew what to expect.

The tussle of a lifetime was only a short taxi away.

Why couldn't he understand her job required keeping flyers healthy for future missions? *Her* mission demanded more than simply slapping a Band-Aid on a sucking chest wound so some jet jock could finish out the day with his ego intact.

Flyer egos.

Those required more technique in handling than a vasectomy in a cold room.

Maybe if she'd mastered the art of navigating aviator psyches earlier, her marriage might have lasted. Logic told her otherwise. Dual military careers were hell on even the most compatible of couples. She and Andrew hadn't stood a chance.

At least her parents had restrained themselves from spouting a litany of I-told-you-so. No big family secret, she sucked at relationships. Had from the cradle. Give her a textbook anyday. The dependability of science, rules, regimen offered her a lifelong security blanket against being hurt, and she was smart enough never to bare herself to anyone again.

Snowflakes caught and lingered on her eyelashes while she watched the jet circle then land. As the cargo plane taxied closer, battle damage revealed itself. Runway lights glared on half-dollar-size chinks and dings under the wings and along the tail. Like the edges of a twisted soda can, the ragged metal gaped.

Kathleen shuddered inside her jacket. She knew it was rare for larger combat planes to land without holes. That didn't lessen horrific images of the wreckage that one better-aimed scrap of flak could cause.

The C-17 taxied to a stop, parking beside a line of other planes, engines whining, silencing. Wind howled from the rolling hills, stirring a mist of snow from the evergreen forest surrounding the flight line.

With trained precision, crew chiefs swarmed the plane. A refueling truck squealed to halt. BDR—Battle Damage Repair—began their assessment and patching. All joined to prep the plane for its next mission while she patched the flyers.

The side hatch swung open, and Major Lance Sinclair bounded down the stairs to wait by the rail. Kathleen squinted, searching for her patient. What kind of shape would he be in? Did he need a stretcher?

The jet's doorway filled, sealing closed with a body as Tanner Bennett eased into view. Halogen lights glinted off his golden-blond hair, shadowed the bold lines of his bronzed jaw, his square chin and a twice-broken nose that somehow added a boyish appeal. He ducked and angled sideways to clear the hatch, had to for his leather clad shoulders to fit. Slowly he tackled the steps, his gloved hand gripping the rail for support.

Her breath hitched, a glacial gasp of air freezing a path to her lungs. At the oddest times his incredible size caught her unaware. She knew his vitals. Six feet five inches. Honed 238 pounds. Good cholesterol and blood pressure as of his last physical recorded in his chart stowed inside the ambulance.

Chart stats didn't come close to capturing the magnetism of the man.

He hadn't lost one bit of his brawny charm that had so enchanted fans during his four years on the Air Force Academy football team. Then when he'd chosen service to country over a seven-figure NFL income with the Broncos— Even she had to admire him for that.

Not that it would garner him special treatment from her.

Kathleen inhaled a deeper breath of chilly air to banish a warm hum in her stomach that she wanted to attribute to sleep deprivation and too much coffee.

Tanner shuffled over to her, pain etched in the corners

of his eyes, skin pulling tight around his bumpy nose. "Hey, Doc, what are you doing out so late?"

Sympathy pinched her right on her Hippocratic Oath. Poor guy had to be in agony. Of course, experience told her he wouldn't admit it.

She pushed away from the ambulance and pulled herself upright, still no more than eye level with his chest. Strands of hair blew across her face, making Kathleen wish she'd had the time for her more professional braid. She tipped her face up and met Tanner's sapphire eyes dead-on. "I'm taking care of flyers who won't take care of themselves."

He turned to look back at the plane, the twist stopping midway when he grimaced. He jerked a thumb over his shoulder, instead. "Is somebody hurt in there and I missed it?"

Yeah, she had a tough one on her hands tonight. "Your wit has me in stitches."

"I can tell."

"Trust me, hotshot, I'm laughing. Just not with you."

Getting him into the ambulance wouldn't be an easy sell. The man was as stubborn as he'd been at the Academy his freshman year, making her junior year as his training officer a challenge from start to finish. Twelve years hadn't changed them, only their jobs.

He began to turn. "Well, then, time for me to go—"

"Legal point of reference, my good Captain. Your body belongs to the United States Air Force. If you mistreat it, say you get sunburned—" a frigid gust of wind mocked her example, whipping her hair across her face "—if you can't perform your duties because of that recklessness, that's abuse of government property and grounds for a court martial."

"Geez, Doc. Do you keep the Uniform Code of Military Justice in your bathroom?"

"I happen to have a UCMJ travel edition right here."

She patted her zippered thigh pocket over her wallet and comb. "They issued them to all the good officers. Didn't you get yours?"

"I was probably stuck waiting in sick call that day." He raised his hand with a barely disguised wince and flicked aside her strand of hair.

At his touch against her cheek, his eyes widened, then narrowed, colliding with hers. Her face warmed with the curse of a redhead's blush, her skin firing even hotter on the exact spot his gloved fingers lingered. They'd never touched in any way except professionally since that one moment at the Academy....

His arm dropped to his side, and she exhaled a proverbial storm cloud into the cold air.

Kathleen backed up but not off. "Okay, hotshot, let's cut the chitchat. I'm cold and I'm tired. I've got rounds at six and sick call at seven. If I'm lucky, I'll manage three hours of sleep tonight. Let's get you into the ambulance and evaluated."

Tanner shifted right then left as if trying to look around the snow-dusted tarmac without turning. "Uh, where's Cutter?"

Kathleen bristled even though she wasn't in the least surprised. Tanner Bennett had been dodging appointments with her since she'd been stationed in Charleston a year ago. She wanted to attribute it to narrow-mindedness on his part about being treated by a female doctor, but she couldn't. He never objected to seeing the other female flight surgeon when Cutter wasn't available.

Only her. "Cutter's not on call. You'll have to make do with me. Now step up, and let's take a look at that back."

Ready to end the whole awkward incident, she reached to brace a hand between his shoulder blades. His muscles contracted beneath her fingers into a sheet of pure metal beneath leather.

He lurched away, flinched, then stared at her hand as if it were a torture device rather than an instrument for healing. Stepping aside, she gestured forward for him to precede her into the ambulance.

Tanner looked from her to the ambulance and back again. His eyes glittered like blue ice chips. "Not a chance."

"Pardon me?"

He skated a glance toward the crew bus where Lancelot and Tag waited, then ducked his head toward her. "No way." Tanner's voice filled the space between them with a low rumble. "I'm not climbing up there in front of everyone."

Each word puffed white to swirl between them, caressing their faces, linking them in an intimate haze.

Making her mad as hell.

"Am I supposed to pitch a tent in the middle of the tarmac and examine you out here? Or maybe you can haul yourself back inside the plane." She jabbed the space between them for emphasis—and to disperse those damned distracting breathy clouds. "Zip your ego in your helmet bag, hotshot, and use your brain. You need to be in the hospital, not standing out here freezing your boots off arguing with me."

He blanched. "The hospital?"

"If this is anything like last time—"

"Sorry, Doc. Not gonna happen." He pivoted slowly on his boot heels and lumbered toward his aircraft commander. "Hold on, Lance. I'm outa here."

Kathleen hooked her hands on her hips, a quiet rage simmering. "Bennett."

He ignored her.

Forget simmer, she was seething. "Bennett!"

Tanner held his right hand up and kept walking, if his shuffle-swagger could be called that. Frustration fired within her until she could almost feel the snowflakes steaming off her. Of all the thick-headed, arrogant stunts he'd—

Reluctant remorse encroached on her anger as she watched him struggle to board the bus.

But what could she do? She couldn't force him to seek treatment if he wouldn't admit to a problem. If she were a gambler, she would bet he hadn't even been the one to place the call for a flight surgeon in the first place.

Not that she was one to waste her money, time or energy on chance. Logic served better.

And more faithfully.

Kathleen clambered back inside the ambulance, her exasperation over his senseless testosterone dance igniting again. Logic told her Tanner Bennett wouldn't be able to roll out of bed by morning, and she was the flight surgeon on call until noon.

She slammed the ambulance door shut. Hard. With any luck the big lug would oversleep and someone else could treat his wounded back and tender ego.

Too late, Kathleen recalled she'd never believed in luck any more than chance.

Chapter 2

Two hundred twenty-three. Two hundred twenty-four.

Tanner counted the tan cinderblocks in the wall for the eleventh time that morning. Not much else to do since he couldn't move. His reach for the telephone fifteen minutes ago had left him cursing—and shaking.

He cut his gaze toward the clock, not risking more than half a head turn.

The time—8:30 a.m.—glowed from the clock in the dim room, the only other light slanting through a slight part in the curtains.

He sure hoped Cutter had gone on call at eight.

After waking and realizing he couldn't haul his sorry butt out of bed, Tanner had shouted for Lance in the next VOQ—Visiting Officer's Quarter. Their rooms, connected by a bath, were close enough that Lance would have heard had he been around. No luck. The telephone call to the clinic had been a last-ditch resort.

Where was Cutter? Didn't the guy ever check his messages?

Tanner hiked the polyester bedspread over his bare chest. Even the small movement hurt like a son of a gun. How long before it let up? Lying around left him with too much time to think. He preferred action, needed to be back out on the flight line.

The flight line.

Images of Kathleen O'Connell looking mad enough to chew rivets blindsided Tanner when he didn't have any chance or the physical capability of ducking.

Had he actually touched her?

Awash in postbattle adrenaline, he'd found her fire stirred his, as well. With a will of its own, his hand had swiped that silky strand of hair away from her face.

Surely the impulse was only combat aftermath, emotions running high. He didn't think of her that way.

But he had before.

Tanner's head dug back in his pillow as if he might somehow dodge memories he couldn't suppress. His first day at the Air Force Academy, he'd seen Kathleen walking across the parade ground, vibrant, toned and radiating a confidence that had found an answer within him. Every hormone in his eighteen-year-old body had roared to life.

Until he'd noticed she wore a beret with her uniform, the distinguishing symbol of an upperclassman.

Relationships between upperclassmen and freshmen-doolies were forbidden. Grounds for expulsion. And he wasn't throwing away his career for anyone.

Maybe later, he'd thought....

Later she'd become his training officer and his own personal ticket to hell. Training officers were universally resented by the doolies they hammered into Academy material.

Tanner had stuffed his hormones into his footlocker and concentrated on getting through his freshman year.

Becoming a pilot meant everything to him, and he wouldn't risk it.

Something that hadn't changed in twelve years.

Footsteps echoed in the hall. Closer. With a light tread that launched a wave of foreboding in Tanner. Unless Cutter had lost about seventy pounds and developed a decided glide to his walk, those footsteps didn't belong to him.

Two quick raps sounded on the door.

Foreboding death-spiraled into certainty. "Yeah. Come in."

The door swung wide, revealing Kathleen O'Connell.

His libido crashed and burned. And damn, but it was one hell of a plunge.

She lounged against the door frame, wearing lime-green scrubs, instead of her regular forest-green flight suit. Cotton hugged gentle curves her bulky uniform usually disguised. Her leather flight jacket hung loose as she hooked a hand on one shapely hip. "Well, good morning, hotshot. How's the back?"

Did she have to sound so chipper, look so hot? Small but fit, her tight body tugged his gaze into a slow glide he didn't have the reserves to resist. She came by those taut muscles honestly. More than once over the past year, the two of them had pitted themselves against each other doing sit-ups during physical training.

A stethoscope dangled around her neck, nestling between breasts that were as understated and damned irresistible as the rest of her. Apparently, the attraction hadn't left after all, only slipping out of formation while waiting to rejoin without warning.

Time to pull out the old footlocker and replace the padlock on his hormones.

A strange thought taunted. Could their arguments have been a way of rechanneling his lust? *Damn it all.* "Figures you would be a morning person."

Kathleen's wicked smile creased her blue cat eyes. "And with next to no sleep. Imagine that? Come on. Hop up and let's go to breakfast. What? Having a little trouble moving are we? Hmmm." She pressed a slim finger against her pursed lips. "Guess that's to be expected when someone ignores his doctor's advice. Word around the water cooler has it that you even skipped out on your last chiropractor appointment."

Tanner tapped precious energy reserves to tuck his good arm behind his head casually. "What are you gonna do, bludgeon me with your pocket edition UCMJ manual?"

"My, we're cranky today. Just think, you could have been languishing in a Demerol daze as we speak. But, nope. You had to play the tough guy."

"Doc, your bedside manner sucks."

Her smile tightened. "Chalk it up to sleep deprivation. Two house calls in less than twelve hours qualifies as more TLC than you're issued, soldier. In the civilian world I could have financed a summer home with the overtime you're demanding."

He might as well have been a freshman again, pumping push-ups over some infraction. She wasn't going to cut him any slack. "And you've opted to take it out of my hide, instead."

"Sounds like a plan to me." She smoothed her already immaculate hair. No sneaky strands slipping loose today, her red mane was swept back into her traditional French braid with the short tail secured under.

Tanner frowned. When had he started noticing how she styled her hair? She'd kept it cropped at the Academy, he remembered that much. Until he'd seen it loose on the flight line, he hadn't given much thought to its longer length hidden inside that braid.

Now he couldn't think of anything but wild red strands wind-whipped around her composed face.

Kathleen uncrossed her feet and flicked on the overhead light. "While the conversation is positively stimulating, I've got other patients to see. Ones who want to get well. Sit up and let's take a look."

"Might as well get it over with." Contracting his stomach muscles toppled a domino effect to his back that left Tanner straining not to whimper like a kid. And now he couldn't get his arm from behind his head.

"Bennett?" Compassion darkened her blue eyes. "You can't sit up, can you?"

He offered silence and no movement as his answer, all the concession his pride would allow. As much as he wanted to snap at her, he couldn't. His innate sense of fair play insisted he'd brought this on himself.

"Time to call for a stretcher." She turned on her heel, her tennis shoes squeaking against the tile.

"No!" Tanner arched up. And promptly fell back, his hoarse groan echoing.

Kathleen closed the space to the bed in three quick steps. "Deep breaths. Look at me, Bennett. Focus and breathe until it passes. Try to relax or you'll make it worse. No need to fight everything in this world, hotshot. There you go, in and out. Breathe."

Her voice talked him down, like flying by instinct when the instruments were shot and he couldn't see beyond the clouds. He locked on the timbre of her throaty voice and let it work through the fog of agony.

"Better?"

"Yes." He offered the clipped word rather than risk even a nod.

She braced her hand on the headboard and sighed. "I'm not going to be able to talk you into a stretcher, am I?"

"No."

"Even if I tell you walking out of here could delay your recovery?"

Man, she fought dirty. Lose air time or lose face. Hell or Hades. Same thing.

Almost.

He could grit his way through recovery. Regaining face…

Tanner opened his eyes, wasn't sure when he'd closed them, and allowed himself to gaze straight up into her blue eyes, eyes as clear as an ocean sky. "I can't roll out of here on a stretcher, Doc. I have to fly with these guys again. Trust in the air is everything, could make the difference in a split decision that costs somebody's life." Frustration snapped his restraint. "O'Connell, come on.…"

"Okay."

Shock immobilized him as much as his back. "What?"

"If we can haul you out of this bed, and if you can put one foot in front of the other, I'll allow you to walk out of here under your own power. No doubt that flyer ego can manage more miracles than modern medicine."

He searched for sarcasm in her words, in her eyes.

Better not look at her eyes.

Back to her voice. Not a note of sarcasm, just resigned logic.

"Thank you." Gratitude mixed with respect. He understood how difficult backing down could be.

Then he realized he owed her, an uncomfortable thought at best. He would have shrugged it off if he could lift his shoulders. He joked instead, a safe barrier against free-falling into her eyes. "Do you think we could act like I've got some shrapnel in my butt? It would make for better stories around the Officer's Club."

Her laugh, low, throaty and her one unreserved trait, filled his senses. Like a drag of one hundred percent oxygen from his face mask, it invigorated him, left him slightly dizzy.

She chuckled again, dipping her head until he could see

every tuck of her braid. Each perfectly spaced weave called to his fingers. He wanted to untwine that restrained fire until it poured over his hands.

Silken fire. He wanted it with a pulsing force that threatened stirrings within him farther south.

And he didn't have anything more than a thin bedspread between his naked body and total exposure.

Kathleen gazed down at the 238 pounds of bare-chested man under the rose-colored spread and wondered if she would ever understand Tanner Bennett. Or her own reaction to him.

It went against every principle ingrained in her to let him walk out under his own compromised power. She told herself it was part of treating the ego as well as the man. Keeping the big picture in mind. A really big picture.

But she knew that wasn't her real reason.

She kept remembering the Academy doolie. She'd given him hell as his training officer. No sports jock would warrant special treatment from her, just as she accepted no special treatment for being a woman.

He'd never caved.

Even if she didn't agree with his tactics, she had to admire his warrior spirit. To crush that would be to the detriment of the Air Force.

So her decision was for the Air Force. Right? Not because he looked up at her with those sapphire eyes in which mingled determination and boyish charm.

She extended her hand. "Maybe you can try sitting now."

"Sure." He waved away her hand and inched up on his elbows, paling to match the bleached sheets.

"If you can."

"Of course I can."

More spirit than sense.

"Come on, Bennett. You need help getting up. There's

nothing wrong with admitting it's too hard. Here, let me give you a hand.'' She reached for his arm.

He pressed back into his pillow. ''Doc!''

''What?''

Tanner imprisoned her wrist. ''I don't think you want to go there.''

''Huh?''

''I don't have anything on.''

His bare chest suddenly looked all the more exposed, sporting nothing more than his dog tags and a medal nestled in a dusting of golden hair.

''Nothing?'' Her wrist screamed with awareness of skin-to-skin contact.

'''Fraid not.''

Kathleen tugged her arm free and smoothed her braid, willing her composure to follow suit. ''Oh. Well, I'm a doctor, your doctor. It's nothing I haven't seen before in your flight physical.''

''Not like this you haven't.''

Her hand paused along the back of her head. ''Pardon me?''

''Doc. I'm a man. It's morning.''

She could feel the color drain from her face until she, as well, no doubt now matched the sheets. ''Oh.''

''Yeah, oh.''

Kathleen looked at the television, the minifridge, the cinderblock walls, anything to keep her gaze from gravitating to where it had no business going. Finally she simply spun on her heel before gravity had its way and her gaze fell straight down.

''Okay, Bennett. Let's find you some sweats.'' She faced the dresser, rather than the man with a chest as broad as one. ''Which drawer?''

''Top shelf of the closet.''

Kathleen yanked open the wardrobe door. The musky

scent of leather and cedar wafted straight out and into her before she could untangle her thoughts enough to ignore it. His flight suit and jacket dangled from a hook inside the door like a ghostly shadow of the man. Her hand drifted to caress the butter-soft jacket, well-worn and carrying perhaps the slightest hint of his warmth.

What was it about Tanner Bennett? With any other flyer, she would have shrugged the whole thing off while helping him into his boxers.

Not with Bennett. All she could think about was his big, naked body under that blanket, and her lack of professionalism infuriated her.

She couldn't have thoughts like this.

Yanking her hand away, she arched up on her toes to reach, searching by touch since she couldn't see into the top shelf. She would pull it together, damn it, get him dressed and turn his case over to Cutter.

And if Cutter let Tanner slide?

Her hands hesitated in their quest. What if Tanner played the friendship card, enabling him to plow back out into combat before he was ready? Her fingers clutched a pair of sweatpants.

Flashes of the battle damage from Tanner's aircraft flashed through her mind—twisted metal. Her medical as well as safety training had stockpiled too many graphic images of wreckage.

Her ex-husband had expected strings pulled. Being married to a flight surgeon entitled him to special treatment, didn't it? Her ex had played that trump card with one of her workmates, and it had almost cost him his life. Thank God, he'd flown an ejection-seat aircraft.

Kathleen knew what she had to do. She understood her job, and no hormonal insanity on her part would interfere with performing her duty for the flyer entrusted into her care.

She yanked free a pair of oversize gray sweatpants and shook them out in front of her as she spun to face Tanner. ''Okay, hotshot. Let's get you suited up.''

One hundred forty-two.

There were one hundred forty-two ceiling tiles in his sparse infirmary room. Tanner squinted. Or were there a hundred forty-three? The walls wobbled through his mellow haze of drugs.

Not mellow enough to iron out his irritation.

Before, in his VOQ room, Kathleen O'Connell had shed her compassion like unwanted cargo. With cool professionalism she'd helped him dress beneath the privacy of the blanket. He might as well have been a eunuch for all the effect the awkward situation had on her.

Then she'd grounded his sorry, sweatpants-clad butt and parked him in the infirmary—indefinitely. If he had to watch one more minute of the Armed Forces Television Services, his head would explode.

He tried not to think about his crew flying without him. What if the next mission carried the golden BB, the missile that took them down when he wasn't there? How the hell would he live with wondering if he could have prevented it? Not more than a couple of hours ago, the television had announced a C-17 crash out in California. If something like that could happen on a routine mission…

The television show changed to a service announcement full of holiday cheer. ''Jingle Bells'' or maybe ''Silver Bells'' swelled into the room. His twin sister had loved carols—

Tanner silenced the television with a thumb jab to the remote.

Definitely too much time to think.

Losing a family member sucked no matter what. Losing

that person during the holidays carried an extra burden. The anniversary of her death never slid by without notice.

Tara had been Christmas shopping at the mall, for crying out loud. How could he ever forget that? They'd always gone gift hunting together in the past since his job had been to look out for her.

That Christmas he'd been at the Academy.

And some slime in search of a lone female had lurked, waiting in the back seat of Tara's car. The bastard had kidnapped her. Beaten her. Raped her. Then thrown her unconscious body into a snowbank where she'd died. Alone.

Tanner flung aside the remote, welcoming the stab of pain from the violent gesture. Damn drugs had turned him morbid, lowered his defenses until he couldn't halt the flood of memories.

The cops had found Tara's car later, her packages still in the trunk. She'd bought her twin brother a St. Joseph's medal.

Tanner gripped the silver disk around his neck and steadied his breathing. He'd learned a bitter lesson that Christmas—never, never leave your wingman.

A solid knock on the door pulled Tanner back to the present, and he embraced the distraction. He wouldn't have even minded seeing his hard-hearted doctor. "Yeah. Come in."

The door swung open and Major Grayson "Cutter" Clark strode through, wearing a flight suit and a cocky grin. "Hey, pal. Check out the nifty nightie they issued you."

Tanner shifted in the cotton hospital gown. Damn thing didn't fit right anyway. "About time you decided to drop in. Where were you when I needed you, bud?"

"Sorry, but I wasn't on call. Only just now heard the news over at the clinic. I thought for sure O'Connell would have you in traction. Too bad. I had the big piñata joke all ready to go.''

Tanner snorted, then winced. He could always count on crew dog camaraderie to lighten his mood. ''Don't make me laugh.''

''Builds character.'' Cutter snagged the clipboard from the foot of Tanner's bed. He flipped pages. ''Hmmm. Good stuff she's got you on. Demerol, no less. You must have wrecked yourself to be hurting through all this.''

Tanner grunted. ''A day off my feet and I'll be fine.''

''Then you and O'Connell can tangle it up again.''

Thoughts of her dressing him slid right through that Demerol haze. ''What do you mean?''

''Your set-to on the flight line last night is all the talk around the briefing room.''

''Great.''

Cutter sank into a chair, hooked his boot over one knee and dropped the chart to rest on his leg. ''Don't get your boxers in a twist. Nobody expected anything different from the two of you when O'Connell showed.''

''What do you mean?''

A brow shot right toward Cutter's dark hairline. ''You're yanking my chain, right? Your arguments are legendary. Tag once suggested tying you two together, gladiator-style, and just tossing you into the arena to have it out. Two walk in. One walks out. Colonel Dawson giving that signature thumbs-up and thumbs-down of his.''

Laughter stirred in Tanner's chest, begging to be set free even though he knew it would drop-kick him right between the shoulder blades.

''Stop! No more jokes.'' A chuckle sneaked through anyway, punting his muscles as predicted until he groaned. ''Did she send you in here to torture me so I would laugh myself into traction?''

"Sorry." Cutter smirked as he resumed flipping chart pages.

Tanner sagged back on his pillow. The gladiator image began to take on an odd fantasy appeal in his drug-impaired mind. At least the drugs offered a convenient excuse. Damn, but Kathleen would have made a magnificent warrior goddess. That woman never needed anyone.

The ultimate loner. Tanner's muscles tightened in response. That loner mind-set proved a threat to the crew mentality essential to his Air Force doctrine. The Air Force, the team spirit, was everything to him.

Never leave your wingman.

Tanner raised the bed higher, ignoring even thoughts of discomfort. "Can't you do something about this? Get me outa here and back in action with my crew. Man, you're one of us. You have to know how crazy this is making me."

While all flight surgeons specialized in treating flyers and their families, a handful of those doctors were also flyers themselves. Cutter being one of the few. Tanner couldn't help but hope that might nudge the scales in his favor. "Well?"

"Sorry. Can't help you, my friend. I've seen your chart. I know your history. O'Connell's dead-on with her diagnosis, and there's no mistaking her notations."

"Figures I lucked into the one doctor on the planet with perfect penmanship." Time to invest in an Armed Forces Television schedule.

"Yeah, you are lucky. Lucky she didn't string you up like a piñata. We flight docs don't take well to having our orders disregarded. If I were you, pal, I would start thinking up an apology."

"The piñata sounds less painful." Deep down, he knew he owed her better than that. She'd kept him in the game years ago when he'd wanted to quit.

"Kick back, pal. Take care of yourself. You were only weeks away from leaving your crew, anyway. You should be up to speed in time to upgrade."

Should be. The words didn't comfort Tanner any more than the Demerol.

What if the grounding became permanent? What would he do without his wings? His mother swore his first word had been plane. While other kids drew puppies and trees, he'd already perfected his own depiction of Captain Happy Plane. "Six weeks is a long time in a war. If something happens and I'm not there…"

Cutter closed the chart. "I hear you, and I understand what you're feeling. But there's nothing I can do."

Last down and his field goal had fallen short. Tanner scrambled to salvage what he could for the rest of his team. "Look out for Lance. Okay? Make sure he gets a solid copilot."

Cutter stilled. "Is there something I should know about?"

"Nothing specific. He's just not…up to speed. He and Julia are having trouble again. Deployments and stress messing with another Air Force marriage—" Tanner stopped short. Hell of a thing to say to a guy only weeks away from the altar. "Oh, hey, sorry, bud."

"No sweat. Lori and I know what we're up against. Nobody said Air Force life was easy on the family. It's going to be work." A full-out smile creased all the way to his eyes. "She's worth it."

Tanner gave his friend an answering smile. "Congratulations."

Cutter nodded, then thunked the bed rail with Tanner's chart. "Now get well. Lori'll kill me if my best man falls on his face halfway through the ceremony. Look on the bright side. You won't have to haul yourself across the

Atlantic on a civilian flight to make the wedding. You can head back on the tanker with me next week.''

''Great. Nothing like sitting in the back seat.'' Tanner's hands already itched to be in control.

From the day he'd drawn that first airplane, he'd known he would be a pilot. Forget he was a poor kid working two after-school jobs to help support his single mom and twin sister. Course set, he'd achieved his goals, Air Force Academy, pilot. He'd never wavered in his focus. Except for the night he'd heard his sister died.

The night he'd kissed Kathleen O'Connell.

Chapter 3

Kathleen hovered in the doorway of Tanner's hospital room, unable to draw her gaze away from the man who had filled her thoughts too often that morning. Flat on his back, he took up the whole bed. A dimple flashed in his unshaven jaw as he laughed with Cutter. Tanner's exuberance for life hadn't dimmed, even after a downing injury and a hefty shot of Demerol.

She watched the two men talk with their hands, typical flyer "talk," their hands flying tandem aerial maneuvers.

Her guard perilously shaky of late, she envied them their camaraderie, the easy exchange apparent in most flyers. She knew better than to blame their exclusion on her being a woman. Years of growing up the misfit in her family had left her with the assurance she simply didn't get it. Relationships. Her ex had confirmed the conclusion through his lawyer.

So she stood alone in the hospital doorway, feeling too damn much like the little girl who perched in trees with a book about bugs. All the while peering down at a blanket full of her sisters and their friends having a tea party picnic.

Tanner's laughter rumbled out into the hall. Teams and partnerships bemused her. She understood in theory, but in practice…she couldn't make it work. The flyers respected her yet didn't include her. Her nickname—or lack of one—being a prime example.

Flight surgeons were sometimes given honorary call signs, like Grayson "Cutter" Clark or Monica "Hippocrates" Hyatt. Kathleen was just "Doc," the generic appellation afforded any doctor who hadn't received the distinction of a naming party.

Not that she wanted to change herself just to be a part of some flyers' club. Flying solo offered fewer risks.

Before she'd helped Tanner into his clothes, she'd regained her objectivity, barely. She wouldn't let her guard further crumble, regardless of how cute he looked in that incongruous hospital gown.

Kathleen rapped two knuckles on the door just beneath a miniature Christmas wreath. "Hello, boys." She gestured to their flying palms. "Shooting down your watches with your hands again?"

Tanner started, looking up at Kathleen in the doorway. A painful twinge worked its way through the Demerol, but he resisted the urge to wince.

Her half smile, wry though it was, shook his focus. His hands stopped aerial maneuvers and landed on the bed. "Hi, Doc."

Cutter glanced from one to the other, his brows pleating. "Did it just get chilly in here? Time for me to punch out." He passed the chart to Kathleen on his way to the door. "I'll check in with you both later."

Her smile faded as Cutter left. Disappointment nipped Tanner. Too much.

He wanted to bring that smile back. What a crazy

thought. Must be the drugs again. Regardless, Cutter was right. Kathleen—

Kathleen?

Tanner frowned, and refocused his thoughts. *O'Connell* deserved an apology. "I'm sorry about last night."

"What?" Still no smile in sight, not a surprise since her face looked frozen with shock.

Tanner inched up. "I shouldn't have given you hell on the flight line. It's not your fault my back's out. Are there some torturous tests you want to run so I can pay my penance?"

Her gaze skittered away, and she flipped through his chart, avoiding his eyes. "Just follow the recovery plan."

"I intend to be a model patient."

"Music to my ears."

"The sooner this is over, the sooner I can get back on a crew. I don't expect you to understand, Doc."

Her head snapped up. The diamond glint in her eyes could have cut glass. "Why not, hotshot?"

"Hey, I'm trying to apologize here." He raised his hands in mock surrender. What had he done this time? Not that either of them ever needed much of a reason to argue. "The least you could do is be gracious."

Hugging the chart like a shield, she pulled a tight smile again. "Pardon me. Must be something else this 'Doc' didn't learn in medical school. Apology accepted."

"Great."

"Thanks."

"Fine!"

A cleared throat sounded from the hall just before Lt. Col. Zach Dawson knocked on the open door with exaggerated precision.

The Squadron Commander. The boss. Tanner wondered if a plague of locusts might be next, because his day couldn't get much worse.

Lt. Col. Dawson ducked inside. "Hey, you two want to fire it up some more? I don't think they heard you in Switzerland."

Kathleen popped to attention. "Good afternoon, Colonel."

Tanner sat as straight as he could, mentally cursing the hospital gown. "Colonel."

"Captains." The Squadron Commander nodded. His Texas twang echoed in the silent room as he ambled to a stop at the foot of Tanner's bed. "So, Doc, when're you going to cut my guy here loose?"

"Overnight in the infirmary should have him back on his feet, ready for desk duty within twenty-four hours. Two weeks on muscle relaxants. I'll reevaluate then, but he'll likely be on flying status again within four weeks. As long as he keeps up with his chiropractor appointments, there shouldn't be a repeat."

The commander shot her a thumbs-up. "That works."

Tanner studied his boss for signs of impatience over the lost air time and found none. No gripes or pressure to get him into action? Unusual for Dawson. "Thanks for stopping by, sir."

"Just checking on one of my men. And having O'Connell here saves me arranging a meeting later." The commander plucked a metal chair from the corner and straddled it, his arms resting along the back. "Doc, how about pull up a seat and let's chat."

Eyes wary, Kathleen lowered herself to the recliner by Tanner's bed. "Yes, sir?"

The commander scrubbed a hand along his close-shorn hair, taking his sweet Texas time. "See, I've got this morale problem in my squadron, and that concerns me."

Tanner frowned, sweeping a hand over his face to clear away the Demerol fog. "Sir?"

"Morale is the glue that bonds a unit. And when there's

a problem in that department, say infighting among my officers, especially in front of my enlisted folks, it needs to be addressed.''

Their flight line incident. Cutter had said it was the story of the day, apparently for everyone. Icy prickles started up Tanner's back that had nothing to do with pinched nerves.

The commander pinned Tanner with his deceptively easygoing stare. ''Bennett, what's the first thing I do when I've got dissenting fliers who need to establish camaraderie?''

Those icy prickles turned into a veritable shower. He knew where this was headed, and it didn't bode well for either of them.

''Well, Captain?''

Tanner voiced the inevitable. ''You send them TDY as a group.''

Dawson shot him a thumbs-up worthy of Caesar at gladiator games. ''Exactly. A little temporary duty together is just the ticket.''

Kathleen's light gasp tugged Tanner's gaze. Every last drop of color drained from her already pale face until freckles he'd never noticed popped along her pert nose.

Lt. Col. Dawson continued as if Kathleen's telling gasp hadn't slipped free. ''Get away from the rest of the squadron. Work together. Ride together. Eat together. Play together. Spend every waking hour with each other until things settle out.''

It wasn't the waking hours that worried Tanner. ''And what will be our official function during this TDY?''

''I'm sending you two to check out a C-17 accident. Put all that money spent sending you to safety school to good use.''

''Crash? I heard something about one on the news earlier. No details released though.'' Tanner shed his own concerns, nothing in comparison to a crash in their small and tight flyer community. Any accident was personal. "Did anyone die?"

"No fatalities."

Tanner swallowed a relief stronger than the meds pumping through him.

"It's a test crew," the commander continued. "Only minor injuries to the loadmaster. Baker's crew, Daniel Baker."

"Crusty's crew?" Tanner exchanged a quick look with Kathleen.

The commander frowned. "Problem?"

Kathleen straightened. "We all attended the Academy together. But no, sir, that shouldn't be a problem."

Tanner wished he could be as certain. The last thing he wanted was to write up a fellow flyer—a friend.

Folding his arms over his chest, Tanner clenched his jaw shut before he said something reckless. Why couldn't he have kept his mouth closed on the runway the night before?

The commander cleared his throat and resumed the brief. "It happened last night while you were airborne. The crew was running a test mission, dropping a two-pack of Humvees. The drop went bad and ripped the ramp right off the airplane. A lesser crew would have bought it."

Or a crew that was off its stride from losing a team member.

Dawson canted forward. "So I've volunteered you two to head on over to the site and join the investigation team. See if you can figure out what went wrong. Perfect timing with Bennett being grounded for a month. You can even spend Christmas together. I call that downright serendipitous."

Serendipity stunk. The flicker of horror on Kathleen's face told him her feelings flew the same path.

But the deed was done. The best he could hope for was a good locale, one of the bases where they could lose them-

selves in recreation after hours. Away from each other.
"And where was this test mission being flown?"

"At Edwards Air Force Base."

In the middle of the California desert. Tanner slumped
back on his pillow.

Lt. Col. Dawson pushed up from his chair and swung it
back against the wall. A steely warning flashed in his silver
eyes, belying his laid-back attitude. "Lighten up, Captains.
This will make for great reading in your performance reports. If memory serves, and I believe it does, O'Connell's
got a major's board coming up. Soon, right, O'Connell?"

Kathleen's jaw flexed before she nodded.

"Thought so. This accident should be a snap to wrap up.
Investigations can speed right along if the team's working
together." Dawson's head cocked to the side. "Or they can
drag on for weeks. Hear that, Bennett? Weeks. I sure would
hate to reschedule your upgrade slot. Again."

Tanner pulled a weak smile. "Me, too, sir."

"Good enough, then. I've already submitted the paperwork for your tickets back to the states. Be packed and
ready by tomorrow night." He dropped a hand on each of
their shoulders. "Captains, consider yourselves tied to each
others' side for the next month."

The commander nodded and loped out of the room,
shooting them both a final thumbs-up just before the door
eased closed. How appropriate, since Kathleen looked as if
she wanted to feed him to the lions.

Two walk in. One walks out.

Diplomacy, diplomacy, diplomacy, Kathleen mentally
chanted with each rapid stride through the Frankfurt airport,
Tanner shadowing her. Less controversy translated into a
speedier resolution to the accident investigation.

She wasn't risking another embarrassing "conference"
with Lt. Col. Dawson, especially so close to her major's

board. At least she could use this investigation to prove once and for all she could keep work separate from her personal life.

Focus on facts, not emotions. Her carry-on bag weighed heavily on her shoulder, packed full of faxed files for the case. Reviewing them on the plane would get her that much closer to finishing. And offer a good distraction from the insane attraction she couldn't avoid any more than Tanner's bobbing shadow, which was swallowing hers as they charged down the airport thoroughfare.

Kathleen wove through the international throng, foreign languages bombarding her from all sides. Turning sideways, she edged past a cluster of Goth teens with alabaster faces and black lips. Tanner's arm shot ahead protectively as he put his body between Kathleen and the mass of opaque fabric and pierced body parts.

Her independent nature, combined with the inclination to argue, trickled whispers of irritation through her. She squelched the urge to bristle. In the interest of diplomacy and being polite, she angled a grateful glance over her shoulder. "Thanks."

"No problem," said her ever-present shadow.

Sure their travel plans were identical, but she hadn't expected him to stick so close to her. Of course, an international airport wasn't the safest place for military personnel, thus her decision to fly in civilian clothes. Not that anyone would mess with her personal bodyguard. He sidestepped a group of airline pilots and attendants, French perhaps, given their jumbled exchange.

Tanner's bout with a pinched nerve hadn't slowed him one bit. He'd rejected all medication but a mild muscle relaxer. A dose of Flexeril and he'd bounded out of bed to report for duty.

He definitely looked fit now.

She would have expected civilian clothes to steal some

of Tanner's charisma. Her ex had seemed to diminish when he shed his flight suit, leaving something of himself behind and making her wonder how much of the man was real.

Not the case with Tanner. The man made the flight suit. Or the sports jacket in this case. His dark blue coat stretched over broad shoulders along with a white button-down left open at the collar. Neatly creased Dockers completed the conservative look. The clothes could have belonged to any number of traveling businessmen filing past in the crowded terminal.

The man, however, was one of a kind.

Kathleen plowed forward—smack into a group of boys. The wind knocked out of her, she gasped for breath as she righted her footing. Her vision cleared, and she assessed the wall of bodies, older teenagers, carrying oversize military issue bags and looking scared. New recruits from the states. "Sorry, soldiers."

"No problem, ma'am," one of the recruits answered.

Tanner gripped her shoulders, guiding her out of the traffic flow until she leaned back against a display window outside an airport gift shop. "You okay?"

"I'm fine."

His brow furrowed. "You're sure?"

"Yes! I'm sure! No need to make a big deal over getting the wind knocked out of me." She smoothed her hands down simple blue cotton pants, suddenly feeling underdressed.

Her hands hesitated midstroke. Why should she care about her appearance? Even if she were interested in impressing a man, it certainly wouldn't be with her wardrobe. She left those ploys to her mother and her sisters. She felt confident in her femininity, so much so she didn't need pumps and push-up bras to bolster her morale.

After years of trying to wrangle a spot in line with her perfect sisters, Kathleen had learned not to compete with their weapons. Better to make her own statement, in her own way, on her own terms.

Lights glistened off Tanner's golden-blond hair, caressed his freshly shaven jaw as he gazed down at her, genuine concern in his eyes. Kathleen fidgeted with her pearl stud earring.

Okay, maybe she wouldn't have minded a little lip gloss. She tried to scoot aside. "I'm fine. Really."

Warm and heavy, his hands hesitated on her shoulders before sliding away in a tingling trail down her arms.

Distance. She needed a moment to recoup with him out of her personal space. "How about you go on ahead to our gate and I'll meet you there later?"

"I'm not in any hurry."

"No, really." Why couldn't she shake him? "I want to pick up some postcards for my family."

"Go ahead. I'll wait."

"You're kidding, right? Don't men hate standing around while women shop?"

"Not this one." Tanner's muscled arms folded over his chest.

"Okay, Bennett, what's up?"

"What do you mean?"

"You haven't let me go anywhere alone except the bathroom since we stepped out of the cab."

He shuffled, paused to look around, then faced her with narrowed eyes. "An international airport is a dangerous place for any military person. Might as well paint a bull's-eye on our backs for terrorists."

Reinforcing Tanner's warning, cops lined the walls, nothing unusual for the airport, but it still gave Kathleen pause even understanding the risks. Armed police forces in green uniforms and jackboots carried machine guns over their shoulder. Guns with the paint worn off as if they'd been used. Often.

"You've been protecting me from unknown terrorists?" She couldn't decide whether to be irritated, amused…or oddly touched.

He shrugged, almost masking a slight wince. The movement knocked his jacket askew, leaving his left lapel flipped up. She knew she should just tell him.

Should.

Instead, her hand crept up and smoothed the coarse, warm fabric. A slow swallow slid down his neck. "Kathleen…?"

"Your, uh, lapel."

"Yeah, right. Thanks."

She resented like hell the nervous twitters buzzing through her. "It's just strange seeing you like this, I mean not in a flight suit."

Tanner ran a finger along his shirt collar. "Gotta admit, I prefer the bag myself. But this is safer."

"Safer? Ah, a businessman disguise. I guess I never thought about it in that much detail."

"Too many deployments for me not to think about it. I can't do much about the haircut, but I make changes where I can." His palm fell to rest over her fingers that still gripped his jacket.

Heat crawled up Kathleen's face. *Oh, God.* Had she really left her hand there all that time? "Thanks for worrying. But I'll be fine."

He didn't move.

"I don't need a baby-sitter." She yanked her hand from beneath his, her wrist still tingling from a touch no longer there.

Tanner eyed a passing couple in trench coats. Muscles rippled with tension beneath his coat until the couple passed—a baby gurgling and waving from the man's backpack kiddie seat. Kathleen sagged against the wall with relief, then stiffened.

Damn! Now he had her doing it.

Protectiveness was all well and good, but this guy was becoming downright smothering. Or was that because his large body closed off the rest of the world from view until she only saw miles of chest and eyes so blue they could hypnotize?

Snap out if it! she chastised herself. ''Just because I don't obsess doesn't mean I'm clueless about airport security overseas. It's not like I'm wearing my uniform.''

He snapped. ''You might as well be.''

She snapped back. ''What's wrong with my clothes?''

''Those blue pants and shirt look almost identical to a uniform. Your hair's even tucked up according to military regs.''

''Since when did you join the fashion police?''

''Cute, O'Connell. Real cute—'' He hauled in a breath and held his hands up into a *T*. ''Time out. Let's not draw attention to ourselves by fighting.''

Of course he was right, but his comment about her clothes still stung. What had Lt. Col. Dawson been thinking with his crazy plan?

Diplomacy. Diplomacy. Dimple.

Dimple?

Tanner stared down at her with a half smile dimpling one cheek. ''Come on.''

''Huh?''

Tanner's smile spread until the second dimple tucked into his other cheek. ''We're going to get you a disguise.''

Kathleen followed, not that she had a choice since he wouldn't let go of her hand. His playful grin had further rocked her balance. Sure Tanner joked with everyone else around the squadron, but he saved his irritation for her.

Not now. He turned that boyish charm on her, full power, as he dragged her toward the crowded gift shop. ''Let's start with the military bag. It's got to go.''

"But I can't—"

"Trust me. Hmmm." He flicked through a rack of dangling tourist tote bags with expert shopping hands. No visual skimming the surface of the display for this man. "You need a big one. Got a color preference?"

Kathleen eyed the door, then resigned herself to the inevitable. "Why ask me? I'm a fashion fugitive, remember? Color coding is beyond me."

"No preference." He unhooked a fuchsia bag, logo blaring—I Did Germany Bavarian Style. His eyes glinted with mischief. "Since you don't care, how about this one? Ah, so pink isn't your color after all?"

A reluctant smile played with her lips. Her sisters had dragged her out like this before, but shopping hadn't seemed half as entertaining with them. "Not my first choice, no."

Although it had definite possibilities as a Christmas gift for her mom.

Her poor mother never had quite understood her G.I. Jane daughter. Holiday dinner talk inevitably turned to gift offers for a makeover or color coding—or invitations to join the family medical practice. Kathleen had learned to smile, nod and make her own choices once she walked out the door. She was just too different, a real changeling in their midst.

"How about this, then?" Tanner passed her a beige canvas tote with a big heart declaring I Love Germany. "Better, *mein Wienerschnitzel?*"

My veal cutlet? Kathleen groaned, then laughed as she swiped the bag from his hand.

He tugged the tag off and placed it on the counter by the cash register. A twirling jewelry stand towered beside her. Tanner reached past, bypassing the gold. He untangled a thong cord with a nutcracker charm hanging and draped it around Kathleen's neck. Rocking back on his heels, he spread his hands.

"Oh, yeah, that does it." He quirked a brow, grabbing a pair of matching earrings and dancing them in front of her face. "Want these, too? My treat."

"Maybe next visit."

Snagging a feathered cap, he plopped it on her head. "Or how about a hat. No?"

Tanner replaced it on the hook. Carefully crouching for a lower display, he began stacking items on the counter while the clerk rang them up. He pinned a Go Frankfurters button to the tote. A miniature beer stein key chain dangled from the handle. Three bars of Toblerone chocolate spiked from Kathleen's bag.

An unknown imp sprang to life within her, and she pulled a pocket protector full of pens from the display wall. Tanner's brow creased.

She dropped the plastic pen case on the counter. "Businessman garb for you."

He rewarded her with another smile. "You learn fast, *meine* toaster strudel."

That grin and a few words shouldn't have the power to bring such a heady rush of pride. Geez, it wasn't like she'd dug out a bullet under battlefield conditions. Still, she couldn't stifle an answering smile when he slid his pen holder into his shirt pocket.

After adding a German phrase book and map sticking conspicuously in view, Tanner slid his wallet free.

"Hey, wait, Bennett. I can't let you pay for all of this."

"Of course you can. It was my idea."

"No, really." She reached into her new canvas tote. "I can—"

"O'Connell. Stop. I've got some German marks to use up." He tossed down a stack of bills before he grasped her hand. "Consider it payback for those house calls. Not exactly a down payment on a summer home..."

His hand eclipsed hers just as the sensation of his touch enveloped her senses, completely, until she could only feel the warm rasp of his callused skin. Her hand twitched free, only to fidget with her nutcracker necklace. "Thank you."

"My pleasure."

She laughed, the sound tighter than she'd intended. "Decking the uptight doc out like a tacky tourist? I'm sure it was."

Genuine concern wiped away the laughter in his eyes. "Kathleen, I wasn't making fun—"

"I know." And that scared her more than if he had. Needing that distance, soon, she flicked a finger on his jacket over his pocket protector. "Now that I've got my own spy disguise, let's find our gate."

Kathleen spun on her heel and charged for the door, away from the temptation of this strangely enticing playful Tanner. Somehow this man posed an even greater threat to her peace of mind than the cranky patient and workmate.

Workmate. How could she have forgotten her number-one rule? No more relationships with flyers.

"O'Connell!" Tanner called. "One more thing."

Kathleen stopped, braced her shoulders and her resolve before turning, only to find Tanner a single step away. Heat curled through her despite Tanner's co-worker status.

"What?" She was powerless to move as she watched his big hands ease toward her, hypnotized by the thought of him reaching for her.

"Your hair." His hand snaked behind her neck and gently tugged two pins. The short tail fell free. His movements deliberate, he untwined the rubber band, fingers combing through one notch at a time.

The man bombarded her senses, when her defenses were

shaky at best. His methodical attention to her hair dried all the moisture from her mouth.

Staring up at him with unblinking eyes, she found herself studying his face with a new perspective, personal rather than professional. Her fingers yearned to explore that bump in his nose, the crook having been set ever so imperfectly.

How long did it take to unbraid hair, for crying out loud? His torturously slow progress, those hands whispering against her scalp, sent shivers prickling down her spine.

The craziness had to be a by-product of abstinence. She didn't miss her ex-husband, but she certainly missed regular sex. That had to be the reason her body responded to a man she respected but wasn't quite sure she even liked.

Her mind taunted her with how much she'd enjoyed his impromptu shopping spree through the gift shop. And she couldn't recall ever being so turned on by a guy simply playing with her hair.

His fingers massaged her scalp as he swirled her hair forward. She barely managed to bite back a moan. His pupils widened in response.

Enough.

Forget camaraderie. This had to stop. Kathleen stepped back.

"Thanks. I can finish." She combed her shaking hands through her hair, the strands suddenly unbearably sensual caressing her neck. "Okay now?"

"Perfect."

His tone, low and intimate, sent a fresh wash of shivers all the way to her toes. Tanner's chest rose and fell, faster, each speedier respiration telling Kathleen more than she could handle about how much she affected him, as well.

She wanted her uniform back, with all the protection and distance its familiarity offered.

The loudspeaker crackled, announcing flights, theirs ending the list. Christmas carols replaced the droning voice.

Tanner's head cocked up to the sound, his face hardening with an intensity that nudged concern past her own needs.

She couldn't stop herself from asking, "You okay?"

He looked down as if he'd forgotten her. Not very complimentary since her every tingling nerve still remembered his touch.

"Yeah, I'm fine." Tanner palmed the small of her back. "Come on, Mata Hari. Let's make tracks."

She shielded her senses against the heat of his hand. Why turn sappy just because they'd actually laughed together and he'd bought her a few tourist tokens? It wasn't like they had anything between them except a common alma mater, years of bickering...

And one unforgettable kiss.

A kiss she prayed Tanner *had* forgotten. If not, they had larger problems than unraveling the crash of an aircraft worth $125 million.

Chapter 4

Tanner shifted, turned, shifted again but still couldn't manage to wedge himself comfortably in the microscopic airline seat. He would have better luck stuffing the drink cart through the tiny window beside Kathleen.

Flipping another page in his paperback, he tried to ignore his grumbling stomach. In the past five hours, he'd only eaten a cardboard croissant sandwich, five tiny bags of pretzels and two of Kathleen's Toblerone bars. He stared across the aisle with envy at the kid snoozing the flight away.

Tanner's hand itched to grip the stick of his C-17, to fly, instead of being chauffeured around in a civilian air taxi. He second-guessed every whine and drone of the humming engines.

Being a passenger stunk for him on a good day. This wasn't a good day. His back hurt, his stomach was snacking on itself. And Kathleen looked so hot he couldn't even enjoy the latest techno-thriller novel.

Tanner gave up trying to read or get comfortable and

studied Kathleen, instead. She fitted in that confined space, no problem, working her way through a stack of files on the seat between them. He sometimes forgot how small she was, probably not more than five foot four.

Dwindling light filtered through the oval window, glinting off the thin wire frames of her reading glasses. They gave her a schoolmarmish air that proved curiously sexy, like her standard tight braid.

Her hair.

Tanner slammed his book shut and rubbed his palms together as if that might dispel the lingering sensation of her hair sliding between his fingers. The lingering scent of her minty shampoo on his hands. Caving to the temptation to untangle her braid had been insane. But she'd looked so cute in her tourist getup. So unusually approachable.

Like now.

The window light sparked off her free-flowing hair. Threads of gold shimmered through the auburn. Kathleen retrieved another file from the stack, the nutcracker necklace swaying between her breasts. Settling back, she compared the columns of figures on one page with another.

She'd always been the studious type, a real curve buster who set a high bar for others to match, and heaven knew he enjoyed competition. Other than those glasses and the longer hair, she didn't look much different from the Academy cadet who'd hunched over textbooks in the library.

The woman he'd kissed until they both couldn't breathe.

Did she remember? The thought that she might have forgotten jolted a dangerous frustration through him.

Suddenly he had to know. He had to have an acknowledgment of that moment, even if they never intended to repeat it. Maybe then they could defuse the attraction lurking between them.

"Do you ever think about Academy days?" The question fell from his mouth, and he didn't have the slightest desire to recall it.

She didn't answer, didn't even twitch or move to acknowledge she'd heard him. But her gaze stopped scanning from side to side along the page. Slowly she slid her glasses off and turned to him, her eyes wary. "Sure."

His stomach took another large bite out of itself. "Really?"

"Of course. I spent four years of my life there."

"Yeah." Not what he was looking for in the way of a response, but then O'Connell had never been easy. "I remember sharing a couple of them with you."

"Uh-huh." Cool professionalism plastered itself right over the wariness. Kathleen shoved her glasses back on her nose. She whipped a file from the bottom of the stack and dropped it in his lap. "Check out the crew's training reports while I review their seventy-two-hour histories prior to the crash."

"Okay." He opened the file and thumbed through the pages. Determination kindled within him, fueling the same competitiveness that had carried him across the goal line more than once.

It was only the first down. Be patient. Hang tough. Wait for the opening.

He read through the contents of the thin manila folder, then thumped the stack of papers in front of him. "Training reports look good. The copilot busted a check ride two years ago, only hooked the test on something minor, though, nothing reckless enough to wave a major red flag about."

"Isn't the copilot kind of young?"

"Compared to me? Yeah. But I pulled time as a C-130 navigator first." Which made him all the more anxious to speed through the upgrade from right-seat copilot to aircraft commander flying left seat. He had to establish an uncomplicated working relationship with her to prove his professionalism to the Squadron Commander.

Tanner stacked the training reports and slid them inside their folder. Time for his next play, a surprise sweep around to her blind side. "It'll be good to see ol' Crusty again once we get to California. Remember how he used to catch hell from you about his sloppy uniform?"

"Uh-huh." She plopped another file in his lap. "Take a look at the pilot's seventy-two-hour history. It says here Crusty only ate burgers and dill pickles for two days before the flight. That seems odd, like he's forgotten something. Who eats nothing but burgers and pickles?"

Second down. Stopped short of the ten-yard gain. Damn it, he would make all the time in the world for the case, after he got one thing settled.

With her head bowed over the file on the seat between them, he could see a third color threading through her hair. A deeper shade of copper mixed in with the red and gold. She glanced up. Her blue eyes shone as clear as the sky whipping past that tiny window, taunting him with a small peek when he wanted the wide open expanse.

"Bennett? Burgers and pickles?"

He regained his footing before he lost critical yardage. "Oh, uh, yeah. Crusty's a bachelor. That probably explains it."

"If you say so." She scribbled a note on the top corner and flipped the page as a mother and toddler eased out of the seat in front of them.

Tanner shifted his legs from the aisle to let a woman hurry her child toward the bathroom. Minimal privacy established, he stretched his legs again. "Back at the Academy, whenever Crusty saw you coming, he would untuck his shirt or scuff his shoes, anything to catch your attention. Sure enough, you would stop and chew him out. He really had a thing for you."

''Apparently, he got over it.''

Time to press. ''He had to get over it. The whole doolie-upperclassman taboo.''

Her hands faltered. The paper shuffling stopped, and he thought he had her. Finally she would say something about the night that should have gotten them both kicked out of school.

She glanced toward him, and it was all there for him to see. The memory of that kiss scorched her mind as much as it singed his. She stared back at him, drawing him into her sky-blue eyes filled with memories. Filled with hunger. With fire.

Twelve years ago the two of them had been brimming with need and seriously lacking in sense as they'd fed on each other. Mouths meeting, hands almost as frantic as her breathy moans, sweet sounds that had eased the roar of pain in his head.

Tanner canted forward, his hand reaching. Still he remembered the glide of her hair against his skin. He couldn't resist her healing warmth now any more than he could then. ''Kathleen—''

Her eyes shuttered like clouds in front of his windscreen blocking the sky. Without a word she returned to the open file on her knees.

But her eyes weren't scanning. Her spine couldn't have been any straighter if she'd snapped to attention.

He slumped back against his unforgiving cement-slab seat. The woman had defensive moves that would garner serious bucks in the big leagues. He wasn't going to get anything out of her this way.

She'd obviously done a better job at putting aside the past than he had. As if he could ever forget any of it. Of course, that night had been...beyond hell, and she'd been there for him.

Forget a touchdown. Punt the ball and salvage what he could. "About that night. I never had a chance to say—"

She slapped her file closed. "Bennett."

"What?"

"Save the apology."

He stared at her blasé face, her tight jaw. He hadn't planned to apologize at all. He owed her a big fat thanks for dragging him through the worst night of his life. "Kathleen—"

"It was one kiss twelve years ago." She flung half the stack in his lap. "We've got work to do. Look over these maintenance records."

Her bland expression didn't fool him for a minute. The slight tremble of her hands told him so much, an understated sign that screamed a clear message coming from this restrained woman.

He'd won. She'd admitted she remembered, and it had dogged her as much as it did him. Now they should be able to jettison all the sparks arcing between them.

Except he still wanted her. A woman who played by the rules scorned rule breakers like him and wouldn't pass up the chance to ground his butt permanently if he misstepped.

Maybe Kathleen had the right idea. Reviewing pages of maintenance reports was a hell of a lot less frustrating than acknowledging those memory missiles lobbing between them.

Yet his gut told him otherwise, and flyers learned to follow their instincts. If he and Kathleen didn't figure out a way to face the attraction and move on, it would keep tracking them, waiting until their defenses were lowered.

Then it would blast them both right out of the sky.

The Fasten Seat Belts light switched off with a *ding*. Kathleen slid the folders into her I Love Germany bag and readied to disembark. Ready? She was beyond ready to end the transcontinental journey and Tanner's persistent questions about their good old Academy days.

Eleven hours total in the air, broken by a three-hour layover in New York, had wasted her resistance, and they still had a ninety-minute drive to Edwards ahead of them. Their flight from New York to California had been packed. They no longer had the neutral zone of an extra seat between them.

Exhausted and more than a little irritable, she'd spent the past four hours with her body molded from shoulder to ankle against Tanner. Masculine heat and musk saturated right into her. His every muscle-rippling move, and he shifted way too often for her comfort level, left her swallowing a case of sodas from the drink cart.

Not that it helped moisten her dry mouth. She didn't bother deluding herself that it had anything to do with cabin pressure.

He moved in his seat again, stuffing the doll-size pillow behind his head before his snores resumed. Poor guy. That tiny airline seat had to have made a mess of his back. At least he'd finally acknowledged his mortal status a few hours ago and downed a couple of muscle relaxers.

Kathleen studied the big lug sprawled asleep in his seat, his broad chest clearly outlined even under the drape of an airline throw blanket. The man had a great body, always had. She would have to be blind not to notice. And she would be crazy to do anything about it—other than occasionally admire the view.

One muscled leg extended out in the aisle, with the other knee wedged against the seat in front of him. Figures he's a sprawler.

Probably a bed hog, too.

Whoa, girl! Those kind of thoughts could just hike right on back into her subconscious, because she had no intention of exploring them further. She had a case to solve and a promotion to secure. No way would she let another hotshot flyboy interfere with her career.

Especially one with such damned distracting dimples.

Kathleen started to reach for his shoulder and he shifted, flinging his arm across her lap. His hand rested, palm up, searing her leg through her cotton slacks.

She forced her breathing to regulate.

Just a normal hand, five fingers and his Academy ring. Except that hand flew planes with the same finesse he'd used to scramble her brains back in the airport with a few caresses to her head.

What would those callused fingers feel like exploring her bare skin? Her heart rate kicked up a notch.

Scooting her leg from under his hand, Kathleen gently nudged his foot with hers. "Rise and shine, hotshot. We're here."

He jackknifed upright, eyes wide as he woke without hesitation. At the sharp movement he paled, and a curse slipped free with enough force to make her wince.

"Are you okay?"

"Take off your stethoscope, Doc. I'm fine. Just slept crooked and moved too fast." He shoved aside the pillow and blanket and stood, stretching. His arms arced over his head in a muscle-rippling reach.

She tore her attention from his chest.

Couldn't she display a little sympathy without him turning defensive? Given the thrust of his jaw, apparently not. "If you're sure."

"I'm sure." He hefted his bag from the overhead storage.

"Fair enough. I'll put away the MD." Kathleen shoved aside her hurt feelings and shrugged her bag onto her shoulder.

She wedged into the crowded aisle behind Tanner as he turned sideways to fit through the narrow passageway. Did his slow swagger hide genuine pain? He needed bed rest, not an eleven-hour flight in a cramped airline seat.

Had he been home in Charleston, one of his girlfriends would have been pampering him, plying him with eggnog and TLC. Who was he seeing now? Tiffani, Brandi or some other woman with a name ending in an *I* with a heart over it.

Kathleen inched forward, mentally kicking herself for thoughts that bordered on petty. Tanner wasn't a bar hound collecting a different bimbo every week like some crew dogs, such as her ex-husband or Lance Sinclair before he married. Gossip and her own observations revealed Tanner had a relationship pattern.

She didn't want to ponder overlong on why she'd bothered to listen to gossip about his love life.

All stories ran the same path. He held steady for six months to a year. Then one of them broke it off for any number of lame reasons.

Another common thread ran through it all. The Brandi, Tansi, Candi types were all needi—*needy*. And no doubt about it, Tanner was a man who thrived on watching out for people. His protectiveness in the German airport had only been a sampling.

Kathleen had been born taking care of herself. She'd never needed rescuing, except for two brief moments. Once when she'd fallen out of a tree as a kid and sprained her wrist, and later in a rock climbing accident that had left her with a broken ankle. Both times the helplessness had been hell.

Much like Tanner must have felt in the infirmary.

The thought blindsided her, tangling her feet for a startled moment. Who would have expected she could find a common bond with Tanner Bennett?

They approached the cheery flight attendant by the cockpit. The woman bestowed an extra bright smile with her "bye-bye" for Tanner.

He ducked to clear the airplane doorway, barely disguising his wince. Kathleen resisted the urge to stroke a comforting hand over his broad back. He would likely accuse her of plotting another hospital stay.

So what if her name didn't end with a sweet and softening *i*? That didn't mean she couldn't offer a little compassion when someone deserved it.

Her bedside manner did not suck, damn it.

She winced. All right, maybe she wasn't the soft and cuddly type like her mom and sisters. She'd learned long ago to stick with what she knew and did best, then no one would be disappointed.

Kathleen locked away her conciliatory remarks. For this trip she wasn't Tanner's doctor. She wasn't his Academy bud. And she wasn't the woman who would tend to his aching back. She was nothing more than his workmate.

Her hand skimmed down the nutcracker necklace that weighted like a ten-ton reminder of Tanner's hundred-watt smile.

Tanner crossed his arms over his chest and braced his feet as the shuttle bus plowed around a corner toward the rental car building. The ever-present L.A. smog battled with misting rain to haze out visibility. Drizzle streaked the windows, the overcast sky mirroring his mood.

Kathleen hadn't released her grip on the seat in front of them. There wasn't a chance the bus driver's haphazard speedster techniques would fling her against him. The stubborn set of her jaw and white knuckles told Tanner she wouldn't budge if they hurtled into a three-car pileup.

He'd made her mad, not unusual, except he had no idea what he'd done this time. The comments about their Academy days? Maybe. But she'd handled it, stopping him dead with a chilling stare. He couldn't dodge the notion that he'd hurt her feelings somehow.

That bothered him more than any of their bickering.

The shuttle bus squealed to a shuddering stop in front of the rental car building, puddles sluicing up onto the sidewalk. Tanner followed Kathleen's stiff back and trim, too-enticing hips all the way inside.

Wasn't she going to talk to him? They couldn't resolve anything if she wouldn't speak. That woman had the silent treatment down pat.

He would wait her out.

Not that he'd ever been the patient type.

Just hang tough. The ninety-minute drive to base would likely stretch into a couple of hours, thanks to rush hour traffic.

Oddly, he missed sparring with her. Mental boxing matches were something he shared with Kathleen alone. The women he dated had always been more agreeable, yet something about Kathleen's bristly manner put him at ease and fired him up all at once. One of their lively exchanges would spark up a dreary day.

Kathleen advanced in the line to the garland-strewn counter. One of the twenty androgynous agents droned, "Driver's license, proof of insurance and credit card, please."

Tanner reached for his wallet.

So did Kathleen.

Uh-oh.

He sensed her silent treatment was about to come to an abrupt end. Anticipation churned inside him as it did during those last sixty seconds before take off.

His hand twitched on his wallet. "I always drive on TDYs."

"So do I." Kathleen flung her canvas tote onto the counter and began digging for her wallet in earnest.

"And I'm going to look like a real chauvinist if I say I want to drive, anyway." Tanner tried to keep his tone light, a smile in place, but suspected the annoying tic in one eye might give him away.

She planted a hand on the counter and perched her other hand on her hip. "I'll make this easy on us. Who has the rental car on their travel orders? Military joint travel regs state that's who is responsible for the car. Need me to cite the reg?"

"Ah. The regs."

"They're there for a reason, Bennett." Kathleen pivoted on her heel and fished out a file just as Tanner yanked his orders from his carry-on. She opened the file.

The small flash of victory in her tired eyes said it all.

Damn. More right-seat copiloting for him. Stepping back, he raised his hands in surrender. "Chauffeur away."

At least Kathleen didn't gloat over her win, merely passed her driver's license and military travel orders to the impatient clerk.

Outside, Tanner frowned at the overcast sky. Sixty degrees and drizzling, the weather would make for a miserable ride out. They wouldn't even reach base before dark.

Keys jingling with her brisk walk, Kathleen wove between lines of cars. Tanner kept his eyes off her backside this time. The last thing he needed were thoughts of those slim hips taunting him for the next two hours in the car. As long as he kept his distance until she cooled off and started talking again, he would be fine.

Then he saw "it" in a deserted corner of the lot.

Their car. If it could be called that.

How could he have forgotten? The government always opted for econo-class compacts. If he managed to wedge himself inside, there wouldn't be an inch to spare between them.

Kathleen unlocked her door, tossed her luggage on the

back seat, then paused halfway in, staring over the roof at Tanner. "What now?"

He looked back and tried not to notice the mist dampening her shirt. "I wonder if they have anything smaller."

Her brow furrowed as she glanced around the lot, cars starting and departing at a regular pace. "I don't think so."

"No, really. They must have a scooter back there. It would probably be more comfortable."

Compassion softened the defensive edge in her eyes. "I'm sorry, Bennett. But you're going to have to hang in there for another couple of hours." She glanced at her watch. "I can authorize you another dose of medication in fifteen more minutes."

Great. Just what he needed, hours alone, mega-relaxed with her in that shoe box with her wet shirt and those sympathetic eyes. The double dose of meds would have him saying God only knew what. Not a chance. "My left leg won't fit in there, much less the rest of me. We're going to have to upgrade."

"We can't."

"Because?"

"Regulations. The government only authorized us for a compact. We aren't Fortune 500 travelers, you know."

"Then I'll pay the extra."

"That's not in accordance with our orders. And if we aren't in compliance with those orders and we're in an accident, we're not covered." Her lips pulled tight with that oh-so-proper schoolmarmish look that never failed to make him want to do all sorts of very improper things with her.

"You really do memorize this stuff."

She shrugged apologetically. "We're expected to be good stewards of the government's money."

He had to rent another car. Preferably one with a large console between the driver and the passenger. "Put your calculator away for a minute and be practical."

"Looking for special treatment?"

"I'm looking for leg room."

"Good thing you're not driving, then." She swept her hair off her face. "You'll have extra space in the passenger side."

That simple glide of her hair stirred his tired body when reserves were nearing empty. Hours of uninterrupted Kathleen had him so on edge he needed to jog, swim laps, anything to burn off the tension twisting inside him. A tension that had the annoying habit of settling right below his belt.

A tic started in his eye again. "Sticking my head out the sunroof doesn't sound appealing."

"Last time I checked, they didn't offer rental tanks." Hands on her hips, she threw her shoulders back.

Which gave him an unrestrained view of her damp blouse. The thin cotton became transparent when wet, revealing the edges of a lacy bra.

Tanner closed his eyes, rubbed the bump on his nose and reminded himself how the twice-set crook had occurred because he'd charged in before thinking.

They could have been right back out there on the flight line again, sparring through their frustration. If he didn't watch out, he would be running his hands through her hair, over that blouse.

She would look up at him with those blue eyes that made him want to fly right inside without thinking about the consequences. If she didn't slap him first.

This had to stop. Ignoring the attraction hadn't worked for the past year any more than it had twelve years ago. His attempt at discussing the problem obviously hadn't been direct enough. They had to get this out in the open and get over it. His hand fell away from the bump on his nose. Forget worrying about impulsiveness.

Fourth down and only one second left on the clock. Time for a "Hail, Mary," pass. "Damn, you're hot when you pout."

Chapter 5

Kathleen choked on the retort she'd planned that suddenly wasn't worth a damn. "What?"

Tanner dropped his luggage on the cement and rested his arms on the car roof. His lazy blink belied his laser-sharp stare. "I said you're really hot when you pout."

She clutched her open door, a logical move since her world was suddenly tilting off center. If only she weren't so exhausted. She didn't have the mental edge to battle with Tanner right now, not when the past hours spent rubbing against him had left her edgy and restless. "Did you take too many of those muscle relaxers?"

"Followed your orders to the letter, Doc." His head cocked to the side. "I had a lot of thinking time back in the infirmary, thanks to you, and I figured something out."

"Please share your Demerol delusions." Kathleen pulled her lips into a tight line to keep from saying something she might regret.

His gaze hovered along her mouth for a second too long before he continued. "We don't like each other much."

That hurt. More than it should have. More than any of Andrew's countless digs.

And that made her damned mad.

Tanner shouldn't have the power to tweak feelings she hadn't realized could still be pinched by a careless comment. "So now you're a rocket scientist as well as an ace pilot."

He pushed back from the car and lumbered around the hood toward her. "But we've got this…chemistry thing between us."

She didn't bother to deny it. What would be the use? Hadn't she already tried that on the plane?

He stopped in front of her. She kept the open door between them like a shield. Thank goodness for the drizzle cooling her body or she would definitely be overheating by now. "Your point?"

"Most folks who don't get along just play nice and stay clear of each other. That doesn't seem to work for us, and it's because of that chemistry. When it gets to be too much, we snap. The tension's gotta go somewhere. We fight to blow off steam."

Tanner rested his hands on the door beside hers, not touching. How small her hands looked next to his on the canvas of a teal door. One slight move and his hand could eclipse hers in callused heat.

She struggled not to yank her hands away and step back. His head angled right. Mist clung to his hair. Droplets sprinkled his skin just begging for her to taste away. If he leaned two more inches, if she arched up on her toes, their mouths would meet.

Of their own volition, her lips parted. "We fight because we want each other?"

Was that husky voice really hers?

"Yes, ma'am, we do."

The breath from his words kissed her mouth as surely as

if he'd placed his lips there. The heat lingered, excited. "And?"

"Now, as I read it, you don't want to do anything about the attraction."

Was there a hint of a question in his voice? Did she want there to be? And if she even insinuated as much, she could easily find out she was mistaken. She'd misjudged her husband's intentions more than once.

What was she thinking? The last thing she needed was to crawl in bed with Tanner Bennett. She forced her voice not to quiver. "Of course I don't want to pursue it."

He winced as if he'd pinched a nerve all over again. "Well, you can't be any clearer than that."

Her fingers itched to cover his. "Tanner—"

"No. It's okay." He ambled back, his arms extended as he held the car door. "I agree, and I don't expect you to feed my ego. We just need to clear this up. I tried to talk about it back on the plane, but, well, subtle's never been my strong suit."

His hand shot up to forestall her automatic retort. She bit back her tank-being-more-subtle comment and waved for him to continue.

"We have to get along for the next few weeks. We can't rip each other's head off whenever hormones kick in. If we're fighting all the time, we'll never figure out what went wrong with that plane."

Her mind churned through his words. Fighting *all* the time equaled turned on all the time.

He was turned on by her *all the time?* She definitely didn't need to know that. "All right. Truce."

"We'll start fresh."

She nodded. "Sounds good."

"No more snapping and firing up our hormones."

"Right."

His arms crossed over his chest. "I'll start by apologizing for whatever I did to make you pout."

Starch crept right back into her spine. "I don't pout."

"O'Connell, that counts as a snap." A dimple creased one cheek. "Breaking the rules already."

"Who says you get to decide all the rules, Captain Hotshot Pilot? I'm the rule expert. Remember?" His smile deepened, damn him, and she stomped her foot. "And I do *not* pout!"

Creases fanned from his eyes as a suspicious light twinkled. "Turning you on that much, am I?"

She almost shot into the car and drove off without the conceited lug. Then the twinkle turned so outrageously mischievous, her anger drained away. "You're teasing me."

He shrugged, but she recognized the playful Tanner from the airport, the lighthearted Tanner who made everyone smile. He was treating her like one of the guys.

Well, not exactly the way he would treat the guys, but he was joking with her in his own infuriating way.

A smile tugged at her cheeks, laughter tickling her mouth and finally bubbling free.

Tanner's low chuckles joined hers. "Time to lay down our arms and declare a cease-fire. I must say, Captain O'Connell, you've been a worthy adversary."

"You're a formidable opponent yourself, Captain Bennett."

"For a hotshot pilot."

She clapped a hand over her mouth to stifle the next laugh. "Did I really stamp my foot?"

"Not that I saw."

"Very noble of you."

"All in the interest of no more snapping."

No more arguing. No more sparks. No more heat to suppress and try to ignore.

No chance of ever exploring it.

An odd melancholy stirred deep in her stomach. Her eyes met his across the door, held. Remnants of his low laugh still brushed the air, wrapping around her, dispelling a chill she'd had long before she stepped out into the dreary parking lot.

Apparently, he could upset her equilibrium without laying a finger on her.

Her smile faded. "It's a long drive in, and it'll be dark soon. We really should get going."

Tanner nodded, backing away before turning on his heel to store the luggage. He folded his body into the car while she tucked herself behind the steering wheel.

His leg pressed against hers.

Kathleen looked at the floorboards and couldn't find an extra inch for escape. Masculine heat and musk saturated her senses, just like on the plane.

The sooner she left, the sooner they would be through. She reached to release the parking break in the middle.

Her knuckles rubbed a long, very long, very torturous, path over Tanner's thigh. The cotton fabric of his pants rasped along her every heightened nerve.

Kathleen's foot twitched on the brake. "You know, Appendix O, section C of the Joint Travel Regulations does indicate that if the car doesn't meet requirements we may be authorized a different-size vehicle appropriate to the mission. Given your size and medical history…"

Tanner was already reaching for his door. "Wouldn't want to land me back in the hospital from hours spent in this shoe box."

"Right." Kathleen ripped the keys from the ignition. "The midsize over there would save the Air Force money in the long run."

"See. We're already learning to agree."

"Absolutely."

"I'll get the luggage while you change the paperwork."

"Great." Kathleen threw open her door and sprinted through the rain for the Hertz desk. Even as she ran, she knew a minivan wouldn't offer enough space. She couldn't escape the memory of Tanner's warm laughter sweeping over her like a lover's caress, making her want more.

Not that it could ever matter. She might want him, but she would never need him, not like the women he seemed to prefer. Being vulnerable just wasn't worth the price.

The next morning Tanner slid on sunglasses to dim the piercing desert sun. Beside him, Kathleen sipped her coffee and drove, predictably five miles an hour under the speed limit on a highway where most people sped like demons.

He refused to let that cloud his mood. Face tipped into the gritty breeze whipping through the open window, he decided the wide-open skies offered a good omen for a new day. He and Kathleen had found a safe middle ground, and he intended to keep it.

Along with the help of a great big armrest console between them.

Tanner inhaled the chicory scent of his coffee to override the mint wafting from Kathleen. He drank his Jamaican breakfast blend and resolved to be productive.

Their ride into base the night before had been tense at first, then easier as they'd debated the merits of great historic generals. For once, their combative natures had found a positive outlet in a discussion on Alexander the Great, another good omen as they began their case.

The morning meeting with six other members of their investigation team from different bases had been spent divvying up interview subjects. Since Kathleen's toxicology reports weren't due in from the labs for another couple of days, she and Tanner were partnered for the day.

First on their agenda—check out the subcontractor who'd modified the electromechanical release device on the

C-17's load ramp. Another whole day with Kathleen. Lt. Col. Dawson's plan was well underway. Tanner still couldn't decide if the idea was inspired leadership or reckless endangerment of their sanity.

Tanner focused on the landscape outside his window, rather than the too-tempting view just beside him behind the wheel. Rain from the day prior had coaxed color from barren cracks. Flowers now bloomed in a surprise splash of color. Clumps of Joshua trees and creosote brush seemed to stand taller.

The sun glinted off a shallow sheen of water on a dried-up lake bed. Plastic shark fins dotted the expanse, bringing a welcome smile to Tanner's face at the tradition he'd often viewed during countless TDY's to the base. Squadrons at Edwards AFB kept those fins ready to use after every rain.

Military folks worked hard, but they also played hard as a safeguard against the stress. Joking offered a pressure valve for the grim realities of their world, combat missions and even the ever-present risk of a crash on any flight.

Like the one they were investigating.

It could have been worse. Twisted metal. A burned-out hull. Nothing left to identify the crew but the extra set of dog tags inside boots.

The cause couldn't remain a mystery, otherwise, it could happen again. To him. To his friends.

Tanner shrugged off the depressing image and allowed himself an unreserved glance at Kathleen for distraction. Her tourist getup a thing of the past, she wore her flight suit, those fire-red strands tucked away in her regular braid.

An image of her in the airport sneaked into his thoughts as she did too often lately. His mind's eye remembered her tentative smile when she'd passed him the pocket protector full of pens.

She didn't smile often, something he hadn't noticed before. How did she blow off the steam that accompanied her high-pressure job? She needed to smile more often.

Tanner knocked back the dregs of his coffee, then smiled, lifting his empty cup. "A good omen."

"What?" She replaced her disposable cup, before readjusting her hands on the steering wheel. Positioning at precisely ten o'clock and two o'clock, of course.

He suppressed a grin at her manual-perfect driving. He understood her better now, and understanding the opponent gave him an edge. "We both like coffee. The sun's shining. All omens that it's going to be a kick-butt day."

"Omens." She gave a decidedly unladylike snort. "I'm more of a make-your-own-luck kind of person."

Of course she was, being a scientist. It made sense. Maybe he needed to help her understand more about the flyer mind-set as well. The sun seemed to wink in agreement. Or could that be a mocking gleam?

"Flyers are superstitious. We hang on to good luck charms, perform all sorts of rituals before we fly. Rabbits' feet, lucky coins, a bar coaster. Our pockets rattle with the stuff. One guy I know is convinced if he eats sardines and crackers for breakfast before a flight he won't get air sick."

She shot him a wry smile. "Alert the AMA." The wind snagged at her hair, finally freeing a lone strand. "And his reasoning behind this?"

"On his first training flight he was the only one in his class not to hurl. Now he's certain it was because of the sardines he ate that morning. It's become a mental thing. You can be sure that if he doesn't eat those sardines, he'll be puking his guts out by air-to-air refueling."

She winced, laughing softly. "Lovely."

The stray lock streamed across her face, catching on her mouth.

Tanner trained his eyes on a cactus so he wouldn't surrender to the temptation to smooth back her hair. "Don't diss the mojo, lady. We've seen it go bad for no reason too often not to hang with those traditions.''

"Okay, so you know a few superstitious guys. You find superstitious people in any walk of life.'' She hooked the strand behind her ear.

Tanner relaxed in his seat, temptation safely tucked away for the moment. "Not this many. Have you noticed we always get into the plane on the left? Even if there's also a door on the right side, we still only use the left one. Fighter planes have the ladder rolled up to their left.''

"There has to be a logical reason.''

Figures his scientist partner would say that. "We think it's a carryover from cavalry days since you always mount a horse from the left, but we're not certain. Not a chance will anyone test it by breaking the tradition. Those rituals offer reassurance. Confidence in the air is everything.''

Her eyes distant, Kathleen scrunched her nose, those few freckles more apparent in the morning sun. "Funny, I watched Andrew climb into that fighter at least a hundred times, and I never gave the left-side thing a thought.''

Jealousy launched an ambush, downing Tanner when he least expected it. "Andrew?''

Kathleen's knuckles whitened around the steering wheel. "My ex-husband.''

Ex-husband? So much for omens and knowing his opponent, good signs and a great day. Tanner could have sworn his mojo rode the morning breeze right out the window. "You were married?''

Kathleen drained her coffee to give herself time to phrase a response. How could she have let Andrew's name slip? It had to be all the research and paperwork on crashes that brought Andrew to mind. With her emotions stirred into an uncontrollable swirl, she'd slipped.

She didn't hide the fact that she'd been married. However, once she'd reclaimed her maiden name, her colossal mistake wasn't something she enjoyed discussing. She'd allowed herself to relax her guard and enjoy the Tanner Bennett everyone else knew. Big mistake. One she planned to rectify. "A lot of people have been married."

"Not me."

An opening for a subject change and she intended to leap all over it. "How come?"

"Uh-uh. You first." His feet braced against the floorboards as if driving the car—or flying a plane. "You were married to a fighter pilot?"

Given the thrust of Tanner's determined jaw, Kathleen knew there wasn't a chance she could dodge his questions. Even in the passenger side, he drove in theory. This guy didn't give up control with ease or grace.

Better to keep her answers simple and factual, then move on to safer discussions like leadership traits in Alexander the Great. "Yes. For two years."

"What happened?"

"There wasn't room in our bed for me and his ego." She paused, then mumbled, "Not to mention his girlfriends."

Tanner stayed silent so long Kathleen pulled her eyes from the road to glance over at him. He stared back, and she didn't have to see through his sunglasses to know his eyes weren't smiling.

His brows pulled together. "I'm sorry."

A sympathetic Tanner was even more tempting than an amusing Tanner. Kathleen focused on the road, a safer place to look, anyway. "I was, too, but not anymore. It's over, and I learned from it. Life's about learning from our mistakes, right?"

"Sounds like he was the problem. What mistake did you make?"

"Falling for a hotshot pilot."

Her peripheral vision caught the ripple and flex of muscles along Tanner's legs as his feet worked the floorboards again. When he didn't flash back with a smart remark, she found her own words bubbling free with unusual chattiness.

"I don't do relationships with pilots anymore. Call it my own mojo if you will. Besides, with my job it isn't wise to mix the personal and professional." She couldn't help but wonder who she was trying to convince.

His hand fisted on his knee, twitching. Like flying a plane?

Tanner was thinking too much, and that didn't bode well for her. She'd found he packed quite a brain behind those jet-jock glasses. Time to turn the conversation around before he had her sharing things she would undoubtedly regret. "What's your ritual? Or are you a lucky charm kind of guy? What do you cart around in those pockets?"

That stopped his pseudo flying. Tanner's hand unclenched. "A St. Joseph's medal."

A pulse throbbed faster in his temple. Apparently she'd hit an untouchable subject, and the last thing she wanted was to press for emotional confidences.

Silence stretched for five passing telephone poles before she looked over at him. Not a smile in sight. She wished she could see behind his glasses. Flyers wore those tinted lenses like shields over their souls. No one could peek inside without permission.

Sure, she knew the practical, medical reason most aviators wore sunglasses. Flying above the pollution put them past filters. Their eyes became sensitive from being over-radiated, thus the need to wear sunglasses even when on the ground.

It offered another in a long list of stresses put on aviator bodies. They shrugged it all off, shielding their aches and pains with sunglasses and a laugh.

Except he wasn't laughing now. What ache was he hiding? And did she truly want to know?

She'd tried to comfort him years ago, and it had left them both with a cargo hold full of baggage. Better to stick with safer topics. "Your turn."

He scrubbed a hand across his jaw, swiping away his frown. "What?"

"Why haven't you married one of those perfect women you date?"

"Excuse me?"

"Sorry. Childish remark." One that sounded too much like jealousy. So much for safer topics. Tanner had a way of wrangling things from her without even trying. "Suffice it to say, you date women just like my sisters, which pushes another button for me. But we're talking about you. Why aren't you married yet? Lovin' the bachelor life too much?"

His fingers drummed along the console between them. "I'm not against marriage. Just haven't figured out how to make the long-term thing work yet."

"Ahhh, commitment shy."

His drumming fingers picked up speed. "I'm not hiding from it. I'd like to get married someday, have a few kids. Someday, but no rush. It's important to get it right—" The drumming stopped. "No offense."

"None taken. I totally agree. No one *wants* to go through a divorce." No way would she subject herself to that hell again. "So you want a marriage like dear old Mom and Dad had."

"My mom wasn't married to my father."

"Oh." Kathleen shot him a quick glance. She'd wedged the old flight boot in her mouth with that one. "Sorry. I didn't mean that the way it sounded."

"No offense taken. I've never met my father. Apparently, parenthood at eighteen didn't appeal to him. He skipped out, leaving my teenage mom pregnant with twins."

God, what must he have overcome to make so much of himself after such a rocky start? She'd had a secure childhood, full of far more advantages than Tanner had been given as a kid. Her father and mother had both been a part of her life and loved her, even if they didn't understand her life choices. "I'm sorry."

"Don't get me wrong. This isn't some sob story about a bad childhood. My mom did a damn fine job taking care of Tara and me."

Tara. His sister who'd been murdered in a carjacking attack. Kathleen didn't know all the details, but she'd been there firsthand to witness the aftermath for Tanner. He hadn't worn sunglasses over his eyes in those days.

Clearing his throat, Tanner pulled his elbow back in the car. "We always knew we were loved, but it was hard for Mom going it alone. If I ever get married, I need to be sure it's forever, for my wife, for the kids."

Tanner with kids, now there was an image. Too easily she could see the big playful lug with a little girl on his back and a chubby-cheeked baby crooked in one arm like a football. She and Andrew had talked about children near the end. The conversation hadn't gone well at all. "So you break off a relationship when you realize it isn't going anywhere?"

Rather than just continuing to use the woman for sex as Andrew had done.

There was a certain amount of honor in Tanner's method, at least. It still galled the hell out of her that her ex had slept with her the night before he'd served her with divorce papers.

Tanner shrugged. "I've always thought I should treat women with the same respect I would want some guy to show my mom and my sister."

Kathleen kept her eyes on the road, not that it helped.

The sincerity of his words, the inherent honor, twined around her.

Scared the starch right out of her flight suit.

Almost against her will, she whispered, "You're a nice guy, Tanner Bennett."

Slowly he stuck his head out the window, looked left and right.

"Tanner? Is something wrong?"

He ducked his head back inside and grinned. "You paid me a compliment. I'm just checking for an eclipse or some other natural wonder. Maybe a bolt of lightning to strike the car."

Apparently, heavy discussions had been canceled, and she exhaled her relief. Tanner's good mood was infectious. She couldn't stop her answering smile. "Those superstitions again. I called you nice. I didn't submit your name for sainthood."

His low chuckle rumbled along the breeze. "There's the O'Connell I know and admire." His laughter faded. He swept aside a strand of hair from her jaw. "You know, Kathleen, just because flyers are alike in some ways, doesn't mean they're all scumbags like your ex."

The easy camaraderie faded with his laughter, his words. His touch.

She never should have told him about Andrew. With what could be weeks left to spend together, she needed to keep her guard up.

Intellectually she understood what Tanner said about flyers being different, but maybe she harbored a few superstitions after all. Because seasoned soldier that she was, she still couldn't find the courage to test her luck on that one.

Chapter 6

Tanner watched Kathleen's pinky tap the turn signal as they neared the Palmdale Testing Facility. He'd watched her a thousand times before, wanted her, admired her, been mad as hell at her. But he'd never been so confused.

She'd been married. It shouldn't surprise him. Of course she would have had a life during the nine years after she'd graduated and before she'd been stationed in Charleston.

Kathleen had been married. No big deal.

Yet, it changed something—something he couldn't quite target. He'd carried an image of her for years, had grown comfortable with that, and now it had changed.

He'd always seen her as a solitary woman. She dated, but quietly and nothing serious. Apparently, she'd been serious once. Tanner couldn't help but wonder about the man who'd gotten through to Kathleen O'Connell.

A fighter pilot. Tanner swallowed a curse. Couldn't she have at least chosen a crew dog?

Rivalry between the different airframes was common.

Bomber, fighter, cargo aviators—they all collected reasons why the others were bottom feeders.

Camaraderie within the unit was important. He'd thought Kathleen was one of them, a flight surgeon for the cargo guys. Maybe that was what had his shorts in a knot, her momentary defection to the other side. Yeah, that was what had him frowning.

Not the thought of some other guy dragging down the zipper on Kathleen's flight suit.

Tanner bit back another curse. They'd definitely spent too much time alone together. He needed distance. Soon.

The investigation was too important. To some it might seem like a simple case of an airlift drop gone bad. No fatalities. But it was more than that to him. A certain amount of Air Force honor rode on this. He'd heard the whispers of crew cover-ups. Let the press get ahold of that and morale would self-destruct.

Looming ahead was the factory, a sprawling lone structure at the end of a dirt road. Cars filled the parking lot. The main building towered, a warehouse with gleaming white siding and metal framing. Brick add-ons fingered off to the sides, three stories tall with office windows along the top floor. The warehouse, located twenty miles from the base, ran tests on minor parts subcontracted out by major manufacturers.

The best thing he could do for Lance, for all the others, was keep his head on straight and find out what the hell went wrong, so it wouldn't happen again. It wasn't the same as flying combat, but at least he would be doing something. If the warehouse held those answers, he would find them.

Gravel crunched under the tires as Kathleen pulled precisely into a spot marked Visitor. One slim leg at a time, she stepped from the car.

Time to implement boundaries. Tanner joined her outside. "I ran into Crusty at the coffee machine earlier, back at the squadron."

"Oh?" Wind howled across the desert, tearing the door from her hands and slamming it closed. "What did he have to say?"

"Nothing much, not in the middle of squadron. We're going to meet later for a beer over at the Wing and a Prayer Bar and Grill."

"Good thinking." She tucked the keys in the leg pocket of her flight suit before following Tanner up the walkway. "Should I bring my tape recorder or just a notepad?"

And spend an entire evening together? Not a chance. "You're kidding, right?"

"About what?"

He tugged open the heavy steel door. "It's better if I meet him alone. You know, Doc. Crew dog to crew dog."

Her eyes narrowed. "Right. This *doc* definitely understands."

She shot through the entrance without another word, her determined stride kicking up a miniature sandstorm. What had he done now? He was only trying to plow through the investigation as fast as possible.

And avoid spending more time with her.

Tanner shrugged through a kink in his back brought on by an uneasiness that had nothing to do with a pinched nerve.

Inside the factory, the main warehouse gaped into a wide-open space. Tanner pulled off his sunglasses and hooked them in the neck of his flight suit.

Metal rafters webbed the ceiling over workstations. The rattle of machinery, grinding metal and repetitious clanging mixed a ragtag chorus with the low drone of Christmas music.

Jingle Bells gone rogue. How appropriate for his lack of holiday spirit.

From beside a workstation, a man stepped forward, wearing khakis and a red polo bearing the test facility logo. With a full head of prematurely gray hair, he might have been mistaken for older, but Tanner pegged him at around forty.

The man's easy swagger carried him across the warehouse toward Tanner and Kathleen. He squinted, staring at the name tags on their flight suits. "Captains O'Connell and Bennett from the base investigation. I heard you two were on your way." He thrust out his hand. "Quinn Marshall, head of this little corner of the testing world. What can I do for you?"

Tanner stepped up and returned the firm shake, trying to place why the man's name seemed so familiar beyond just a line item in a file. "We could start with a tour of the facility, while you give us a handle on the testing process."

"Certainly. Happy to do what I can to speed this along, so you folks'll clear on out of my work space."

"That's what we're hoping for. While we're walking around, we'd like your secretary to make copies of some files. We'll need all the test data on your modification for the load ramp's cargo-release system." Tanner watched for any hint of hesitation, a flash of reluctance, and found nothing.

"Of course." Quinn Marshall snagged a phone from the wall, punched in a number and clipped out instructions. Replacing the receiver, he nodded to Tanner and Kathleen. "All set. Follow me."

As Kathleen strode past, her minty fragrance lingered, distracted, so much so that Tanner almost missed the scowl pulling her mouth into a tight line. What had her twisted now? And why was he letting her moods crank a new knot in his back?

No way did he need to waste time, energy and waking thoughts, not to mention sleeping ones, on Kathleen. He forced his attention to Quinn Marshall's tour guide explanations.

"The modification in question on the C-17 load ramp has ten parts. Each of those parts was tested before being installed on the plane. Stress tests. Repetition tests. Heat tests. Then they were X-rayed for cracks."

Marshall pushed open a door, revealing a room about half the size of a football field, dominated by what looked like a huge pizza oven. A vent funneled heat to the outside, but the place still dripped with sweltering humidity. And that humidity now carried the distinctive scent of Kathleen's shampoo.

Tanner skimmed his finger along the neck of his flight suit and wandered toward the mammoth oven—away from Kathleen. "Nice roomy setup you've got."

"Square footage is cheap in the desert." Quinn stopped by a temperature gauge, thumping the dial. "Here's where we run heat tests. The spectrograph gauges ensure the metal heats evenly. It shows the purity of the metal."

Kathleen tugged a notepad from her leg pocket. "Every part goes through this before it's installed?"

"Absolutely."

"So if there's an undetected problem with one, there could be a problem with all of them."

"In theory."

Frowning, Kathleen nodded as she jotted notes on the pad. She walked alongside Tanner while they toured the warehouse room by room. Tanner peppered Quinn Marshall with questions. Kathleen scribbled pages of notes.

Tanner listened, yet couldn't stop his mind from winging back to his crew. He might be out of action, but he tracked his squadron's missions. At that moment supplies were being off-loaded in a Sentavian refugee camp. Without him.

What if one of those planes had a defective part and it kicked in on this mission or the next? He thought of recent flights with Lance, how he'd hauled Lance's butt out of the fire more than once. Tanner shifted from foot to foot restlessly. If he wrapped this up in a few days, he could be back in action for a full month before upgrade....

Except for his back.

He wanted to put his fist through a wall. Which would probably throw his back out. Kathleen would toss him in the infirmary before he could say "upgrade slot."

Quinn completed his tour, ending in the main hallway of the brick office sections. "The copies you wanted should be ready by now. Detailed test data...." He pointed through the door to a slender man talking on a cell phone by the soda machine. "All signed by that guy over there. The defense department inspector."

Kathleen thumbed through her notes. "Randall Fitzgerald."

"Right."

Tanner assessed the man by the vending machine—late thirties, clean-cut with suspenders. A government paper pusher worth interviewing later.

Pencil poised, Kathleen nodded. "So, Quinn, how long does—"

Tanner jerked his attention from the government inspector and snapped his fingers. "Quinn! 'The Mighty Quinn' Marshall. I knew I'd heard your name before. You used to be on active duty, a C-130 pilot back in Desert Storm."

Quinn's chest puffed. "A lot of years ago."

Kathleen flipped her notebook closed. "I'm going to find a ladies' room while you boys shoot down your wristwatches with your hands."

Quinn nodded absently. "Yeah, sure, straight ahead past the soda machine, then right."

"Thanks."

Tanner's eyes trailed Kathleen without his consent. Even constrained in a braid, Kathleen's hair gleamed like a beacon in the dreary factory as she paused by the defense contractor. What was it about that woman?

An evening with his buds at the Wing and a Prayer and he would be back on track.

"What's the deal on her?"

Quinn's voice pulled Tanner's attention, if not his eyes. "She's the flight surgeon on the investigation team."

"No. I mean is she married? Seeing anyone? What?"

Tanner's gaze darted back to The Mighty Quinn. The answer fell free without hesitation. "She doesn't do relationships with pilots."

"Pilots!" Kathleen stepped out of the shower and kicked the boots lying on the bathroom floor. Too bad they didn't have a certain big, blond hotshot inside them.

Cinching her towel tighter around herself, she scooped the uniform off the tile floor. She stuffed it in her laundry bag and wished her frustration could be as easily discarded.

She hadn't accumulated years of medical training only to be banished from crew-dog interviews or to take notes, while Tanner and The Mighty Quinn talked airplanes. Give the doc a pat on the head and send her on her way. Kathleen whipped off her towel and flung it in the tub.

Willing her temper to fade, she slid on ivory lace underwear, her secret indulgence. She hadn't grown up in a house full of fashion-conscious sisters without picking up a few preferences of her own. Expensive matched sets of underwear nurtured a corner of her soul in need of pampering.

It also became her little secret she carried beneath her uniform. She would play by their flyers' club rules, compete wherever they set the bar, but she would do it as a woman.

She might not have a name like The Mighty Quinn, Bronco or even Crusty. But she knew who she was, and

Tanner Bennett could take a flying leap off his own load ramp if he thought he could eclipse her.

Let him have his guy-talk meeting with Crusty. She'd scheduled her own investigative appointment with the government inspector, Randall Fitzgerald. Their little chat by the soda machine had netted more information than the entire tour through the factory.

Kathleen shrugged into her cream satin shirt, buttoning slowly. No way would she let Tanner's towering presence overshadow her tonight.

From the closet she unclipped and pulled free her favorite pants. Brown leather. One leg at a time she eased them on, savoring the sensation of the supple leather sliding over, then clinging to her. No need to tuck in her shirt as it stopped an inch below her waistband. She could enjoy the night breeze slithering the satin across her bare skin.

Kathleen slipped on low leather pumps and her standard pearl stud earrings. Nothing flashy like her sisters. No pouring on the charm like Tanner. Just herself, and damned if she planned to stand in the wings.

One spritz of perfume in her open neckline and she finger combed her damp hair, ready to leave. Let the desert night air dry it on her way to meet the inspector.

At the Wing and a Prayer Bar and Grill.

Tanner shoved open the door to the Wing and a Prayer, shooting a thumbs-up thanks over his shoulder to the friend who'd given him a ride. The aviator hangout was parked at the intersection of the middle of nowhere and the ends of the earth. The clapboard building sported the tail of a plane sticking out of the roof.

Cactus Christmas lights glowed around the door frame, offering a festivity he chose to ignore. Laughter and clanking bottles foretold the crowd he would find inside the always-packed bar.

He wouldn't wonder what Kathleen had decided to do with her evening. This was about getting his head on right again, while snagging time with Crusty to ferret out the straight scoop about what had happened on that flight.

Military and civilian locals alike gravitated to the bar decorated with Air Force test memorabilia dating back to the 1940s. Pieces of crashed aircraft—shell casings, metal skin off planes, busted flight instruments, propellers—covered the walls in the same way fishermen mount their prize bass. Straight ahead, a wide-screen television blared nonstop aviation movies for those who opted for a table rather than the bar off to the left.

He wove around the dark wooden chairs in search of Crusty. Tanner sidestepped table after table with crews and…

Couples.

Why hadn't he ever noticed how many couples congregated in this bar during his other TDY visits to Edwards? He'd always thought of it as more of a crew hangout. Apparently not.

Maybe he only took note now since he was between relationships himself. He liked having a steady woman in his life, regardless of what Kathleen might think. Okay, so his relationships usually self-destructed after about six months, but that didn't mean he hadn't tried.

Damn it, he wasn't commitment shy.

He could almost hear her snort of disdain over the clank of beer bottles.

"Bronco!" a male voice shouted from the back corner.

Tanner pivoted and found Daniel "Crusty" Baker waving from two tables over. Wiry and an inch shy of six feet, Crusty looked as if he'd just rolled out of the sack. A rumpled flight suit, crooked patches and a severe case of bedhead marked the guy as slack.

Appearances were deceiving. Reputation labeled him a

sharp pilot with solid air sense that had gained him a chest full of medals for his flights over Afghanistan.

Tanner thumped his old classmate on the back. "Hey, bud! How's it going?"

"Bennett, my man." Crusty finished stuffing French fries in his mouth, then swiped his salty fingers down his flight suit before shaking hands. "I see you're still determined to pass up the big bucks and ball-field glory with the Broncos for a pair of silver wings."

"What can I say? The job comes with a leather jacket and cool toys."

"That it does."

Tanner waved for the Santa-clad bartender and ordered two beers. During their Academy days, Crusty had worked in the football video lab, taping games for later analysis. Tanner had spent more than a few hours with his classmate while Crusty spun tapes, as well as fantasies about their training officer, Cadet O'Connell.

Geez, couldn't a guy even go out for a beer without that woman creeping into his thoughts?

Crusty gripped his long-neck bottle like a throttle. "So you're here to hang me out to dry."

Tanner leaned back in his chair. "Should I?"

"What do the after-action reports tell you?"

"Not much, but my Squadron Commander says your hands brought the plane down safely."

Scratching along the neck of his flight suit, Crusty knocked his squadron scarf farther askew. "That doesn't mean they're not going to try and pin this on me by claiming something happened earlier."

"Did it? Hey, we're human. All it takes is for the airspeed to be a little off during the drop, the wings cranked—"

"No!" Crusty snatched his beer from the table. "Damn

it, they always want to blame it on the pilot. It's easier than admitting they screwed up somewhere higher in the chain."

"I hear you." He understood too well, and it tore at him. A part of him sided with the brotherhood, didn't want it to be a career-ending crew mistake. "I don't want it to be your fault, but we gotta figure this one out before it happens again."

"Check the in-flight tapes." Crusty tipped his beer, nursing a long swig.

"Wish I could." Tanner eased his chair back on two legs. He searched his friend's eyes and waited.

Crusty lowered the bottle from his lips. "What?"

"The tapes are blank. Demagnetized. Erased. Do you have any idea how that happened?"

The other pilot thumped his bottle back on the table. "They're gonna hang me out to dry."

Nothing but frustration showed in Crusty's eyes. More questioning wouldn't pull anything from him. Better just to reestablish the friendship in hopes the guy would come to him if he had something to spill later. Tanner slugged him on the arm. "Hey, bring it down a notch, bud. Let me buy you another beer. Catch me up on what you hear about the mess over in Sentavo."

"Yeah, you bet." Crusty shrugged his shoulders and shook the tension out of his arms, rippling his wrinkled flight suit. He gestured for a drink, but didn't look away from the bar. His gaze stayed fixed just over Tanner's shoulder.

Tanner twisted in his chair, looking.

Finding.

Her.

Kathleen stood silhouetted in the doorway.

His chair thudded all four legs on the floor in a teeth-jarring landing. No flight suit for her tonight, she'd changed.

Man, had she changed.

Brown leather pants molded themselves to her every curve. They sealed over her trimly muscled calves, up her thighs to cup that bottom he'd tried not to watch all day. Her hair flowed in a fiery curtain around her face, brushing the collar of her satin shirt. Scorching his eyes from across the smoky room.

She leaned over the bar to place her drink order. Her blouse inched up, baring a thin stripe of skin along her back. Twelve years hadn't dimmed the memory of how soft that skin felt beneath his hands, how warm.

Crusty whistled low between his teeth. "Well scuff my shoes and untuck my shirt, she still makes me want to stand up and salute."

Tanner didn't even have to think about his response as he turned back to his college pal. "She doesn't do relationships with flyers."

"Ah, so that explains why she's sitting next to him."

"Him who?" Tanner twisted in his seat again, heedless of any leftover wrench in his back.

Kathleen hitched a hip onto a bar stool next to a man in civilian clothes. The government inspector. Randall Fitzgerald.

The guy's Christmas tree socks matched his tie and suspenders.

Tanner's fingers twitched around his untouched long-neck. Kathleen canted forward as if listening to something the man said, then laughed. The husky timbre dive-bombed Tanner's weakened defenses from clear across the room.

Hadn't they agreed to ignore hormones for the good of the investigation? So what was she doing sidling up to Inspector Happy Tie just because he wasn't a flyboy?

Her hair shimmered with the toss of her head. Inspector Randy reached.

He touched her hair.

Tanner's muscles bunched.

Slowly Randall Fitzgerald grasped the stray strand and hooked it behind Kathleen's ear.

Tossing money on the table, Tanner never looked away from the bar. ''Been good talking with you, Crusty. Catch you at the squadron later.''

Tanner didn't wait for the reply. Before he could rub the bump on his nose as a reminder for caution, he plowed across the bar, straight for his redheaded partner.

Chapter 7

Kathleen scooched back on her bar stool and sipped her lemon water, a much wiser way of removing Randall Fitzgerald's hand from her hair than breaking the guy's fingers. Randall skimmed his knuckles across her cheek anyway, before grasping his vodka tonic.

Of course, survival training *had* provided her with at least four different techniques for snapping a pinky.

Not that there was anything wrong with him—a nice guy, well groomed, intelligent. She just wasn't interested in anything other than an informal interview, and she hadn't lead him to believe otherwise. Perhaps he needed another reminder.

Kathleen twirled her straw. "How long have you been working at the Palmdale facility?"

"Five years." The gleam in his eyes matched the fluorescent ornaments painted on his Christmas tree suspenders.

Randall dragged his bar stool closer. Of course, he could have been clearing space for the drunken duo plopping down to "fly" the stick and throttle attached to the bar. She decided to give Randall the benefit of the doubt.

"So you like it there?" She watched him for visual clues while she sipped her water.

"Sure. It's a great job. No office politics, since the boss is a million miles away." Randall loosened the knot on his evergreen tie, then leaned an elbow on the bar. "I'm made of free time if you'd like a personal tour of the local hot spots."

Kathleen's smile became pained. The next thing she'd know, this clown would be asking her if she preferred waffles or pancakes for breakfast.

It wasn't fair. Two guys exchanged beer and small talk and it furthered an investigation. A man and woman did the same and it became some kind of mating dance.

But she could handle him. She hadn't hung out with flyers for years without learning a few polite brush-offs. Keep it professional at all costs. Never give an inch. "What exactly do you do out there at the plant?"

"I verify that all the parts are tested, sign for them, then the government takes possession of them."

"Uh-huh." She motioned for a water refill from the bartender by the throttle-style beer taps. "And then?"

Apparently good ol' Randy mistook her interest for impressed fascination. The guy sure did love to talk about himself. Rather than set him straight for pride's sake, Kathleen simply listened and filed information away to sort through later when her head wasn't pounding.

At least her headache wasn't Randall's fault. That pain had a certain blond pilot's name all over it. She'd seen Tanner when she'd stepped in the bar. How could she miss him? He could fill a room with his presence in a way that had nothing to do with his shoulders.

Even with her back to him, she still felt him. Felt the irritatingly predictable awareness that buzzed from her toes right up to the roots of her hair whenever he came near. She started to look over her shoulder just as a shadow fell across the bar.

A broad-shouldered shadow.

The buzz increased to a rippling jolt of heat, like a near miss with an electrical outlet.

A thudding heartbeat later, Tanner stopped beside her and thrust his hand toward Randall Fitzgerald. "Hi. Captain Tanner Bennett. I don't believe we met earlier at the testing site."

The inspector bolted to his feet. "Randall Fitzgerald, government inspector."

"Yes, so my reports tell me." Tanner gripped the inspector's hand, and Kathleen had to give Randall credit. The man didn't wince.

Tanner reached behind Kathleen's back, bracing a palm on the bar. The heat of his arm, his chest a whisper away from her shoulder, embraced her.

What the hell was he doing?

Tanner fingered a lock of hair on her shoulder. "Are you about ready to leave? We've got an early start tomorrow."

"No." She edged her head away until the strand slid free. When had her hair grown so darn long?

"Are you sure? You didn't get much sleep the past couple of nights." His voice lowered to husky intimacy.

"I'm fine." Or she would be after she killed him. First she would stake him out in the desert, slather him with his own honeyed words and set the ants loose.

Then she would kill him.

Kathleen decided not to dignify his comment with an explanation about how her sleepless nights were a by-product of a late-night visit to the flight line followed by a transcontinental trip home. No need to encourage Randy into thinking they would be sharing those waffles. And the only waffles for Tanner would be dumped on his head. She understood ants loved syrup.

Randall tightened his tie. "Time to call it a night, then. I have an early call myself, Captain Bennett."

"Nice meeting you, Randy."

"You, too. G'night, Kathleen." He didn't even hesitate on his way out the door.

Kathleen pivoted on the bar stool until she faced Tanner eye to eye. "What was that all about?"

"What?" He cocked his head to the side, keeping his arm possessively placed behind her back.

"Don't play dumb jock with me, hotshot. I know you better than that." She shoved his hand off the bar. "You ran the guy off with your macho territory marking."

"I thought you would be glad."

Anger must be cutting off the blood supply to her brain. "Run that one by me again?"

"The guy was hitting on you." The air carried a full measure of musky Tanner and seasoned leather.

"That's your problem because…?" She propped one elbow on the bar, for distance as well as steadying. She couldn't even put on her leather jacket anymore without thinking of him. "I'm thirty-two years old, Bennett. I can handle myself, thanks all the same."

"Excuse me for trying to help. It's obvious he wasn't here to discuss metallurgy and quality control."

"Do you think I don't know that?"

Tanner straightened, his face blank. "So you *were* meeting him here—socially."

"No." She lowered her voice, which forced her to move closer in order to be heard, but not overheard. "I was asking some informal questions, just like you planned with Crusty."

"Crusty wasn't playing with my hair." Tanner advanced

a step. Her knees brushed his thighs. "That guy had his hands all over you."

Kathleen resisted the urge to hop off the bar stool. She held her ground and didn't move, not that she had any choice. Her only other option to avoid contact would be to part her legs.

Not a chance.

Her whole focus narrowed to her tingling knees, and that royally ticked her off. Her hormones would not rule her. "I was handling it just fine until you shouldered your way over here and all but whizzed on his leg. Geez, Bennett! My job places me in an almost exclusively male world, traveling in close quarters with men on a regular basis. Do you think none of them have ever hit on me? Let me tell you, hotshot, I've picked up more than a few skills in turning down a guy without making him mad."

Tanner's eyes honed from pale blue to steely gray in a sharpening flash. "Who's been giving you trouble?"

The need to shout at him almost overwhelmed her. Holding her ground wasn't working. "I do *not* need a bodyguard."

She yanked her purse off the back of her chair and leaped from the bar stool. Her knees forgot their job for one wobbly second before Kathleen regained her balance. She jammed her purse strap over her shoulder.

"Kathleen, now hold on—"

"Let me make one thing clear, Bennett, in case you were wondering." Her voice rose with each word, and she was too frustrated to care if the whole bar heard her. "I'm mad as hell at you right now. Mad. Angry. Furious. *Not* turned on!"

She spun on her heel and stalked toward the exit.

Her slam rattled the glasses over the bar. Tanner stared at the closed door and resisted the urge to charge out after her and finish their argument.

Jangling glasses silenced. Only the television's low drone filled the room. The bar full of faces trained on him.

A low whistle pealed from Crusty, like a dropping bomb, followed by a growling explosion. "Way to crash and burn, my man."

Tanner didn't bother answering. He traced his thumb over the bump on his nose and counted to ten—then twenty.

She wasn't the only one mad. Although he wasn't sure what made him angrier, her blasé response to the aptly named "Randy's" overtures or the fact that workmates hit on her far too often.

Either way, Tanner's temper stirred like the rumbling percussion of Crusty's imaginary bomb. But another confrontation with Kathleen would only lead them into saying things that would make work even more strained in the morning.

Better to sit, bolt back some buffalo wings and watch the movie. He did not need to extend their discussion to a parking lot.

A dimly lit parking lot.

An image of Kathleen, vulnerable as she walked to her car, exploded within him. She might be smart as hell and capable beyond reason, but so was his sister. None of that had mattered to a man twice her size with a gun.

Regardless of how much Kathleen infuriated him, she was his partner. His wingman.

And he'd let her leave. Alone.

"Damn." Tanner sprinted for the door.

"Damn." Kathleen thumbed the unlock button on her key chain for the third time and it didn't open the car. "Damn. Damn. Damn him!"

Slumping against the silver Ford Taurus, she sucked in

calming air. The chilly desert night did little to help cool the hot swirl of emotions.

She wanted to scream. She needed to cry. But she wouldn't do either because of a man ever again.

How would she get through the next day, much less weeks working with Tanner? God, she wished she could have that neutral ground back.

Staring up at the twinkling sky, Kathleen blinked away frustrated tears that blurred the stars until any wishing became impossible. The key weighted down her hand. Even her shoes seemed ten pounds heavier. Sighing, she palmed the door unlock button again and shoved away from her car.

Only to see another just like it.

Scanning the willy-nilly parked cars, Kathleen counted five silver Ford Tauruses in the lot, apparently the military rental car of choice.

Her shoes lost ten pounds with her laugh.

She finally spotted her car among the others parked in a haphazard cluster. As she walked, a coyote howled in the distance.

A shiver rippled through her. From nerves, the chill or just plain anger, she didn't know. She stole one last look at the stars, overly bright without the smear of smog diluting their brightness. Their intensity granted her peace if not wishes.

Wishing on a star was superstitious, anyway.

She shook free thoughts of superstitions before Tanner charged back into her mind.

Finally the key chain worked as advertised, activating interior lights as her car doors unlocked. She refused to feel guilty over leaving Tanner at the bar. He'd found his way there. He could find his way home. She reached for the door handle.

A hand fell on her shoulder.

Her fingers convulsed around her keys. Fear burned over her for three interminable seconds.

Then instincts brought chilling numbness. Training assumed command of her brain.

Kathleen rammed her heel on the foot behind her. Her elbow pumped back into a rock-solid stomach. A gratifying swoosh of air huffed over her just before a burly arm banded around her stomach.

She forced down panic. *Think.*

The keys. Set off the car alarm.

She juggled the keys in her hand, grappling for the right button. Sweat slicked her palm. The keys jangled to the ground.

Fear rolled over her in earnest. Use it. Channel it. Go for the groin.

A hand vise-gripped her wrist.

''Kathleen.''

The masculine voice dimly pierced her narrow focus.

''Kathleen! It's me. Tanner. Stop before you turn me into a gelding.''

Tanner.

She sagged against his arm. His corded muscles relaxed. Fear had skewed her senses until she hadn't even considered it could be him. Tanner. Who'd taken too damn long in announcing himself.

Kathleen spun around and found him directly behind her. His face was dimly distinguishable in the poorly lit parking lot, but no doubt about it. With the aid of a harvest moon, she could see him well enough. She should have known when she'd leaned back against him, except she'd been too damned scared to death.

She wanted to gut punch him, but hesitated at the last second because of his back. If he ended up in the infirmary, he would get pain medication.

He didn't deserve it. The jerk should hurt for scaring her.

"Tanner."

"What?"

"This." She grabbed his pinky and bent it back. She'd taken men to their knees with the move at survival camp and considered the option now.

"What the—" He stumbled a step but stayed on his feet. "Geez, Kathleen! That hurts."

"Good!" She flung aside his hand. "You scared the hell out of me! Don't you know better than to sneak up on someone like that?"

His brows slammed down into a foreboding scowl. "Don't you know better than to walk through a dark parking lot alone? You didn't even check inside the car before you reached to open it."

"So you were teaching me a lesson?" Her voice rose as postadrenaline shakes set in. "Protecting me? Well, I'm not interested in participating in your testosterone tango tonight."

"This has nothing to do with testosterone, lady, and everything to with common-sense safety. What would you have done if it hadn't been me?"

"Broken your nose. Poked your eyes out." Shards of fear still scratched at her insides, not that she would admit it to Tanner. "Gelded you."

"Maybe. If you were lucky. But maybe not. Why take that chance? I outweigh you by over a hundred pounds."

"So size matters after all?" Kathleen suppressed a wince as her mouth ran away with her yet again. Damn but she was tired of being a victim to her emotions around this man.

The normally lighthearted Tanner didn't even crack a smile. "I'm not in the mood for jokes."

"I'm just playing by your rules."

"You don't get it, do you? You were so zeroed in on your anger at me, you didn't think about blasting out here alone. You forgot the most basic Air Force rule. Never, never leave your wingman.'' His head tipped back, displaying an unrestrained view of his flexing jaw. His throat moved with a long swallow before he looked down at her again. "Answer one question. Why didn't you shout?"

"What?" Confusion muddied her anger. "Shout? Back at the bar? I tried to keep our argument low-key for the sake of the investigation."

"No. When I caught you around the waist. Or even earlier when I put my hand on your shoulder. Why didn't you scream for help?"

"Oh. Because…I was just…" She scrambled for a reason…and came up blank. She didn't know why. For once she had no quick comeback for Tanner, and she didn't like the uneven footing.

Time to retreat and regroup. Kathleen scooped her keys from the gravel. "Forget it. I refuse to fight with you tonight."

His arm shot forward, blocking the driver's door. "I didn't put my hand over your mouth, something a mugger wouldn't be so generous about. You never made a sound. Just dug your heels in—granted you dug them into my boot—and fought the battle by yourself when help could have been three cars down. Why?"

The intensity of his eyes held her with a power that frightened her, stirred her, immobilized her in a way that had nothing to do with Tanner's size. "Let me go, and we'll talk more in the morning when we're both calmer."

"We'll talk about it now." His other palm pressed against the car as he bracketed her with his arms. "One in every four rapes takes place in a public area or in a parking garage."

His sister. Kathleen sagged against the quarter panel. How could she have forgotten his sister had died in a carjacking attack? That explained his overreaction, made it forgivable.

Kathleen's anger dissipated like rain on a thirsty desert floor. ''Tanner, I'm—''

''Sixty-eight percent of rapes occur between six at night and six in the morning.'' His voice deepened, every word faster, heavier. ''Seventy-five percent of female rape victims require medical care after the attack.'' He jerked a thumb over his shoulder toward the bar. ''At least forty-five percent of rapists are under the influence of alcohol or drugs.''

''Tanner!'' She looked into his eyes, silver-flecked sapphire eyes glinting with tears. Still as full of pain as they'd been twelve years ago. All the defenses she'd built against him fell away, leaving her way too vulnerable to a man she already had trouble resisting. ''Tanner, please—''

''Every two minutes in America a woman is sexually assaulted. Over three hundred *thousand* women a year.'' Tanner's forehead fell to rest against hers, his breathing bursts of ragged emotion. ''I won't let another woman—you—be a statistic, damn it! I won't.''

His hoarse vow sliced through Kathleen. The healer within her couldn't resist this wounded man any more now than that night in the Academy barracks. No matter how she tried to tell herself she would ache for *anyone* in so much pain, she knew otherwise. Tanner had a way of stirring her emotions that no one had ever matched.

She couldn't turn away from those glistening eyes.

Kathleen cupped his face in her palms and once again silenced him with her lips.

Chapter 8

The roar inside his head quieted. And just like twelve
years ago, Tanner welcomed the forgetfulness offered in
Kathleen's kiss. Except this time the roar had been brought
on by her, the fear of her being the one trapped, hurt. Dead.

He cupped the back of her head. Anchored her to him.
Anchored himself in the moment with her intoxicating heat.

His fingers stroked through her hair while his tongue
stroked through her mouth. Minty shampoo tempted him
outside, the sweet flavor of lemon and Kathleen inside. He
tasted, drank the sweet assurance that she was alive.

Man, was she alive.

Her arms looped around his neck, and she kissed him
back. Really kissed him. No question about whether she
wanted this or not.

His gut-twisting fear for her eased, leaving in its place a
raw hunger for Kathleen, one that he'd shoved aside for far
too long. He didn't stand a chance of battling it now, not
when she tangled her tongue with his. Nipped his bottom
lip. Lightly moaned into his mouth.

Her toned body pressed against his—as closely as she could, given their height difference. Impatient to feel all of her all over him, Tanner cupped her bottom and lifted.

Warm leather and softness filled his hands. Groaning, he pulled her closer. Her legs locked around his waist.

Did this woman have to be so damned perfect?

He lowered her to sit on the hood of the car. Gently, carefully. He couldn't forget how small she was.

Not that she seemed concerned.

Kathleen tightened her legs, strong and taut around him, and she nudged closer, closer still until she fit. Who'd have thought leather could become that hot without melting?

Her breasts, small, firm, perfect, pressed to him, beaded against him in an unmistakable invitation. No way could she miss his throbbing reaction to her, either. And still she didn't pull away.

With surprising strength and purpose, her fingers gripped his shoulders, arms, face. His hands trembled with the effort to keep his touch gentle, thumb brushing over her cheekbone.

He'd wanted her for so long, had endured more dreams about this woman than he could count, and here she was. Hotter, better, sweeter than any dream.

And she was in his arms. His. He smoothed his hands over her hair as if he could brush away the image of another guy's hands on her.

A car roared past, honking. "Hey, you two!" a man shouted out the window. "Get a room!"

Tanner mumbled his frustration through kisses along her jaw. However, the driver of the car had an excellent point. Once he got Kathleen all to himself...

"Stop, Tanner." She gasped against his cheek, but the words came between her kisses, which didn't show signs of slowing. "We've got to stop."

Kathleen's trembling voice whispered past his increasing need to take her. Now. In a bar parking lot.

Reason edged a bit further into his consciousness, and Tanner reluctantly tore his mouth away. Her neck made a logical resting place for his face while he regained control. Of course breathing the scent of undiluted Kathleen offered almost as much satisfaction as tasting her.

His late-day beard snagged against her satin. Skin or her shirt? Both so soft, how could he tell?

But this wasn't the place.

He peeled his body from hers, allowing himself to touch her only by cupping her shoulders. She looked in need of the support. Her eyes cloudy, she swayed under his hands. Massaging the satin over her skin, Tanner promised himself the pleasure of gliding that shirt off her body later. Then those leather pants that had been torturing him all evening.

All evening?

Thoughts of having Kathleen had tortured him for years. Now that he would finally have her, he didn't intend to rush. Yeah, he looked forward to removing those leather pants, but with torturously slow precision, discovering, tasting, sinking into a fantasy he'd never expected to live out.

He forced a laugh to ease an ache that made his back's stint seem like a cakewalk. "Good thing one of us has sense."

Her tremulous smile faltered until it collapsed like a marionette with cut strings. "Sometimes those IQ points are a real pain."

"A few minutes delay won't kill us."

"Delay?"

"Yeah, until we get back to my room. Or yours. Doesn't matter to me." His fingers tightened on her shoulders. "It'll be worth the wait."

Kathleen stopped swaying. "I don't think you understand."

Tanner stroked his thumb along her neck. "Then explain."

"This can't happen." The rapid beat of her pulse beneath his thumb belied her words. "We can't finish."

"Can't finish?" He searched for indecision in her eyes and found a cargo hold full. Tanner advanced a step, slid his hands down her back and studied the mouth he planned to take again in another second. If holding her, kissing her was all he could have tonight, then fine. It would be enough. For now. "Then we'll just keep not finishing."

Her hand shot toward his chest, stopped, didn't touch. "No. I mean never."

His pinky started throbbing right along with another larger part of him. He backed two steps away from the tempting image of Kathleen perched on the hood. "Okay. I hear you. But why? And don't toss me that 'no pilots' line. We've known each other too long for it to be as simple as that."

When she didn't answer, he scrounged for the right words. He was trying like hell to be reasonable, sensitive...persuasive. The woman worshiped logic, after all.

"I want you, Kathleen. Hell, it's no secret I've always wanted you, and it's tearing us both up to the point we can't work." Tanner watched her grow still. And she wasn't arguing. He forged ahead. "We're both adults. Neither of us is seeing anyone else. What's to stop us from getting this out of our system once and for all?"

She sat at least four inches taller. "Get me out of your system?"

Uh—oh. "That's not what I meant."

"What did you mean?"

"Not that."

"Then what?"

He shifted from one foot to the other, checked out the stars for guidance, found none. "It's not like we're looking for anything long-term. You know you'd want to kill me inside a month.''

"A week. Then we'd still have to work together.''

He cupped her face with his palm. ''But it would be one hell of a week.'' She tensed beneath his hand and he started to pull away. ''Fine. You're right.''

She stopped his hand with hers and held it to her face, pressed a slow kiss in his palm, before lowering it. ''I'm sorry.''

Damn, he deserved to have his other pinky twisted. He needed to quit thinking below the belt and remember this woman deserved better from him. He'd been a hormonal cretin from the minute he'd seen her sitting with the randy inspector.

''Tanner, if it helps, I'm just not a casual sex kind of woman. No matter who the guy is.''

''It does help. And it doesn't.'' At least he didn't have to worry about Randall Fitzgerald anymore.

''Maybe I'm crazy, but somehow I got the idea you weren't into casual sex, either. Something about treating women the way you would want some guy to treat your mother and your sis—'' She screeched to a halt, but not soon enough. ''Oh, God, Tanner. I'm sorry. I wasn't thinking.''

The already cool night chilled another ten degrees.

In the wake of the icy shower of her words, Tanner heard the low rumble start in his ears. If he let that roar build, it could too easily lead him into begging for the forgetfulness only Kathleen seemed able to offer. ''Forget it. It doesn't matter, and you're right. Enough talking. Time to down a couple of those muscle relaxers and pack it in for the night.''

Tanner extended his hand to help her from the hood.

She didn't budge. ''Did you drink anything?''

''No, Doc.'' He shouldn't be surprised by her logical

concern about him mixing medication and alcohol. But he resented her ability to think clearly when the lingering effects of their kiss still had him on shaky ground. "I ordered a beer for appearances with Crusty and didn't touch it."

"Okay."

Then Kathleen surprised him.

She dropped the keys in his hand. "I'm not in any condition to drive now."

Kathleen ignored his extended hand and hopped from the hood. Her head high, spine rigid, she made her way to the passenger side. He would have thought Kathleen unaffected if it weren't for the keys in his palm and the small dent in the hood of the car.

She might be right about them not finishing anything tonight. But she was wrong about expecting him to back off.

Kathleen might have the IQ of a rocket scientist, but she'd missed the mark this time. They couldn't walk away from what they'd started. Chemistry like that didn't come along every day.

They were going to finish it. Before it finished them.

Kathleen wanted to finish it, longed to take it all, but feared the whole pot of java wouldn't jolt her to life after her restless night. Standing beside the lobby coffee machine, she replaced the carafe on the warmer and resigned herself to making do with the measly twelve ounces in her travel mug.

A corner of her hopeful brain had decided she'd exaggerated her response to Tanner all those years ago. One kiss and she would know the truth.

The truth had not set her free.

The truth had her by the jugular, and she didn't know how to shake loose. Kissing Tanner had been nothing like twelve years before. She couldn't possibly have remembered the intense reaction and still allowed herself to become so close. Almost friends. Vulnerable.

Which was why she had to forget about their lip lock of the prior night. If kissing him could turn her into mindless mush, then making love with him would zap every ounce of control she'd cultivated.

Heavy treads sounded from the stairwell just before the lobby door opened. One flash of golden-blond hair and already her heart pumped a hummingbird's pace. Kathleen turned away, busying herself with selecting the perfect napkin from the drink cart.

"Good morning, Kathleen." Tanner reached past her shoulder for a cup, then the pot, never touching. Just too close for her to ignore.

Kansas would have been too close.

She sidled away, downing a scalding gulp from her mug as she eyed Tanner over the lid. Would he be angry? Men in a testosterone snit could be testy. She wasn't feeling all that pleasant herself.

Worse, what if none of it mattered to him? Lighthearted Tanner could shrug off anything, including one parking lot turn-down from his least favorite flight surgeon.

With a familiar gleam in his eyes, Tanner returned her stare over the top of his cup. She'd seen it the last time he'd headed into combat, and she knew that look. Focused determination.

Focused on her.

He hadn't forgotten. Tanner hadn't shrugged one second of their kiss off those broad shoulders.

A rogue shiver of unwanted excitement prickled over her. Followed by numbing determination. He might be circling, but she intended to set boundaries with impenetrable defenses. They had two weeks to wrap up the investigation before Christmas. She intended to be home in time to finish her shopping.

Kathleen reached into her left breast pocket. His gaze trailed her every movement as she withdrew a slip of paper. He didn't linger.

He didn't need to. Her memory supplied plenty of details about her breasts pressed to his rock-solid chest. Another steely hard part of him pressed—

She set her jaw and offered him the scrap of paper. "Here."

Tanner took it without touching her. Not that he needed to. "What's this?"

"A chiropractor appointment. Yours. We should be finished checking out the wreckage with Quinn and Crusty in plenty of time for you to make it this afternoon."

His thumb worked over the print as if that might erase the time. "I assume this is non-negotiable."

"You got it, hotshot. Direct orders from your doc." There. Boundary number one. Doctor-patient distancing established. On her own turf, she felt steadier already.

Tanner cocked his head to the side, silent for once as he studied her. Assessing the opponent for weaknesses?

He wouldn't find them.

Slowly he folded the paper and slid it into a sleeve pocket. Kathleen exhaled her relief. Until she noticed the careful manner in which he worked the paper. Favoring his pinky. His puffy, swollen pinky.

Her boundaries surrendered crucial ground.

Kathleen extended her arm. "Let me see your hand."

"What?"

"The pinky I twisted. I need to make sure I didn't break it."

He folded his arms over his chest, holding his cup in one hand, tucking his other out of sight. "You didn't."

"Pardon me if I don't trust you to be honest about your medical condition." She snapped her fingers as she set aside her mug. "Hand, please."

With a you-asked-for-it look, he unfolded his arms. He rested his hand in hers, slowly, precisely, so damned seductively she stifled a tiny moan. His roughened skin rasped against her as it had the night before. Calluses marked him a physical man. That hand could have immobilized her with its strength, yet instead he'd paralyzed her with a gentle caress.

Could do so again.

Scavenging for every professional instinct she'd ever honed, she cradled his hand in both of hers and examined him. Routine comforted her, her science the one dependable thing in her life. She finally released his hand. "Sprained, but not broken. I don't suppose you iced it last night?"

"I had other things on my mind." His eyes deepened from warm blue to something molten hot with memories.

She needed to reestablish those boundaries post-haste before she ended up in full retreat. The ice machine might not be as far away as Kansas, but it would have to do.

Kathleen snagged a paper cup from the table and strode to the machine. Scooping the cup through, she filled the makeshift ice pack. "Stick your finger in this on the way over to the hangar."

He fished the keys from his pocket. "You're determined to make me suffer."

"I'm determined to do my job." Kathleen shoved the cup in his hand. While he was distracted, she snagged the keys from his other hand and spun on her heel, making tracks for the parking lot.

Driving to the hangar, Kathleen found that five minutes dragged on interminably without conversation. She had too much time to think, and her reasonable mind settled on the obvious. She needed to cut ties officially as his doctor.

Not that she planned to pursue a relationship with him. But the attraction had escalated until it interfered with her judgment. That was inexcusable. She'd made the mistake before. While she hadn't been the one to sign her ex-husband's medical waiver to fly, she'd known it was questionable, likely given as a favor to her. And she hadn't said a word because she'd feared kicking another prop from under her already shaky marriage.

Failure was unacceptable.

Sometimes she wondered if she was more upset over facing her family's disappointment yet again than she had been over losing Andrew.

Her hands trembled. Kathleen gripped the steering wheel to steady them, careful to keep her ten-two hand positioning. Middle of the lane. Three miles an hour under the speed limit. In control of her world.

She would contact the Edwards AFB Clinic for a consult with one of their flight surgeons. He could care for Tanner temporarily, and when they returned home, one of the other flight surgeons could take over the big lug's treatment. With her blessing.

For now, she needed to focus on safeguarding the investigation. Her promotion recommendation.

And her heart.

Kathleen pulled into the parking lot outside the airplane hangar housing the damaged aircraft. Planes lined the ramp alongside—a row of fighters, another for trainers, then bombers and airlifters. The airlifters belonged to her.

A rogue thought blindsided her. Did she, plain ol' Doc, belong to them? It had been a long time since she'd wanted to belong somewhere. Solitude seemed safer. "Come on, hotshot. Let's get to work."

Without a word Tanner pitched the ice from his cup onto the cement tarmac. He followed her toward the hangar. It loomed large and "boring brown" like every other hangar in the Air Force. The familiarity of the building only drove home the knowledge that this could have happened any-where, anytime, to anyone of them.

Had, in fact, happened in her world before.

Tanner stopped in front of a smaller door set in the framework of the larger garage-style door. He punched in the combination on the cipher lock.

Inside, the C-17 filled the metal cavern. A bird flapped through the webbing of rafters overhead, startled from its perch by the opening door.

A heavy coating of dust remained on the cargo craft from its emergency landing on a dried-up lake bed. Even towing it to the hangar hadn't shaken loose the caked-on crust.

Kathleen circled the wreckage. While she wasn't a be-liever in things mystical, even she had to admit the wounded plane seemed to hum with memories. Suddenly she understood why flyers and sailors called their crafts a personal "she" rather than an impersonal "it." The em-pathetic physician within her could feel the pain radiating from the damaged aircraft.

She traced a ragged metal edge as if assessing a patient for treatment, for healing. "Explain to me what I'm seeing."

Footsteps sounded, closer, slowing until Tanner stopped just behind her. The fresh scent of his shower, soap and coffee drifted her way with precise navigation. It would be so easy to lean back and let his arm drape around her while they talked. Too easy.

"They were dropping a two pack of Humvees. Two smaller jeeps lashed together on a pallet. The loadmaster lowered the ramp, began the off-load. That's when things went to hell. The pallet started down the tracks fine, but hitched sideways at the last minute, ripping the ramp off."

Twisted metal spoke of a wrenching slash as the craft tore apart. The hollowed belly of the plane held lingering echoes of stunned, perhaps horrified shouts from the crew.

Had it been like that for her husband? Andrew had never told her anything about his crash since their split had immediately followed the accident. Anything she knew came from gossip and a pilfered after-action report. "Once the ramp ripped free, wasn't the problem over? Why an emergency landing in the desert?"

"Losing part of the plane shoots the aerodynamics all to hell. Hydraulic lines and cables to the tail also ripped off, which meant the rudders and elevators didn't work fully." His arm stretched past Kathleen to pat the plane as if consoling a friend. "Talk about a nightmare to land. But even worse to fly. Imagine a lumbering beast swaying in the air. Good thing Crusty was able put her down in the desert when he did or they'd all be dead."

Kathleen shuddered. She wrapped her arms around her waist and reminded herself she should be grateful she'd only ended up divorced and not widowed.

She understood now their marriage had been over long before the actual incident, but that hadn't eased the horror of the news. Her husband had ejected over the ocean. PJs, parajumpers/pararescuemen, had been deployed to recover him. Even with her feet firmly on the ground, she'd been partially to blame for not protesting that waiver.

Of course, the accident had mirrored their marriage, a wreck a long time in the making. Inevitable but unexpected.

She still didn't understand where she'd screwed up along the way with Andrew. She'd tried so damned hard to find that sense of belonging with him she'd never found growing up.

How could she risk the same emotional crash again when she had no idea what she'd missed first go-round? Ever a worshiper of logic, she understood the facts if not the reasons. The need to understand the flyer mind seemed more pressing than ever.

For the investigation, right?

Kathleen looked at Tanner's too-kissable mouth and wondered when she'd started lying to herself. "Okay, so that's how it happened. But I need more than the facts. I can read about those in the report. Help me understand what the crew was thinking."

Tanner shifted to stand in front of her, his hand sliding down the side of the plane. "They were likely flying along, ops-normal. It was a test mission. Maybe they were a little edgy, but not expecting anything out of the ordinary since they'd flown tests with the modification three times before without a problem. Knowing Crusty, he was probably grousing over pulling test duty, instead of being in the action overseas." Tanner darted a pointed look her way as he leaned a shoulder against the plane.

"Message received, hotshot. You're not the only one who would have given me hell about being grounded. Keep talking."

"Then he would have heard the loadmaster curse. Before Crusty could do more than sit up straight, the plane would have jerked under his hands. Then noise. Lots of noise. Guys up front shouting for damage assessment. The loadmaster shouting answers back at the same time. All heavily seasoned with their best swearing. No doubt about it, the tapes would have blistered your ears. And answered a few questions."

Frustration scratched at her already raw emotions. How could he recite all those facts like an automaton? Didn't fear or some kind of emotion come into play for these guys? "You're still just giving me facts. What were they feeling? Thinking about? A life review? Loved ones? What?"

"What did they feel?" His brows pulled together at her illogical request before his face cleared and he pushed away from the plane, closer to her. "For five seconds they were absolutely certain mortality was about to bite them on the

ass. During that time, yeah, they probably thought about
wives, kids, girlfriends, mamas. Then instincts and training
kicked in. For the next thirty minutes, they convinced themselves they were invincible gods who could put the plane
on the ground no matter what the odds said.''

The fire, unmistakable passion in his eyes awed her. This
man lived to fly.

She couldn't resist laying a comforting hand on his arm.
''You're going to be back on flying status soon. This won't
be permanent.''

''I hope so.'' Tanner shrugged off her hand under the
guise of picking up a stray bolt and tossing it inside the
open cargo hold.

She wasn't fooled.

''You will. I wouldn't say it if I wasn't absolutely certain. I know it seems like I came down hard on you, but...''
She pushed free the words she hadn't told anyone other
than a review board. ''My ex-husband crashed because he
was flying on a medical waiver. A waiver I knew was
questionable.''

Surprise flickered through Tanner's eyes but he stayed
silent, thank God. She wasn't sure she could continue if he
stopped her.

''Things were already rocky for us before because of...''
Her voice faltered before she plowed ahead. ''Because of
his inability to keep his pants zipped while he was TDY.
Then he had this chronic sinus problem. He wanted me to
slip him some meds on the sly so he wouldn't miss out on
a deployment. I wouldn't. So he went to someone else, got
a waiver to fly—and crashed the plane. Things went all to
hell for us after that. Basically, I'm such a screwup with
relationships, my marriage ended because of a stupid head
cold. Not to mention my bad judgment in falling for a man
who couldn't respect who I am.''

Tanner advanced a step, reached, skimmed a stray strand of hair from her face. "I'm sorry."

"Yeah, me, too."

His deep blue eyes became nearly translucent, letting her look into his every thought. She didn't find a trace of pity, just genuine sympathy and regret. He'd offered her more of himself with that look and one simple touch of comfort than Andrew had in two years of marriage.

Tanner didn't hold himself back from her, never had, and suddenly that scared her more than getting tangled up again with an aviator stud like her ex.

Chapter 9

Tanner stared back at Kathleen and wondered what thoughts churned in that logical mind of hers. Not that their current conversation had anything to do with logic.

Something sad drifted through her cool-blue eyes, and he hated that another man could still stir that much emotion in her. He wanted to pull her to his chest and stroke that tight braid until whatever twisted inside her eased.

He'd never been good at resisting impulses.

Tanner twined that strand of hair around his finger. He waited for her to object, shove him away, twist his pinky again.

She didn't move, just stood looking as confused as he felt. He drew her forward with a gentle tug to the lock of hair.

Still no objection.

Tanner let her hair slither free and traced his knuckles over her cheek, along her jaw, across her lips. Such a delicate face with petal-soft skin.

He kept his touch light, in part because he didn't want to startle her away, but also because she seemed so damned fragile right now in spite of that iron will. He sketched his fingers down her neck, dipping inside her flight suit to trace her collarbone.

Kathleen blinked twice, quickly, as if trying to keep her eyes from sliding closed. As much as he wanted her, he couldn't make himself hurry through the exploration. He needed to touch her. Had to watch her as they stood caught in something stronger than an impulsive kiss.

Her hand drifted up, taking far too long in Tanner's estimation. Finally she touched him back. One finger trailed down his nose, pausing to rub the crooked set. A brief smile played with her lips. Her fingers brushed his hair back from his brow, once, twice, again even though there wasn't a chance his close-cropped head needed it.

Uncertainty whispered from her eyes. "Tanner?"

He prepared himself for the fact he would have to step away. He hadn't prepared himself for the disappointment. And over what? It wasn't as if they were going to crawl into that plane and have sex.

Although the thought held definite appeal.

A bird flapped overhead, and Kathleen stumbled back a step just before the door opened.

Damn. He'd forgotten about his meeting with Crusty and Quinn.

The subcontractor strode inside, brisk, confident, efficient, just the kind of guy Kathleen should want. "Morning, all."

Crusty ambled past, whipping off his sunglasses. "Sorry I'm late. Overslept."

His spiking bed head verified that.

Kathleen's gaze flickered over his squadron scarf sticking half out of his flight suit. Crusty shot her a wink and tucked it in. "Just like old times, huh?"

Tanner didn't need the reminder he could be hanging an old friend out to dry, anymore than he needed the reminder that Kathleen was still wrong for him. Unattainable.

Quinn splayed a hand on the side of the plane and turned to Kathleen. "I didn't expect to see you here today."

"I'm tagging along with Captain Bennett until my toxicology reports are in." She smoothed back a loose strand of hair. "Let's get to work."

As they circled the plane, Tanner interviewed Crusty and Quinn. Tanner couldn't suppress a grin as Kathleen proved herself more than a tagalong, adding astute questions of her own. God, he enjoyed watching her analytical mind wrap itself around a piece of information. Just like that snug braid and the way her mouth tightened when she was holding herself back, her fast thinking challenged the hell out of him.

Kathleen paused by the ramp, turning to Quinn. Her hands gentled over the ragged metal. "Show me where they installed the modification."

Quinn crouched near the ramp and slid his hands along the inside wall of the plane, near the flooring. "It goes right here."

The subcontractor shot her a tolerant smile. Tanner almost laughed out loud. The poor fool underestimated O'Connell. Tanner stood to the side and watched her work.

Determination lit her eyes, no irritation, just a thinning of her lips. "And it does what, exactly?"

"The pin-pull actuator releases the pins so they move in sync for an even glide down the tracks." Quinn traced the track path, his arm brushing her shoulder.

Tanner's muscles bunched under his flight suit, but he stayed quiet and let Kathleen ask her questions.

"So if one of the pins reacted sluggishly…"

"That would be a problem. But we ran repetition tests at the plant before the part was installed. No problems.

These babies are a beauty.'' The subcontractor's eyes glided up her, lingering on her breasts. ''Works just as advertised.''

Tanner kept his boots firmly planted, when he wanted nothing more than to charge over and put his body between Kathleen and The ''Not-So-Mighty'' Quinn.

Tanner reminded himself she didn't want his help, was in fact handling the obnoxious ass on her own. She'd made it clear she found testosterone dances and jealousy about as welcome as lancing boils.

This time, though, he could honestly say it wasn't jealousy talking. Okay, maybe some jealousy, but with a hefty dose of anger mixed in. Kathleen deserved more respect than Quinn was giving her.

She was an officer in the United States Air Force, a doctor to boot, for crying out loud. Her questions were intelligent and warranted serious answers, rather than the condescending garbage Quinn was shoveling her way.

As if on cue, the subcontractor reached to help Kathleen into the plane, his hand on her back perilously close to being more of a grab at her bottom.

Forget worrying about making her mad. Kathleen would just have to accept she had a partner. Nobody messed with his wingman.

Tanner started forward just as a shadow shifted in his peripheral vision. Like a bandit out of the clouds, Crusty slid up beside him.

In the second that Tanner paused, Kathleen sidestepped Quinn deftly on her own.

Crusty nodded toward the plane. ''Do you wanna take him out? Or should I?''

''Maybe we could tag team him,'' Tanner growled.

''Sounds like a plan. I'm with you all the way, just like the Academy days. Remember when we pushed the F-16 right in front of the chapel?''

A smile twitched. "Yeah. That was a good one."

Crusty chuckled. "Man, was O'Connell pissed. Could have fried an egg on her forehead." His laugh dwindled. He tossed his shoulders back, his wrinkled flight suit rippling. "Okay, Bronco, my man. Let's go. A few well-placed put-downs and we'll set that cretin in his place."

Then take cover before Kathleen exploded.

Tanner cricked his neck side to side twice, almost easing the kink. "I get your point. She can fight her own battles. Damn it, I just want to…"

He stared at his boots, frustration nothing new around Kathleen.

"I know. It's not fair, but that's the way she wants it. We'll only make it worse." Sighing, Crusty forked a hand through his rebellious hair. "Gotta admit, I wasn't much in the mood for fried eggs this morning. Still kind of hungover from last night."

Tanner kept his eyes trained on Kathleen. She'd handled the situation with a finesse she shouldn't even have to consider. He'd almost made it worse by embarrassing her. "Thanks for saving me from making an ass of myself."

"No problem. Just helping a friend."

God, he wanted back in the cockpit where the good guys and bad guys were clear. He turned to Crusty. "Let me help you, too. Tell me what really happened up there."

Daniel Baker didn't answer, but his eyes narrowed. Tanner wanted to believe the defensiveness was a natural reaction. All flyers hated—hell, feared—review boards. "Crusty? Think back. Replay the action tape in your head like we used to do with football videos in the old days. There could have been any number of externals in action. Even a pocket of turbulence might have caused a slight yaw to the side. Not your fault. Just one of those things."

"Nothing happened that wasn't supposed to."

Crusty's set jaw made it clear. He wasn't going to offer

anything. The best Tanner could hope for was a slipup through more direct questioning. "Are you sure your wings were level?"

"Absolutely."

"Maybe you were descending out of a flock of birds?"

"No."

"Climbing?"

Crusty hesitated. "No."

Damn. "No?"

"No." His eyes glinted, camaraderie nowhere in sight. "Now drop it. I'm not going to tell you again, *pal.*"

Crusty spun on his boot heel and joined the duo by the plane. No careless loping. His ramrod-straight back shouted his military training.

Duty warred with Tanner's sense of brotherhood. He'd always seen the two as synonymous. Not today.

His old friend was lying.

Tanner stared up into the rafters as the bird ducked and dove trying to escape. Was he much better than Crusty? He'd been lying to himself, trying to avoid the possibility that Crusty could be at fault, because he didn't want to accuse a friend.

And who was he to judge Quinn for not acknowledging Kathleen's intelligence? Too many times Tanner had ignored Kathleen's advice when he knew full well what a damned smart woman she was. Not to mention he'd spent the whole morning using their time together to work his way into her bed.

He couldn't ignore the obvious. Kathleen O'Connell deserved better from men like Quinn.

She deserved better from him.

Tanner looked down inside the plane and kissed goodbye his fantasy of tangling his body with Kathleen's in the cargo hold. Time to get his priorities in order and focus on

the investigation. No more attempts to wear down her defenses. No more mating games.

He spared one last glance at Kathleen and remembered
the glide of her hair, her satin shirt, her skin against his
hands. Damn, but it would have been one hell of a ride.

Two weeks later, Kathleen gripped the steering wheel
and wondered when her job had become as stale as last
year's fruitcake. Mile after mile of desert road whipped
past—clumps of Joshua trees, an occasional crumbling
adobe mission, seemingly all heading nowhere.

Like all their leads on the C-17 accident.

She should be thriving on the challenge. Instead, she
couldn't stop obsessing over why Tanner didn't touch her
anymore. Not that she wanted him to.

Liar.

The guy who was never at a loss for words now sat
silently beside her, no smiles, no jokes. No touching.

Something had changed between them in the hangar two
weeks ago. She'd gotten what she wanted. He'd quit eyeing
her with competitive determination. Yet the simmer was
still there.

She didn't doubt he wanted her, but they no longer did
anything about it. Not even argue.

Everything had stalled, even the investigation. The team
had shut down for the holidays and scheduled flights out
on Christmas Eve. Not that she particularly cared about
spending the holidays at home. She definitely wasn't looking forward to Christmas alone tomorrow in her town
house.

But maybe the trip to Charleston would restore her balance. And she didn't want to miss Cutter's wedding the
following weekend. Of course that meant more time with
Tanner, since he was the best man.

One at a time, she swiped her sweaty palms down her

crisp jeans. Driving down the monotonous stretch of road offered her too much freedom to sneak peeks at him. Tanner's hand twitched in his unconscious flying routine.

His feet pushed the floorboards like rudder pedals. Her gaze skirted up his deck shoes, bare ankles, over well-washed denim, so white she knew it would be soft to the touch. Smooth cotton encasing flexing steel.

Her stomach lurched. Or was it the car?

"Hey!" Tanner grabbed the steering wheel just before she drove into another rut. "Eyes on the road, Doc."

"Yeah, sorry." She changed the radio station to cover her lapse. The car shimmied and shuddered over another pocket in the narrow side road. "Are you sure this shortcut of Crusty's will get us there faster?"

"Too late to turn back now," clipped the man who'd once been deemed the chattiest guy on earth.

"Maybe you shouldn't trust everything Crusty says."

"I assume you have a point to that remark."

"Some of his answers don't add up and you know it. So let's talk through that, figure something out. I'm not convinced shutting down for the holidays was such a wise choice. We should work on Christmas if we have to."

He dipped his head and stared at her over the top of his sunglasses. "Which general do you plan to yank away from his Christmas turkey to convince that the decision to break for the holidays was unwise?"

"Well, I—"

"We don't have a choice. End of story." He nudged his sunglasses back up.

It was going to be a long ride into L.A. No discussions of Academy days or superstitions. Not even a token chat about military history.

No touching. No kissing.

She should be grateful. She liked order and peace. Right? Except, her life was a mess. She could almost imagine

Lt. Col. Dawson tsking on the sidelines over their definite "thumbs-down" couple of weeks.

Heaven knew, they were trying. Researching. Brainstorming. Pressing for answers until they were easily the least popular couple on base.

They'd put enough miles on the Ford Taurus to earn an Hertz Gold Card membership. She firmly intended to use the upgrade. The once roomy car had become decidedly smaller every day.

Tanner scanned through radio stations, his sunglasses in place and not showing signs of budging anytime soon. Aviator sunglasses reflected the sun, while hiding the man. His biceps rippled with each radio adjustment, straining against his navy cotton polo.

Definitely an SUV in their future.

Kathleen curled her toes inside her tennis shoes, cracking through the restless tension. Too bad she couldn't do that with the rest of her body. Okay, she was frustrated. Sexually frustrated. If she couldn't have sex with him, she was almost desperate enough to settle for her only option for relieving tension with Tanner.

Arguing.

Except the chattiest guy on earth wouldn't even talk to her, much less argue with her. Maybe he needed a push.

She reached for the radio, scanned, passed up an oldies channel, soft rock, country, waiting for something like…

Polka music.

With a satisfied sigh she settled back behind the wheel. Tanner scowled, but stayed silent. She had to give him credit. He endured three accordion stanzas before he nailed the scan button.

Oldies. A droning love ballad about keeping each other up all night.

She tapped scan.

Kathleen thought she heard a low rumble sound in Tanner's chest, but she couldn't be sure. *Scan.* Soft rock again. *Scan.* Hard rock. *Scan.* Country. *Scan...*

National Public Radio. Creating Christmas decorations for under a dollar.

Kathleen returned her hands to ten-two while radio waves filled the air.

"Don't waste your pennies on paper icicles and thready angel hair. Create your own snowy winter wonderland with dryer lint."

Tanner pinched the bridge of his nose.

"With all that holiday family company, you'll be running loads of fluffy white guest towels through the dryer. Put that extra lint to good use. For a candy cane effect, send your favorite red sweater for a tumble. And now for a holiday cheer break, here's the Little Reindeer Choir with—"

Tanner jammed the off button with the heel of his hand.

Kathleen waited for him to say something. A minute ticked by, drifting into another one before she decided he would need more prodding.

She gripped the steering wheel and prepared for a steam-releasing battle. "It's not fair you get to be the god of radios as well as aviation."

"Life's not fair."

"Well, that's really mature."

"Like your radio game?"

"Only trying to fill the silence, hotshot."

"You want the dryer lint lady back? Fine." He punched the button.

The waning notes of "Silver Bells" faded, bleeding over into "I'll Be Home for Christmas."

Her ex had walked out on December twenty-third. Kathleen beat Tanner to the button by half a second. "Listen, Bennett. You've got to stop with the silent treatment."

"I'm staying out of your way."

"You're blowing the investigation."

"Me? You're the one buying into everything Quinn and Randy say."

"Not true at all." She gripped the shuddering wheel and maneuvered the car over another rut before accelerating. "I'm just trying to find answers. Everything about this investigation has been goat rope from day one. The whole team's like an episode of Keystone Cops at their worst. Toxicology reports disappearing. Erased crew tapes. Computer files suddenly plagued by viruses. Something's not right."

"No kidding, Sherlock. But there's nothing we can do about it for another week. Nada. Zip. We've been ordered home for the holidays. Your pocket UCMJ is very clear on following orders. We go home. Eat some pumpkin pie. Then get the investigation back on track afterward."

"Just how are we supposed to do that?"

"Forget it. I'm not going to argue with you." He turned the radio back on.

"Instead, you're just going to brood and sulk over heaven knows what." Her foot pressed more heavily on the accelerator. "Do you think Colonel Dawson won't notice when he comes to Cutter's wedding?"

"Kathleen—"

"Of course he will. This investigation is landing in the toilet, Bennett. If we don't save it soon, we can just flush our careers right along with it."

"O'Connell—"

"No upgrade slot for you, hotshot." With each word, she picked up steam while blowing it off. "You'll be the oldest living copilot in the Air Force. I'll get a promotion recommendation that won't be good for anything other than padding the bottom of the stack. Do you think you're the only one who's frustrated? God knows I don't want to want you, but we've just got to live with this, Bennett, and your silent treatment isn't making it any easier on either of us—

"Kathleen! Hush!"

Well, she'd wanted him to talk. "What?"

"The car's not riding right."

"Huh?" The car shuddered, tugged to the left. Somehow in her anger she'd let the accelerator creep up to eighty. "It's this detour of Crusty's. I knew we should have stayed on the main road."

"Yeah, but— Damn!" Tanner grabbed the wheel just as a tire blew.

Chapter 10

Fishtailing, the car swerved right, then left. Tanner's hand fisted around the wheel as his body strained against the seat belt. The Taurus hurtled off the road.

Tanner's other arm shot in front of Kathleen to brace her. "Drive into the spin, O'Connell!"

"I know!" Her elbow nudged his arm away. "Let go!"

The car pounded over dips and trenches. Damn, but he wished they'd been traveling the more sedate Kathleen speed on the smooth, paved highway.

A second tire blew.

"What the—" His hand reached again for Kathleen. Too late. She slammed against the door. Her head smacked the window.

Her limp body sagged from the seat belt.

"Kathleen!" he shouted. Horror thumped him in the chest harder than the constricting shoulder harness.

The car pinwheeled out of control into a dried-up lake bed.

Forcing himself to block out distracting emotions, Tanner steered. Fly the jet. Don't think about Kathleen slumped beside him.

Damn near impossible.

Grinding metal sounded as rocks ripped at the undercarriage. Focus and fly. He manipulated the wheel by instinct, battling a flat in the front as well as the back. He combated ruts and rocks, tried not think of Kathleen's limp body swaying like a rag doll.

A small pyre of rocks loomed ahead. Unavoidable, but at least it would act as a brake from nature. The car plowed over the stones, jolting the vehicle more than a teeth-jarring landing.

Airbags inflated. Masked Kathleen.

The spin slowed, the car sliding sideways. Stopping.

Dust swirled beyond Tanner's side window. The radio crooned "Jingle Bell Rock" in the aftermath, everything else an echoing silence. Too quiet, as he listened to music and his own labored breathing.

No sounds from beside him.

The airbags began a hissing deflation, spurring Tanner into action. He punched the bag until he could unsnap his seat belt. "Kathleen!"

He flung aside the belt and leaned over the console. Too damned big console. "Answer me!"

She didn't respond. Not even a moan. He cupped her face, afraid to move her until he knew how badly she'd been hurt. "Kathleen, honey, wake up. Come on. Wake up."

He patted her cheeks. Her damp face.

His fingers came away with blood as red as her hair, crimson like the fear darkening his vision. With shaking hands, he examined the cut on her temple. Small, but bleeding like a son of a bitch. "Damn it, Kathleen! Open your eyes. Now! Wake up and yell at me for making you take the detour!''

Still no response. He hung his head, gasping in air to calm his thoughts as well as his heart rate.

Think. Breathe.

His nose twitched. Gasoline hung in the air. Stung his nose, his eyes. Rocks must have torn the undercarriage, causing a leak in the fuel tank.

His head shot up.

The car could blow.

He lunged for her seat belt. Forget waiting, he had to get Kathleen out now and just pray she hadn't broken anything.

Tanner jabbed her seat belt release. Nothing happened. Damn. He grabbed the strap. Mashed the button. Forced it. Still nothing.

For one interminable second, fear for Kathleen and the very real sense of her mortality bit him. Hard. He'd faced death too many times, very recently flying combat missions over Sentavo. All active duty military accepted the possibility of death on the job.

But it wasn't supposed to happen like this.

He would not let her check out because of a flat tire gone way wrong. He had always told himself he could have made a difference for his sister when she'd needed him. Well, he was here for Kathleen now and wouldn't let her die, damn it.

Determination and a hefty dose of adrenaline fired through him. He gripped the seat belt and ripped it from the buckle, his growling shout filling the car. He ignored the raw sting across his palm.

A cloud billowed from the hood. Smoldered.

No time. Worry about injuries later because, damn it, Kathleen would have a later.

He scooped her from the seat, backed out of the car, and

ran like hell. With Kathleen limp and tucked against his chest, he sprinted across the packed sand.

Wind howled, wafting smoke with each gust. A small crackle, then another sounded behind him. He willed his feet to move faster. Farther. He kept his eye on the end zone, praying he'd cross a line of safety before—

An explosion thundered across the desert.

The percussion blast slammed his back. Launched him forward. He twisted just in time to cushion Kathleen's fall with his body.

Damn, but the desert floor was harder than AstroTurf. Stunned from the fall, he struggled to clear the fog.

Kathleen.

Her body sprawled across his. Her soft breasts pressed against him with her every steady, reassuring breath.

She was alive, warm and breathing against him. His arms twitched around her. He cupped the back of her head and gave himself two seconds just to hold her, breathe in the scent of her to chase away the stench of smoke and fear of her dying.

The flames swelled and popped with a secondary explosion. Tanner's fingers tangled in Kathleen's hair, sand and blood mixing in the loose strands shielding her face.

Gently he rolled her from him onto her back. Her ashen face leeched relief from him.

"Kathleen? Kathleen!" He patted her cheeks, snapped his fingers in front of her face. "Wake up, honey. Come on. Don't scare me like this. Wake up or I'm gonna have to carry you all the way out of this desert and it'll screw up my back. Do you hear that? I'll end up in the infirmary, and you can be sure I'll blow off half your instructions."

She stirred under his touch, a small but damned welcome sign he grasped with both hands.

"That's right. Come on, honey. Please wake up."

"Tanner?" she mumbled, her eyes still closed.

"Yeah, it's me." Relief almost knocked him on his butt, but he channeled his thoughts toward her. "Don't move. Lie still until we figure out if you've broken anything. Does it hurt anywhere besides your head? Help me out here, Doc. What should I be checking?"

Her lashes fluttered open, revealing cloudy, unfocused eyes. "Don't wanna be Doc."

Kathleen's cranky grumble brought him laughter along with all that relief. "Not much choice, Doc. We're pretty short on options."

"Hate being Doc. Doc, Sneezy, Grumpy, so Sleepy…" Her head lolled.

Relief took a fast flight out. "Kathleen!"

She blinked up at him. "I want a real name. And a keg party. Like the others."

What the hell was she talking about? But at least she was talking. "Okay, hon. You got it. One keg party coming up."

"Thank you." Her lashes drifted closed.

"Kathleen! Damn it, O'Connell, wake up!" Tanner shouted the hoarse order. He leaned his face inches from hers. "No way! You're not checking out on me now."

His forehead fell to rest on hers. "You don't have to be Doc. Just wake up, Sleeping Beauty, and tell me where it hurts."

He couldn't stop himself from brushing a kiss just beside the purpling bruise. Her lashes flickered open, and he stifled the urge to cheer for good ol' Grimm's fairy tales.

Of course he wasn't much of a prince for this warrior goddess. At the moment he was shaking in his deck shoes and he didn't like the feeling at all. Emotions never got the better of him, at least not since his sister's death. He prided himself on his steady hands in the air and reliable laugh on the ground.

Except he couldn't dodge the notion that he could have

done something. He'd let his guard down, surrendered control, and that could have cost a crucial second. Hell, if he'd been the one driving...

He wanted his objectivity back. He did not want this roaring in his ears every time he thought about Kathleen bleeding. And by God, he would shut it down before he let it distract him again.

Keep it light. Keep it simple. Above all, stay in control.

Kathleen looked up at the looming double shadows swaying above her. Tanner crouched over her, his chest a large blue blur in the polo shirt.

Her head pounded with what had to be a hangover headache of mammoth proportions, and she hadn't even enjoyed the party. She winced, blinked fast, her vision becoming blessedly clearer. "Tanner?"

The hard planes of his face sharpened. His eyes stared down at her as intently as when reading any mission chart. "Yeah. Talk to me, O'Connell. Are you all right?"

"I think so." She flexed her fingers, her feet, warily elbowing up. A small groan slipped between her gritted teeth. Dust powdered the inside of her mouth, a minor inconvenience compared to her throbbing temples. "Except for a killer headache."

He palmed her back. "Okay, easy now."

She forced herself to sit upright without his help. Resting her elbows on her knees, she swallowed down nausea. "What happened?"

"A flat tire, remember? You hit your head when the second tire blew."

"Oh, yeah." She forced herself to breathe evenly. Slow and steady so she wouldn't hurl all over Tanner's big shoes in front of her.

He stroked the back of her neck. God, it felt so good, so soothing. She allowed herself to accept that much comfort, her eyes drifting closed as the pain abated. "Why are we out here, though?"

A breeze wafted past, carrying the acrid odor of smoke and gasoline their way. She sniffed. Her eyes snapped open. She jerked to look behind her and found their car burning steadily fifty yards away.

Nausea frothed from her stomach up her throat. Kathleen clapped a hand over her mouth just before hanging her head between her knees. "Ohmigosh."

"It's okay. We're okay." He gripped her shoulders with a firmness echoed in his tone. "The fuel tank must have sprung a leak when rocks from the lake bed ripped out the undercarriage."

Her breathing ragged, she rested the side of her head on her bent knee, eyes trained on the car. Flames licked toward the sky. Metal blackened to a skeletal mockery of their rental car.

She could have still been inside.

Kathleen raised her eyes to Tanner. "You pulled me out of there?"

He grunted, then shrugged. "No big deal. Just carried you away from the car when I smelled the gas."

Kathleen shuddered. If Tanner had been knocked out, as well, they both would have died. She blinked back tears. A world without his broad shoulders seemed an empty place. Tears burned hotter, became tougher to control, but she would...after she stared at him for another ten seconds to reassure herself he was unharmed.

The vee of his shirt stretched open at his throat, displaying a patch of blond hair against his bronzed neck. What she wouldn't give to rest her head right in the crook for five minutes. Just five. And then she would be herself again. "Thank you."

His eyes collided with hers, and she saw a flash of something. Fear? For her? But of course he would have been worried. He was human after all, a decent man.

Why did she want to convince herself she saw something more?

Then it was gone. His lighthearted dimple kicked in with familiar predictability—along with the power to make her forget about her aching head for a full minute.

He rocked back on his heels. "Couldn't let anything happen to you. Who would I argue with?"

She gathered her tattered composure. She was an Air Force officer, after all. It was time to start acting like one, rather than becoming a basket case because she'd bumped her head. "Keeps you on your toes. Can't let everything in life come easy for you."

"This investigation hasn't been easy."

"You mean working with me."

He looked from the wreckage to his hands. His thumb massaged over a raw patch of skin on the other palm. "Like you said, vintage Keystone Cops."

Smoke-tinged air tickled Kathleen's nose as a sense of whimsy tickled her raw throat. They had actually blown up their rental car. That wouldn't play well with the Hertz folks at checkout.

A giggle sneaked free.

Tanner stared at her as if she'd left her brain back in the car. He thumbed one of her eyebrows and lifted. "Your pupils seem even. What else do I need to check for?"

Kathleen batted his hand aside and laughed harder. Every chuckle hammered her head, not that she could stop even when Tanner scowled at her.

"What the hell's so funny?"

She snorted on a laugh, choked back another before she could answer. "We blew up the car."

"Yes," he said, enunciating with extra precision. "We did."

"Just imagine the look on Colonel Dawson's face when we tell him." She lowered her voice, puffed out her chest. "Sir, we managed to work together on one thing."

Tanner's frown faded into skepticism, shifting to amazement before that dimple tucked in again. "Well, damn. We blew up the car."

A low rumble rolled from his chest, echoing out over the lonely desert. He hooked a forearm on his knee, shook his head and laughed harder.

He'd always had the most infectious laugh.

She let the laughs have their way with her. Who cared if each one carried a slightly hysterical edge? It was safer than crying all over Tanner's broad chest.

One last rogue giggle tripped into a snort. Kathleen pushed a hand to her aching head. "I imagine it's too much to hope for that you have your cell phone in your pocket."

He jerked a thumb toward the smoking car. "It was hooked up to the trickle charger in the lighter. And yours?"

"In my purse. We should have had some of your Lucky Charms for breakfast."

Tanner clasped his hands between his knees, massaging the scratch on his palm, eyes scanning the horizon. "I'm not so sure all this has anything to do with lousy luck."

She tried to sort through his cryptic statement, but couldn't think through the foggy ache. She needed to be checked out by a doctor. "Do you think we're closer to base? Or town?"

"Base, but we're still talking about a helluva haul. We might shave a few miles off if we made a direct path. All the same, I'd rather stick to the road. Maybe someone saw the explosion and has already called for help. If we stay with the roads, we may luck into a car before dark, or at least find one of those old missions we passed heading out. Either way, we've got to walk."

"I figured as much."

He feathered a blunt fingertip over her forehead. "Are you up to it?"

She willed her eyes not to drift shut at that skimming caress. "No choice is there? And don't even offer to carry me."

"Hey, plenty of soldiers carry wounded comrades off the battlefield. No shame in that. You're a hell of a lot lighter than Lance or Cutter." He smiled, but couldn't quite hide the sudden tension between them, a quiet intensity flickering like the lingering flames reflected in his eyes.

He could joke all he wanted, but he had to know she needed a trip to the E.R. Given his need for control, this would be a tough one for him to swallow. She needed to play it straight, because he would recognize a lie. "If I have a concussion, it's better for me to walk. It will keep me alert."

He stared into her eyes as if weighing her words or perhaps checking her pupils again. He must have been reassured by what he saw because he stood, extending a hand to help her.

She gripped his wrist. "Uh, is your back okay?"

"O'Connell…" he growled, his hold twitching around her wrist.

"It better be, because there's not a chance I can carry you out of here, hotshot." She gave him a gentle squeeze and stood.

"I'm fine." His eyes burned with a battlefield determination. "I'm going to get you out of here and to a hospital, Kathleen."

Her smile pulled tight. "How about we do it together?"

"Right." He grunted, dropping her hand. "May as well get started."

Her skin tingled as if she'd singed her palm in the fire. She skimmed a restless hand along her dusty jeans. "What a way to spend Christmas Eve."

"We're both alive. Santa's earned his cookies."

The gruff edge to his response made her recall he'd had worse Christmases. His sister's death had to hit him hard this time of year.

Remembering she had a lot to be thankful for in spite of the hideous day, Kathleen nodded. "Good point."

The road stretched out ahead of her, long, narrow, fading into the horizon. Kathleen wished she had an extra pack of Oreos on hand for hitching a ride on Santa's sleigh.

With her luck so far, they wouldn't reach town until the new year. And the last thing she needed was the temptation of a night under the stars with Tanner.

A coyote howled as the sun inched its way into the horizon. Tanner eyed the crumbling adobe mission in the distance and knew they didn't stand a chance of reaching it until at least an hour after sunset.

The temperature already dipped below freezing. Kathleen's pale face had him ready to fling her over his shoulder and double-time it to the highway. She'd insisted she was fine every time he'd asked, but what else would she say?

Not a damn car in sight all day. Apparently no one else knew about Crusty's detour.

Kathleen trudged beside him. Dogged determination marked her face with an expression he hadn't seen since cross country runs at the Academy. They could have been transported back.

Except for the bruise on her brow.

Across her temple, the purplish stain had spread. The jagged edges of her cut pulled together, no longer oozing but still looking nasty as hell. All because of a simple flat tire.

His brain screamed warnings at him. Two flat tires. That wasn't right. Their string of bad luck went beyond stepping out of the wrong side of the plane or missing a sardine breakfast. Except he couldn't do anything about that now. Just concentrate on getting Kathleen to shelter for the night.

She skirted a creosote bush, her feet tangling as she side-stepped. A fresh fist of dread pummeled him. He had to keep her alert. Talking would help him gauge her state of mind. "What did you mean about wanting a keg party?"

"Huh?" Her eyes shifted from watching her feet to Tanner.

The sunset fingered explosions of vibrant reds behind her, the same awesome shade of Kathleen's hair. He reminded himself that the brightness was merely a by-product of some light refraction on airborne dust and sand. That didn't diminish the view in the least.

"When I tried to wake you after the accident, you kept saying you didn't want to be one of the seven dwarfs. You wanted a keg party. What did you mean about Snow White tapping a keg?"

"I must have hit my head harder than I thought. I have no idea what I meant." She planted one foot in front of the other with each huffing breath. "Did I say anything else?"

"Something about how you didn't want to be Doc, Grumpy or Sleepy. You wanted a keg party."

Confusion smoothed from her face. "Oh."

"What did you mean?"

Her brow furrowed again. With concentration? Pain? Or disorientation.

He tucked in beside her and looped a steadying arm around her waist. "O'Connell?"

"It's silly, really." She didn't look at him. But she didn't pull away.

"Silly is the last adjective I would ever use to describe you."

"Thanks, I think."

God, she felt good against his side, warm, soft…alive. "Talk and let me know you're all right or I'm carrying you. I'll end up back in the infirmary making both our lives a living hell.''

"My name."

He waited for the rest, but she didn't offer up anything more. "You'll need to give me a little more to go on. You're still not making sense."

"Doc. My name. My call sign."

"And? Come on, Doc, spill it." He gave her waist a gentle squeeze, assuring himself he did it in the interest of keeping her conscious. Yeah, right. "Do I have to threaten to piggyback you through the desert?"

"I told you this was silly."

He positioned his other arm as if to scoop her from behind her knees.

"Okay! Okay!" She danced out of his grasp. Returning to her dogged solo march, she trudged two steps ahead of him before speaking. "I never got a real call sign like the other flight surgeons. You know, like Cutter or Hippocrates. I'm just plain ol' Doc. No keg party naming ceremony. Nothing special. Not really one of you."

Tanner took in the proud tilt of her chin when he knew her head had to feel ten pounds too heavy. So many times he'd seen her roll her eyes over what she called "flyer games." He'd never once considered she'd wanted to play along. How could he have missed it? "Kathleen, I—"

She held up a silencing hand. "Stupid, I know, since I set the boundaries in the first place. I'm a loner, and I prefer it that way, so I can't fault the rest of you for not including me. I certainly wouldn't have said anything about it if my brains hadn't been rattled around inside my skull." She pivoted to face him and walked backward. "And I'll deny it if you ever repeat a word of what I said."

He grasped her shoulders, halting her. "I wouldn't repeat something you told me in confidence." He gave her shoulders a squeeze and tried to bring her smile back. "Especially when your brains have been rattled around."

It didn't work and the failure coldcocked him. When had he shifted from wanting to make her mad to needing to make her smile?

Her blue eyes deepened to something closer to the indigo hue of an early evening sky. Chasing nightfall through the clouds had always been one of his favorite flights. He thrilled at the rush he got when hurtling through the shifting colors, as he rode the edge of darkness across time zones. Her eyes flickered with just those deep, rich colors, and he could feel it sucking him in.

Was he chasing or running?

Dipping from under his hands, Kathleen resumed her trek. "I've never been much of a team player, more the track, tennis, swimming sort of person. I go for sports like rock climbing."

Tanner's steps faltered before he regained traction on the cracked earth. "Rock climbing?"

"Yeah, rock climbing." Her lips pulled back into that prissy line. "I'll have you know it's very restful."

He did not need to think about her mouth right now. "I imagine you skydive for fun."

Her lips pulled tighter, sealing any answer from escaping. The silence blared her response, anyway.

"Geez, O'Connell! You do!" As if his heart hadn't been stopped often enough for one day. Did she have to scare the pants off him with thoughts of her rappeling through the air or hanging from a cliff by her fingernails?

She shrugged. "I'm airborne qualified. So what if I like to keep my skills from getting rusty? It's not like you haven't trained for it, too."

"To learn how to get my butt on the ground if the plane won't put me there. Certainly not for kicks." A guy had to have some corner of peace in his life. It couldn't always be about the battle. "This job is dangerous enough, thank you very much. There's nothing wrong with tossing the ball around or sharing a beer with friends in your spare time."

Kathleen stomped ahead. He sure had her talking. Not surprising he'd managed to fire her up in the process. Of course, that was easier than a routine landing.

He pinched the bridge of his nose along the twice-set crook and forced himself to think rather than just react, to remember that his impulsiveness had lead to those breaks.

How could she not know how much the flyers respected her? Yeah, she was prickly, but everyone liked her. She was the one who turned down invitations to join the "flyer games." But damn it, the invitations were there.

Yet she wanted a name.

He'd wondered before how she relaxed, how she let down from the job stress, and now he understood. She didn't, not really. Asking her wasn't enough. She needed a shove to join the fun.

"You know this puts a real crimp in any holiday plans we may have had. Even if we luck into a ride, we're still not going to get home by Christmas." At this rate, they would be lucky to get out of the desert at all, but he wouldn't share that cheery thought with her. "What do you say we do something together? What did you do for Christmas last year?"

"Signed my divorce papers." She continued to pound the sand with her determined steps.

Tanner flinched. He'd landed his size-fourteen foot soundly on a land mine with that one. "That sucks."

"Not as bad as having your husband walk out at Christmastime the year before."

More than a lone land mine, he'd uncovered a whole minefield. Shoulder to shoulder, he walked beside her toward the crumbling adobe church. Silently. What could he say to fix it, anyway?

And why couldn't he just leave it alone? It wasn't his problem to fix.

Except he knew too well how a loss during the Christmas season killed the holiday spirit for years to come. He didn't make a big mourning deal out of it, but the pall hung there all the same.

He'd been relieved when his mom had finally married a few years ago. She'd found a good man who took her away for the holidays. No cookies-by-the-fireplace family traditions, they'd started a fresh slate of memories that didn't evoke those of the past.

Maybe that's what Kathleen needed, a change of holiday pace to set her life on a new course.

She'd always been a loner, but there was an aloofness to her now, more so than during their Academy days. He'd wondered why, finally concluding she'd just grown more uptight over the years. Now he wondered if he'd been wrong.

Kathleen wasn't aloof so much as wary. A cheating husband would do that to a woman, no doubt. Especially one who put as high a price on honor as Kathleen did. Yeah, that ex of hers had done a real number on her.

Of course, a person only had the power to hurt someone if she cared about him. A lot. That Kathleen might still be hung up on her ex shouldn't bother him. But it did.

What was he thinking, anyway? How did he expect to give her some Christmas to remember in the middle of the freaking desert? A fitting setting, no doubt, for a couple of Scrooges hoping to escape the Ghost of Christmas Past.

If the cold and coyotes didn't get them first.

Chapter 11

Darkness hugged her like an indigo blanket, pain thickening the texture to more of a suffocating wool. Kathleen trudged the last few feet toward the crumbling mission. Silhouetted by the moon and a dome of desert stars, the russet stucco church would provide them with shelter for the night.

Thank goodness Tanner had given up trying to make her talk an hour ago. Silently he strode beside her. She didn't have the energy to devote to anything other than keeping pace with the steps he set. Steps she knew he'd adjusted for her, and man did that gall her.

For once, however, she didn't have the will to argue. It was damned embarrassing to be this wasted from what should have been a simple day's hike.

Her head throbbed from the accident. She didn't know about the rest of her, because she couldn't think about anything other than her aching temples. Too bad there wasn't likely to be a bottle of Motrin stored away inside the abandoned building.

A small portion of her brain still operated as a doctor. That little corner of reason told her she should have stopped an hour ago. Not that she really had a choice. She couldn't lie down and sleep on the desert floor while the night cold and coyotes tore at her.

She definitely wouldn't ask Tanner to carry her. Even if she didn't have his back to consider, pride wouldn't let her.

Rather like a thickheaded pilot on the flight line a couple of weeks ago.

Oh, great. Now that little corner of her brain was insisting on being reasonable, as well.

Kathleen pushed through a rickety picket fence and shuffled up the walk toward the half-open doors that hung off their hinges. She stumbled the last two feet to the steps. Adrenaline seeped from her in a steady flow, now that she no longer needed it. Her legs turned to water. She sagged to sit.

Water. Another thought she didn't need. The moist slice from a Joshua tree earlier had left her feeling decidedly green.

"Come on, O'Connell." Tanner crouched in front of her. "You need to get inside out of the wind."

"The wind's blowing?" Her brain must be more muddled than she'd thought. She tipped her face. A strand of hair swiped at her numb lips. "Well, look at that. It sure is."

She tried to move. Survival training told her it would drop to at least twenty degrees by midnight. Not factoring in the windchill. A wind that carried the bay of a lone coyote.

But she couldn't make her legs work.

So why was she floating? And on such a warm cloud that smelled of leather and soap. And Tanner.

Realizing he must have picked her up, she snuggled

against his chest. "You shouldn't be doing this. Did you
at least keep your chiropractor appointment this week?"

"Yeah, Doc."

His half chuckle vibrated against her ear. It held a darker
tone that made her long for his uninhibited laugh. She
wanted to smooth a hand over the worry lining his poster-
boy face. "Not Doc."

"Definitely Sleepy."

"Yep." That niggled at her. Why? "Oh. Remember.
Concussion. Wake me every two hours."

His arms tightened around her. "I won't let anything
happen to you."

Her mouth formed the automatic reply, "I can take care
of myself."

Since she couldn't squelch the need to assert herself, her
brains must not be as rattled as she feared. Reassured, she
nestled closer and simply enjoyed inhaling the scent of
soap, leather. And Tanner. "Every two hours. Wake…
me…."

"Kathleen? Kathleen! Two-hour check. Come on, Doc,
wake up or I'm gonna toss you over my shoulder, kick
some coyote butt, and hike out of this desert."

Tanner's insistent voice pierced Kathleen's foggy need
to sleep. She peeled open her gritty eyes. Tanner loomed
over her as she lay on…

A dusty church pew. How long had she been out?

As she tried to sit up, the dust stirred.

"Achoo!" A sneeze ripped through her. Exploded
through her head. Brought tears to her eyes.

"A-a-choo! Ow!" The second sneeze almost took her to
her knees, but she held up a hand to keep Tanner from
launching into some nursemaid scenario. "I'm okay. Honestly. I'm definitely awake now."

"If you're sure," he said, skepticism infiltrating his tone.

Over his shoulder, she looked around the stark mission. A barren altar table listed to one side. Nooks for statues gaped empty. Moldy whitewash peeled from the walls. No doubt it was a decrepit mess, but the chapel echoed with a majestic peace beyond what could be found in a cathedral full of golden icons.

Kathleen elbowed up, and the world stayed blessedly still, no quivering ceiling. Nausea tickled but didn't overwhelm.

A yard away, a small fire crackled from the middle of a circle of stones. Smoke curled up through a jagged hole in the roof.

Crouching in front of her, Tanner palmed her back until she sat up. "How's the stomach?"

"Better."

He peered into her eyes until he apparently saw enough to reassure himself. "Good."

Kathleen pointed to the fire. "Looks like you've been busy."

"I scrounged up a few supplies to get us through the night. If the pickets run out, we can toss on some creosote brush. It'll smoke like a son of a gun, but we won't freeze. I also carved up another cactus. No luck with food, though. We should easily make town tomorrow. As long as we stay hydrated, finding food's not a concern for now."

The thought of eating caused her stomach to roil anyway. "The fire's great. You get an A plus in survival skills, Captain."

"Those coyotes out front limited our options."

Coyotes. She couldn't stop the shudder tripping through her as she thought of Tanner outside with the coyotes while she'd slept. She hadn't been much of a partner. "How long have I been asleep?"

"I checked you a couple of hours ago. Since you chewed me out, I figured that constituted as a wake-up. Then two more hours now.'' He bared his wrist and tapped his watch. ''I set the alarm.''

The numbers glowed—11:54. Almost midnight. ''What a way to spend Christmas.''

''I've had worse.''

Uh-oh.

She remembered his worst Christmas well. Last time they'd talked about his sister, Kathleen had flung herself at Tanner like some sex-starved woman. Which she was. And weak. Man, was she feeling weak from more than the lingering effects of a bump on the head.

Yet, how could she turn him away if he needed to talk? He'd listened to her morbid tale about her ex. Tanner had far more reason to grieve than she.

And she wanted to hear, to help, to understand him.

Kathleen swung her feet off the pew and leaned back. She would listen to whatever he needed to say, but she would not, under any circumstances, kiss him. ''Tell me about her.''

Deciding how best to answer Kathleen's question, Tanner studied the tilt of her jaw and resisted the urge to check his back. That determined look of hers usually meant he was toast.

The past four hours of watching her sleep, while he set up supplies for the night, had been an odd mix of pleasure and torture. He'd never allowed himself the unreserved opportunity to study her. A pleasure, no doubt.

If he hadn't been so damned worried.

She seemed alert now, her eyes a clear shade of blue, that pretty sky blue that made him want to...

Damn it, she should be in an emergency room, not wrestling him off. He would keep her safe if it meant carrying her the whole way. He wouldn't add another death to his list of Christmas memories.

Tanner shifted to sit beside her on the pew. "About Tara. I never said thank you."

"For what?"

He could still envision Kathleen from that night, see her walking into his room, telling him to grieve for his sister, go to her funeral, but not to drop out of college because of it. His sister wouldn't want that. He'd silenced the words he wasn't ready to hear with a kiss. "For dragging me through that night twelve years ago. For not slapping my face."

For being there for him while he'd cried.

"Anyone would have helped. I just happened to be there."

Remembering just how she'd distracted him, he quirked a brow. "Anyone?"

"Okay, maybe Crusty wouldn't have helped you quite the way I did."

Shock sealed off a response until he saw the wicked twinkle in her eyes. She'd cracked a joke. Well, damn. "Thank goodness you were around rather than Crusty."

Their light laughter swirled with the smoke, lifting, curling through the hole in the roof. He'd never noticed her sense of humor before. She wasn't much for crowds and rousing crew jokes, more of a silent observer. But one-on-one...

Okay, no dangerous thoughts of one-on-one.

Tanner tipped his head back on the pew, the hardwood solid against his neck, and gazed up at the stars peeking through the cracks and hole above. "Did I tell you we were twins? Tara and me."

Kathleen sat silently beside him, a good listener. She always had been. He liked that, had needed it as much as her kiss twelve years ago. "You wouldn't have guessed it from looking at us. Other than sharing the same hair and eye color, we weren't anything alike. She was petite, kind of like you.''

"Petite?" Kathleen snorted an indignant protest.

"But toned," he inserted with a smile. "And stubborn. Man, was she a pit pull."

She twisted on the pew to face him. "I thought you said the two of you weren't alike."

That humor again. He turned to look at her, the pew rubbing along his neck. "Who me? Stubborn?"

Humor, great listening skills and pretty blue eyes. How much could a man be expected to withstand in one night? Tanner shifted his attention back to the sky and lost himself in memories.

"Mom worked long hours, waitressing most nights so she could have weekends off to make it to our games. Tara played, too, softball, basketball, track. We spent a lot of time together at the gym, after-school jobs, at home. She was responsible for making sure I ate. It was up to me to make sure no one messed with her." His voice hitched. "Tara held up her end."

Tanner cleared his throat, sat up, scrubbed a hand across his bristly jaw. Wondered why he'd blabbed all this when he'd only meant to say thanks.

Kathleen's hand drifted to his thigh, offering an odd mix of comfort and arousal. "You've got to know it wasn't your fault. You weren't kids anymore. You were at the Academy when she died."

"I know. What you say sounds logical." He let himself cover her hand with his because she looked so earnest, so in need of fixing his problems. Not because her hand felt so good in his he could almost believe her. "But I knew that by accepting the Air Force Academy appointment I was locked into active duty for four years after graduation. No ball contracts straight out of college. And I knew even then I wouldn't opt for one later if the chance came. So when you're eighteen and already feeling guilty about chasing some aviator dream rather than offering your mom and sister an easier life…''

"Things get muddy."

"Yeah."

Her head bowed, and she turned their hands over, flattened her palm against his as if comparing the size, while she decided what to say next. "Even all those times you made me crazy and I thought you were some jock skating on his blocking skills, I always respected the way you turned down the big bucks to serve your country." She slid her fingers along his. "I've never been much of a gambler, but I'm willing to bet your mother agrees with me. A woman who brought up a son to make that decision would be proud of the choice you made."

One at a time, she traced his fingers—slow caresses, whisper-light, that unkinked his tension stroke by stroke, slowly replacing one with another. He focused on that, not ready to accept her words now anymore than before.

He'd heard her just fine, could even see her logic. But she didn't understand how it felt for a man to realize there were things he couldn't control.

Linking her fingers with his, Kathleen squeezed gently. "You're not responsible for everyone."

Tanner didn't bother answering. She just didn't get it, and he wasn't in the mood to explain. He'd had enough maudlin confidences for one night. He wanted the lightheartedness back, the humor Kathleen had only just started to share with him. Thanks to his preparations while she'd slept, that was one thing about the whole insane day that he could control.

He was going to give Kathleen O'Connell one helluva Christmas to remember.

Kathleen stared up at the overbright stars beyond the hole

in the roof and congratulated herself. She'd done it. She'd listened, comforted him and kept her lips off his.

Heaven knew it hadn't been easy to keep her arms from going around his neck and pulling that ruggedly beautiful face to her breast. She'd offered him her hand, instead.

Of course, there were a few too many nerve endings in her hand and every one of them was screaming on full alert at the moment.

But, by God, she hadn't kissed him.

A persistent beeping tickled her from her self-congratulatory musings. Tanner's alarm? He pulled his hand from hers and silenced the watch.

"I didn't fall asleep, did I?" she asked, worried about time fugues. She knew she'd hit her head hard, likely had a concussion, but she didn't want to consider there might be a more serious injury lurking.

"No, you didn't."

She sagged against the pew.

"I reset it for midnight so we wouldn't miss Christmas."

"Oh. All right." She smiled weakly even though she would have just as soon let the hour pass unmarked.

Tanner stood in front of her. "Close your eyes."

Kathleen sat upright. "What?"

"It's Christmas. While you were sleeping, I worked on a surprise. Now close 'em." The devilish twinkle in his eyes matched that dimple too perfectly.

"Yeah, right. Like I'm trusting you not to play some prank."

He palmed his chest in overplayed innocence. "Who me?"

"Yes, you. Something like gluing Lance's checklist pages together. Substituting the hard-boiled eggs in Tag's flight lunch with raw ones. Changing Cutter's mouse from right-handed to left."

"Hey, that was just a little joke to cheer up Cutter after

he and Lori split last year. Apparently he didn't appreciate my meddling.''

"Not that it stopped you."

"So I threw them together? What's the big deal? It wasn't like you wanted to hang out with me as the flight doc on that rescue mission to Sentavo. Cutter was happy to step in. If Lori just happened to be the relief worker accompanying us…''

Tanner shrugged, the most unlikely overgrown cupid Kathleen could imagine.

"And I fell right in line by jumping at the chance to get off that flight." Kathleen shook her head. "Geez, when did I get so predictable?''

"Predictable? You? Whatever." He tucked his thumbs in his back pockets. "You have to admit though, my plan worked. The Grayson Clark happy nuptials are just days away. Soon they'll all be settled in at Cutter's new assignment in Washington. As you can see, I only use my powers for good. Now close your eyes.''

"All right. But you better be nice or don't bother coming to me for pain meds next time your back's a mess."

"So noted."

Warily she let her eyes drift shut. She heard his footsteps trek to the pew behind her, followed by a rustle and clank before he walked back in front of her. She waited, cautious, but oddly excited by his game.

"Open."

She hesitated, reluctant to end this moment of anticipation or have it ruined by some crew dog prank.

"Come on, O'Connell. No time for a catnap now. Open.''

A bracing breath later she opened her eyes and stared straight into his. Breathing became momentarily optional as he stared back at her, so big, blond and ruggedly handsome, the bump on his nose reassuring in its familiarity. Frighteningly so.

He nodded to the floor. "Well?"

She tore her gaze from his, a task more difficult than a third-year med-school exam. A creosote bush waited at her feet. A decorated bush. From the prickly branches, makeshift ornaments dangled. Flattened tin cans, his car keys, a German mark, his dog tags, a fishing bobber some optimist must have carted along into the desert.

It beat her mother's best designer-decorated Douglas fir, hands down.

Tanner swept an open palm toward the scraggly little bush, his other hand behind his back. "Merry Christmas, Kathleen. Your very own survivalist spruce."

Kathleen slipped from the pew to kneel beside her "tree." "It's wonderful. Where did you find all of this?"

"Around the church. In the courtyard." He dropped to one knee beside her. "There's an abandoned miner's shaft a few yards out back full of garbage, some blankets we're better off not using, even old ropes, cables, pulleys."

"You've been busy." She touched each ornament with reverence, tapped the dog tags until they swayed. "Thank you. This is really sweet."

"Sweet?" He grimaced. "Lady, I'll have you know I'm a honed combat veteran. I am *not* sweet."

"I won't tell."

"Thanks." He winked.

Kathleen winked back. "No problem."

"Close your eyes again."

She plopped on her bottom. "Now comes the prank?"

"You guessed it. Now close 'em again."

She did, and all her other senses promptly kicked into high gear. Tanner's soap mingled with the musky smoke swirling around the old church.

He was watching her. She could feel it, the weight of his

stare, the caress of his eyes along her mouth. Her lips tingled, full and needy. She swallowed, started to flick her tongue across her top lip before rethinking.

Why was he so quiet? If he was going to kiss her, he needed to get to it before she screamed.

"Kathleen?" he called from a step farther away than she would have expected.

She caught herself before she toppled forward. "What?"

"Hold out your hands."

His voice soothed over her like the low rumble of thunder in a spring shower. One of nature's sounds that prompted thoughts of staying tucked under covers and indulging in a sensual cat stretch.

His knees popped as he knelt. He canted closer. Not that she could hear him so much as sense him, feel his heat warm her. He placed something wooden in her hands. Something flat, long…and full of splinters?

"Open."

She looked down at…a fence picket. "Oh."

He stared at her with eyes so intensely blue they matched his well-washed denim. This obviously meant something to him. She didn't want to hurt his feelings, but what was she supposed to say?

Kathleen struggled to figure out his reasoning for giving her what basically looked like a vampire stake. Something to feed the fire and keep her warm? A club for his head next time he made her angry?

Then she saw them. Letters carved in the wood.

A-T-H-E-N-A.

"Sorry I can't offer you an Officer's Club keg party to go with that name," he said, his voice low, so quiet yet intense. "I thought 'Athena' would be a good fit for you since she's the goddess of both wisdom and military victory."

Athena. Kathleen's eyes misted, and it had nothing to do with the smoke puffing from the burning brush.

He lifted a slate shingle with cactus cuttings on it. "This'll have to do for a celebration toast for now, but the keg's waiting at the O'Club when we get out of here."

She nodded, unable to speak without risking a very undignified crying jag.

He ducked into her line of sight. "Hey, if the goddess thing is too un-PC for you, I can come up with something else. We can pitch this one into the fire and work our way down that fence until we come up with a name you like. Your choice."

A tear squeezed free, and she knuckled it away. "No! It's great. Perfect." She sketched a finger along the letters and whispered, "Thank you."

Forget resolutions.

She cupped the back of his neck and leaned forward. Her lips met his for what was supposed to be a brief, thank-you kind of kiss.

Who was she kidding?

It had been one helluva day, and she deserved to have something she wanted even more than her own nickname.

She let her mouth soften under his, cling, just a leisurely sort of kiss, the kind given with ease as if it were her right. For a moment she wanted to pretend. Pretend there would be more kisses given without the need to devour every moment because the pleasure carried a promise of being repeated. Just kiss, enjoy, savor the feel of his mouth against hers.

His fingers tunneled into her hair as he...

Pulled away? She almost groaned in frustration.

Forehead to forehead, he stared back at her. "Kathleen, honey, we shouldn't start this."

Temptation proved too much, and her fingers circled his mouth. "Why?"

''Because you're hurt.'' He kissed her fingers once, twice, his words and mouth apparently at odds with each other.

''Make me forget about it.'' She scratched lightly along his bottom lip. ''This beats a bottle of Motrin any day of the week.''

He nipped her fingertip. ''Wow, lady. You sure know how to stroke a guy's ego.''

''It's not your ego I want to—''

He clapped a hand over her mouth. ''Call me old-fashioned, but we're in a church.''

She ducked his hand and cupped his face with hers. ''There you go, being sweet again.''

''I can guarantee you I'm feeling anything but sweet.''

''Okay.'' She clasped his hand and stood, tugging as she walked backward. ''So we go outside.''

Their arms extended to full reach and still he didn't budge, instead tugged her back down to kneel with him. ''Kathleen, think. Do you really want to do this? Now, when who knows how rattled your thinking might be?''

''Yes, I—''

''We don't have birth control.''

She closed her mouth. Opened it, closed it again before saying, ''Birth control.''

''Our suitcases blew up in the car.''

What kind of twenty-first-century woman was she to have forgotten that? And a doctor, no less. Maybe they could...

No. The last thing she needed was to get carried away in the moment and risk pregnancy. Babies were precious, wonderful, and sadly not a part of her future.

It wouldn't be fair to a child to saddle it with a mother like herself. Andrew had made it clear she was the last woman on earth he would want parenting a kid of his. Why couldn't she be soft as well as successful? He'd presented his case too well.

She couldn't bear to hear those same words come from Tanner's mouth.

Kathleen clutched her gift. "Well, I guess that settles that, then. We should probably chew on some more of that cactus, pile on pickets for the night…"

"Hey, Kathleen?"

"What?" She couldn't disguise her irritation, the flat-out frustration creeping into that single word.

He pushed to his feet, cupped the back of her neck and sealed his mouth to hers for a mind-searing kiss that ended far too soon. Tanner drew his face from hers. "If you still want me once we get to base, I'll jump you before you can say 'Joshua tree.'"

Her mouth turned dry as desert sand.

And, for now, there was nothing left for them to do but go to bed.

Chapter 12

Well, he'd wanted Kathleen in his bed, but this wasn't exactly what he'd envisioned. Tanner shifted on the rock-hard church floor, a too soft and tempting woman slept in his arms, while the wind growled outside.

His arm looped around her waist just below her breasts. Her bottom snuggled against him with tormenting warmth and pressure. Heat surged south with unerring navigation.

The fates had to be laughing their butts off over this one. He couldn't have her, but he had to hold her because of the cold. The fire puffed smoke and dim lighting, but only offered minimal heat. Basic Survival 101 dictated they share body warmth.

It was working. His temp had to be in the triple digits. He'd never wanted a woman more, and he couldn't do a thing about it, thanks to her concussion. It wouldn't be honorable.

The two condoms in his wallet were all but burning a hole in his back pocket. Lying about not having them had been the toughest thing he'd ever done, but he'd run out of options for dissuading her, since she wouldn't take proper care of herself.

After his and Kathleen's kiss outside the bar, he'd promptly invested in a serious stash of birth control, even pocketed two just in case. He would be prepared to protect her.

Who'd have thought protecting her meant turning her down altogether?

His watch glowed in the hazy night. Time to wake her again in a few minutes.

It hadn't been a half bad Christmas. The look on her face when she'd traced those letters on the fence picket had erased a substantial amount of bad memories for him. He knew every Christmas for the rest of his life would include thinking of this night.

If they hiked back to base quickly enough, they should still be able to make arrangements to attend Cutter's wedding. So why the odd sense of restlessness clouding his head?

Kathleen sighed in her sleep, wriggled, sending a fresh throbbing ache through him. He gritted his teeth until she settled again, her head on his forearm, that red hair spilling in every direction over the slab floor.

He checked his watch. Two more minutes left. Close enough. He reset the alarm.

Tanner rested his face against hers, his mouth close to her lips as he whispered, "Kathleen? Time for a two-hour check."

"'Kay."

"What's the date?"

"December twenty-fifth. Early in the morning."

"Good. You can go back to sleep."

"Thanks."

"No problem, Athena."

What kind of wedding had Kathleen had? And why was he hanging out in a church imagining her in a white dress?

More important, why did it make him break out in a cold sweat in spite of the fire-hot female nestled against him?

The woman was messing with his mind with all her talk about commitment-shy men. More likely she was pinning baggage from her ex onto every other guy. "Why'd you marry him?"

He hadn't meant to say it, even half hoped Kathleen already slept deeply enough that she wouldn't have heard him.

"Why did I marry Andrew?" Her groggy whisper caressed Tanner's bare arm. "Good question. Wish I knew the answer."

Her wistful tone tweaked his conscience. Her day had sucked enough without him bringing up her dirtbag ex. Tanner tucked Kathleen closer as if that might somehow insulate her against the memories as well as the cold. "Not everything in life makes sense."

"Too true. I was in the Uniformed Services' med school when I met him. Even then I made a point of not dating flyers. Seemed a dangerous mix, given my job." Her speech slowed and slurred until he thought she'd drifted off. Then she stirred again. "He was a guest speaker for a seminar about flyers and G-force stresses to the body. He spotted me, decided he wanted me. He was persistent. Maybe it had something to do with my last sister getting married. Or maybe my biological clock was ticking with the approaching thirties. Or maybe it was just full-moon madness. I never figured it out, other than that he reminded me of an old college crush at a nostalgic moment. Big, blond and God could he talk."

The world stilled as Tanner's every thought tightened to the woman against him with her head pillowed on his arm. Did she even realize what she'd told him?

"I like a man who talks. Forget the brooding, silent types. I want to hear what's going on in a guy's head, because I'm not very good at guessing and game playing. Problem was, Andrew was a liar. So all that talk didn't mean anything. My fault for trusting him...."

Her back rose and fell with even breaths. He hoped she'd drifted off because he wasn't sure how much more he could stand hearing about her ex before he wanted to pummel the guy for hurting Kathleen. He didn't want to think about the rest of what she'd said. Not yet.

"Tanner?"

"Huh?"

"I know I've already said it, but it bears repeating. Thank you for pulling me out of the car."

He grunted, not at all interested in reliving that moment when he'd thought he wouldn't be able to unbuckle her belt. The raw spot on his hand taunted him with how close a call it had been.

"And thank you for my name."

He winged a prayer of thanks that she was alive to receive it. And he intended to keep her that way. "You're one of the guys now, so don't be surprised when the keyboard on your office computer mysteriously swaps to the Mongolian alphabet."

Her smile brushed his arm as her breathing slid into the even rhythm of sleep. Night sounds echoed around him, desert animals awake and alert in the dark outside. Finally Tanner allowed himself the adrenaline letdown, the battle aftermath that his body demanded.

He'd almost lost her.

Every breath became a struggle, like combating barbells weighting against his chest. A trembling started deep inside him, working its way out. Only his clenched jaw kept his teeth from chattering. He recognized the feeling from near misses in flight and from flying combat.

But the greater intensity this time caught him unaware. His arms shook while he held Kathleen and thought about how close she'd come to dying.

Pushing through the panic, an image of Kathleen eased into his mind. Her smile over "Athena." Her lone happy tear. Her throaty purr when they'd kissed.

The shaking eased as he let his new Christmas memories slide over the old. He pressed a kiss to the top of her head. "Merry Christmas, Athena."

Christmas morning.

For the first time in years, Tanner woke with a sense of holiday expectation. Thanks to Kathleen.

His arms closed on the empty space beside him.

Damn. He would have liked to watch her wake up.

Refusing to let anything blot his mood, Tanner stretched his arms overhead and rolled to his back. Not bad. A few kinks, but no lingering effects from the accident or the night spent on the bare floor.

Where was Kathleen? They needed to get moving if they planned to hit the main road in time to pick up any passing church traffic. He wanted to check in at the E.R. and then with the security police, the sooner the better.

If his suspicions about the screwups and blown tires proved correct, he needed to get his wounded warrior goddess out of the battle, pronto. The commander had only meant for them to investigate. He'd probably never considered they would be in danger from someone trying to cover up the truth. But Tanner would make sure Kathleen didn't remain in harm's way. Which she probably wouldn't like.

Probably?

Better to ease his way into the discussion throughout the day.

"Kathleen?" His voice echoed through the empty

chapel. Rustling sounded from overhead, birds flapping past the opening in the ceiling.

She must have gone outside, likely downing a coyote for their breakfast through just the power of her iron will. He shoved to his feet and dusted off his shirt and jeans.

The creosote bush now perched in clearer sight beside the altar, Kathleen's fence post resting at its base.

Definitely a hefty dose of Christmas cheer charging through the chapel.

Whistling "Jingle Bells," Tanner left the church in search of Kathleen. The mission porch was empty, along with the yard stretching to the fence. Tanner bounded down the steps, scanning the barren horizon beyond. A full-blown tequila sunrise of reds and oranges blazed across the desert, but no sign of Kathleen.

She wouldn't have ventured into the mine, would she? Nothing there but a bunch of rusty tin cans and rope.

Footsteps sounded behind him. From above. On the roof.

Instinct told him he wouldn't like what he found when he turned.

A thud sounded behind him. Silence. Then another. He looked anyway, pivoting just in time to see Kathleen.

In midair.

A rope clutched in her hands, she rappeled from the mission roof. Her tennis shoes thudded against the stucco walls before she pushed off again, silhouetted by the burst of sunrise fire licking the sky.

Tanner's heart stopped for the second time in twenty-four hours. Except this time, her life wasn't in danger because of some accident or threat.

She'd risked her own fool neck out of recklessness.

One misstep, one lingering dizzy spell from her concussion and she would catapult to the ground. He didn't dare shout for fear of startling her, but when she landed, she wouldn't be so damned lucky.

* * *

Kathleen pushed off the side of the building, launching herself into the clear morning sky. Pilots had it all wrong. Who needed a plane? Flying solo offered the greatest rush, rappeling, parachuting, just the air and nothing else.

And she desperately needed that escape today.

Tanner was getting too close. He had her number, and that scared her. The tree, the name, those strong arms holding her through the night. She could too easily lose herself in him.

Her feet thudded against the stucco wall before she shoved herself back into the air. Rope glided through her grip. She needed to do something to work off the frustrated energy. Sex would have been a more satisfying way, but he'd been right to stop them.

She would work off her nervous energy out here. Alone. Rappelling was a lot less dangerous than relationships anyway. The risks were calculated and all her own, affecting no one but herself.

Watching him sleep had been far too enticing. Studying that square jaw softened by sleep, shadowed with stubble a shade darker than his hair. Tracing the outline of his full bottom lip, his brows, his nose.

Slipping free from his arms hadn't been easy. His hold was firm and her resolve was weak.

She was going to cave. Soon. And that whirled a mix of excitement and all-out fear inside her.

If a night spent sleeping in his arms scared her this much, what would a night spent awake in his arms do to her? Worse yet, what would happen to her afterward when one of them walked? Given their histories, she knew without question eventually there would be a foot race for the door.

Her feet pounded the side of the church with more force and less grace than before. She flexed and shoved for the last leap before she had to face Tanner—and herself.

"What the hell do you think you're doing?"

Tanner's shout sent her sprawling on her butt. Stunned, she stared up at the harsh lines of his face tight with unadulterated anger.

She forced a smile and extended her hand for him to help her up. "And who the hell are you to talk to me that way?"

He pulled her to her feet, his gentleness definitely at odds with the ice flecking his blue eyes. "I'm supposed to be your partner. So? What made you do something so crazy?"

"Crazy?"

"Reckless."

She yanked her hand free. "I was scouting for the best way out of here. Good thing I did, too. There's a house not more than an hour's walk due east on another side road."

He jabbed a finger toward the horizon. "That house would have been there a half hour later if you'd taken the time to wake me up. Did it ever cross your lone-ranger brain to take me along?"

"No." Of course it hadn't because she'd been running from him, couldn't stop herself from running now. "In case you haven't noticed, hotshot, I'm not one of your girl-friends needing you to take care of me."

"Excuse me?"

"Oh, come on. You've got to realize every woman you want needs helping, saving, protecting. Like with what's-her-name. Mindi. You took a whole weekend installing new locks on her doors to protect her from some stalker ex-boyfriend."

"That makes me a bad guy?"

"Why not call a locksmith? And it's not just Mindi. It's all of them. Haven't you noticed the protector-syndrome pattern? You don't have to coddle, cosset or save me. I can take care of myself." Even as she rolled through her arguments, she wanted him to step in and disagree. Prove her wrong. "Kind of interesting the past two times we kissed were tied into times you thought I was in danger or hurt."

His eyes blanked, no signs of either the angry or playful Tanner in sight. "I didn't realize your degree included psychology, Doc."

Part of her wanted to recall her words. Except they were true. "What was I supposed to do? Wake you up so you could haul your injured back up there, instead? I don't think so."

"I could have spotted you if you got dizzy."

"I don't get dizzy."

"You're arguing just for the sake of arguing."

"And you're being an ass."

He leaned in until they were nose-to-nose. "You scared the crap out of me, okay? I saw you kick off that roof, thought about your head injury, and I just…"

Tipping his head to the sun, he offered an unrestrained view of the muscles working along his jaw. Her anger deflated. Exhaustion rippled over her in a surprising wave. She was too tired to fight anymore. Too tired of the fight altogether.

She wanted to touch him, but she didn't always want what was best for her, so she kept her hands twisted in front of her. "That's kind of sweet."

"I'm not sweet." A half smile negated his grumble.

"Okay."

"At least try to sound convincing."

"Sure, hotshot." She nudged his foot with hers. "You're not just an ass. You're a bad-ass."

"Damn straight." He gave her a brusque nod, looked down at his shoes, then up at the sky again. His chest rose and fell with a shirt-stretching sigh. "Just take it easy on my heart, okay?"

Shock rooted her feet to the desert sand. "What?"

Tanner lowered his gaze to lock with hers. "Try not to

make it stop again with another stunt before I can get you to an E.R.''

"Oh, yeah, right. I'll try to restrain myself from arm wrestling any coyotes on the way back to base."

"My heart would appreciate that."

Eyes drawn to his, held by his, she wished that house could be another ten miles away so this once-in-a-lifetime Christmas didn't have to end yet. Tanner's simple naming ceremony had been the perfect gift, offering something she'd never expected to find. His choice of names indicated he understood and accepted her in a way her family and Andrew never had. "I guess we should head out."

She didn't move. Neither did he.

"I'm going to miss your mouth, O'Connell."

"Miss me?" She blinked to clear her thoughts. Warmth spread a scary excitement within her at the compliment. "When?"

Tanner winced. "Never mind. I didn't mean to say that yet. We can discuss it later once we've had a big lunch and a shower."

"No. How about tell me now." She crossed her arms and planted her feet. "When are you going to miss me?"

His shoulders lowered with a resigned exhale. "When you stay in Charleston after Cutter's wedding."

"And why would I stay in South Carolina?"

"Because of your head."

"My head's going to be just fine. You're not going to get rid of my mouth that easily, Bennett."

Wait. Back up. She did not need to lead this conversation into discussions about their mouths. Her lips tingled with memories of kissing him, long, deep, hard, not nearly long enough. "I'm afraid you're stuck with me, partner. I'm not checking out because of some silly bump on the head."

"How about because of all these accidents that don't make sense? Missing evidence, now a double dose of flat tires. It's time for you to pack it in and take care of that concussion before something worse happens.''

''This is one of your jokes, right?''

Only the wind answered as Tanner stood his ground, stone silent—a stubborn, immovable rock.

Then his words filtered through. What if the accident hadn't been a fluke? Why hadn't she considered that herself? This opened a whole new path for the investigation. Her mind sped through possibilities she couldn't wait to explore once they arrived back at base.

Except, he didn't intend for her to stay.

''You're serious? You really think I'm going to pull myself off the investigation team because someone may or may not be tampering with evidence? Maybe somebody wanted to spook us a little? The way I see it, that's all the more reason for me to press. I'm onto something.''

''That's my whole point.'' Tanner advanced a step, jabbing the air with a finger. ''*You* shouldn't be on to anything. *We* should be. We. The team. If you won't be a team player, then you're a liability to everyone else.''

His words hurt more than any concussion. Apparently the name and the invitation to be his friend hadn't been genuine. He'd been trying to get her back to Charleston, with the side benefit of working his way into her bed.

And he'd almost succeeded, damn his too charming face. She wanted to bash him over the head with her Athena stick.

Anger whipped inside her to blunt the pain of betrayal. ''You're one to talk about being a team player. You only want to play if you can be the captain. In charge. In control. Even sitting in the copilot seat, you've got to run the mission—forget that it's not your job. You're the one fixing things, like in your relationships. And on this whole investigation, you don't want to work *with* me any more than Andrew ever did. You want me to do it your way, on your schedule, by your rules. Well, I've got news for you, hot-shot. You can't always run the show and still be a team player. Sometimes somebody else is in control.''

Panting in the aftermath, she realized all she'd said. Some of it true, but some horribly harsh and unfair. Just as she started to backpedal, Tanner quirked a blond eyebrow.

''Are you through?''

Ice-flecked blue eyes stared back at her and Kathleen realized he was royally pissed. Not just miffed, or a little angry. Easygoing Tanner Bennett was full-out mad. At her.

She thought about apologizing, but the cold look in his eyes froze the words in her mouth. She settled for a quick nod.

''Good. Because so am I. I'm through trying to work with a woman who takes damn fool chances. I'm through trying to talk sense to you when you flat-out won't listen. And I'm sure as hell through fighting with you today because, unlike you, I happen to care about your health.'' He tapped his watch meaningfully. ''I'm hauling butt out of here, O'Connell, and now that you know, consider me through talking today.''

Kathleen blinked, more than once. She didn't deserve to shed the tears that burned her eyes. She'd taken a stupid risk and acted like a child, to boot. How could she blame him for not wanting to talk to her?

Unwilling to leave her present behind, she shook off the attack of self-pity and hustled back inside the mission before Tanner left without her.

She had a feeling this Christmas was going to be more than just a ''Silent Night'' kind of holiday. Tanner's cold shoulder threatened to extend into a full-blown silent day, night and freaking New Year.

And worse yet, she deserved it.

Chapter 13

Kathleen speared her fingers through her damp hair. A shower did wonders for restoring a person's spirits, especially when she had twenty-four hours' worth of sand, blood and pent-up emotions to wash away. A waterproof bandage over her stitches had enabled her to indulge in that much needed cleansing.

Her hour walk to the farmhouse earlier had been uneventful. Painfully so. Tanner's silence had heaped on the guilt, a silence he'd maintained through their trip to the E.R. and check-in with the base security police.

How long would it take for him to forgive her, if at all? She didn't have much practice in resolving arguments, another by-product of her solitary life. Even when her sisters had started with typical sibling battles, Kathleen had climbed her favorite tree. Once the winds of war had drifted away, she would catapult to the ground.

How odd that Tanner was the only one she argued with. More often, she opted for silence while she followed through on her own plan.

Kathleen went to her closet, thankful she'd left most of her belongings—extra clothes, her line badge, military orders—in her room at the Edwards Inn so she hadn't lost much in the explosion. She slipped into an overlong poet's shirt and black leggings. Her eyes gravitated to the dressing table, straight to the nutcracker necklace dangling from the mirror, her Athena spike propped beside it. She and Tanner had more than arguments and attraction between them now. Those two tokens carried far more memories and thoughtfulness than a hothouse full of roses.

The prospect of experiencing more such moments made her hungry to figure out how to make him forgive her.

Not so hungry, however, that she would compromise her work principles. She wasn't bowing out of the investigation, and Tanner could just get over himself on that one.

But their time alone together was running out. Kathleen didn't intend to waste it in a cold silence deadlock.

At the E.R. Tanner had been on full-tilt grumpy status, pacing the halls, scowling and looking so worried. She hadn't been able to stop herself from hoping that maybe the day, night, New Year wouldn't be a bust after all. Never an impetuous woman, she'd actually found herself asking the E.R. nurse for condoms. Just being a careful, responsible twenty-first-century woman, given how hot they'd been for each other.

Yeah, right. In her heart she knew better.

Waking up in Tanner's arms, she'd worried about being hurt. Now she wondered if there might be larger regrets in store for her if she'd didn't explore their crazy attraction.

Her fingers paused along the buttons. Had she been reverting to days of old, hiding in a tree?

Slowly she slid the top button open again and spritzed cologne in the vee.

Time to catapult off that hidden branch and play out the fantasy that hadn't let her go for twelve years.

The hunger for him had interfered with her work since she'd been stationed in Charleston. No doubt it hindered the investigation. She'd even married the wrong man because he reminded her of Tanner Bennett, something she still couldn't believe she'd admitted in the dark of the chapel.

She needed to find out what drew her to him and what wouldn't let her go. Maybe he was right. They needed to work each other out of their systems. Get over him and get on with her life, because she couldn't go on as she had been any longer. Her ex-husband might have made her wary of men, but her failed marriage hadn't left her immune to them.

Her lips remembered Tanner's heated kiss, his promise to "jump her" if she gave the sign. This was supposed to have been their night. Maybe it still could be if she worked things right. After twelve years of mental foreplay, they would finally give in to their hormones. She turned the thought around in her mind until it settled with undoubted certainty.

Was she scared? Hell, yes.

Was she backing down? Not a chance.

She laced her white canvas shoes and grabbed a purse, not letting herself think overlong on the one that had blown up the day before. Digging inside, she pulled out a set of keys. They glinted in her palm with the same silvery flash she found in Tanner's eyes every time they kissed. She'd planned to pass over the keys to their new rental car as a Christmas token of her own, a peace offering to end his silent treatment.

Maybe her cease-fire offering would evoke a side benefit she hadn't expected.

If she compromised and gave him the cars keys, perhaps she might luck into the driver's seat when it came to who did the jumping.

*   *   *

Standing by the lobby coffee machine, Tanner bolted back a gulp of piping-hot java, as if that might somehow drown his thoughts of Kathleen upstairs, changing.

Dangerous territory for those thoughts, fella.

Their silent ride back to base with a farmer and two turkey sandwiches had been tense, silent and full of regrets. Tanner found regrets as unpalatable as dried-out stuffing.

Already his anger had cooled to lukewarm. Hearing the E.R. doctor pronounce Kathleen fit and healthy had gone a long way toward tempering his mood.

After grabbing more sandwiches from the hospital vending machine, he'd checked in with the base security police. Not that minimal manning for the holidays offered much help, merely taking the complaint and requesting they return on the twenty-sixth. Frustrating, but expected.

Now that he'd showered and changed, there was nothing left for him to do but hang out in the lobby with the coffee machine and the uniformed airman stuck at the check-in desk. The airman peeled back tinfoil from a plate of food while watching parades on the corner television. The kid, probably not more than nineteen, picked at a Christmas dinner his mama must have sent.

Tanner's stomach grumbled for some of that pumpkin pie and a return to the holiday excitement he'd found that morning. Leftovers, like anger, came to a quick end around him. Neither were worth hanging on to—they just spoiled the longer they stayed packaged up.

Now that his temper had faded, what did he intend to do about Kathleen? She wouldn't leave. She'd made that clear as the morning sky.

Which only left one option. It looked as if they would be completing the investigation together.

The more time they wasted, the longer he would have to worry about her. She'd been right after all. They never should have stopped working for the holidays. With three days left until Cutter's wedding, maybe they could plow through and wrap things up for good. No doubt she would be happy to hear he'd backed off having her stay in Charleston.

And if they stuck close together, he wouldn't have to worry about her rappeling from a control tower.

Tanner sealed up a lid on his coffee cup. He would need the extra caffeine with all the work he planned to cram into a short time. Work that would help distract him from thoughts of jumping Kathleen.

"Captain Bennett?"

"Yeah?" He turned to the desk clerk.

"There's a message for you." The airman set aside his fork and pulled a folded paper from under the counter. "From a, uh, Captain Baker."

Crusty had been looking for him? "Thanks."

Tanner started to ask when Crusty had left the message, but the switchboard rang.

While he waited, Tanner read the few scrawled words: *Need to talk with you. Soon. Crusty.*

Folding and refolding the note, he hated the thoughts that charged through his brain. Crusty's obvious evasion. His hostility at persistent questions. Crusty suggesting a detour that would take them off the main road. It was one thing to consider his friend might have been negligent, but that he would deliberately set out to hurt them...

The raw spot on Tanner's palm stung. He could still feel the slick dampness of Kathleen's blood between his fingers. A fresh jolt of anger punted through him.

Crusty was hiding something, and Tanner intended to find out what. Once he had Kathleen safely settled away for the night.

The desk clerk tucked the phone under his chin. "Yes, ma'am. You can leave a message if you want, but he's not in his room because he's standing right here. Would you like to talk to him?''

Kathleen? Tanner reached for the phone, but the clerk was already hanging up. ''Captain O'Connell said she'll be right down, sir, if you'll wait.''

''Thanks. I could use more coffee, anyway.'' It was definitely going to be a long evening. What was she planning? He never knew for sure around Kathleen. It could be anything from demanding her rightful place in the investigation to rappeling off another church tower.

Footsteps sounded in the stairwell—hurried, light treads that slowed on the last three steps before the door eased open.

The determined gleam in her eyes left him with no doubts. She had her sights set on flinging herself off the tallest building.

Yet when Tanner looked deeper into Kathleen's eyes, he found an edginess lurking beneath her determination. She swept a hand down her flowing shirt, treating him to a tantalizing outline of her breasts, before she braced her shoulders and charged forward.

Tanner leaned back against the coffee cart and let her come to him. Better to see exactly where she was headed. He'd given as good as he'd gotten back at the chapel that morning. From past experience, he suspected Kathleen's anger might not be as quick to cool as his.

Her brisk strides drew his attention down to her slim legs. Had she poured herself into those pants? With her baggy shirt flowing below her hips, it wasn't as if she'd left everything out there for display. But the way those pants molded to her calves, her legs might as well have been bare. Her wet hair, the long shirt, made for fantasy material…Kathleen after a shower, wearing only his shirt.

''Hi.'' She cruised to a stop in front of him. With a flick

of her head, she swung her hair into place. Revealing her bandage.

The fantasy image disappeared faster than the airman's food.

"Want some eggnog?" Tanner thumbed toward the milky carafe perched in an ice bucket, then stirred two fingers in the air over a potful of something resembling hot tea with floating dirt. "I'm not sure what's in that other thing there. Looks like somebody forgot to strain it."

"Hot cider. Those are cloves."

"Ahhh. Guess it beats cactus."

She sidled past him to pour a cup of cider. Fewer than three inches separated them as she leaned, shower-fresh and smelling so good his mouth watered.

Work, investigation, pin-pull actuators, load ramps, he mentally chanted to numb his body. It wasn't working.

Then she stepped away. Tanner finished his coffee in one long gulp, watched Kathleen over the rim, assessed his opponent.

Half sitting on a sofa back, she blew into her cup. Imagining those same puffs of air against his neck almost sent him across the room toward her.

He forced his eyes away, down to something safe, like her feet. Damn. She even had sexy feet with slim, bare ankles peeking just above her simple white canvas shoes.

Sexy, restless feet that shuffled, tapped, flexed, before she stopped and crossed them. Nerves looked strange on Kathleen. He'd never seen her wired before. Fired up, yes. But wired, never.

They couldn't work together with this kind of tension. Time to make the peace and set their eyes on work.

"I've been thinking." Tanner barreled ahead, unwilling to watch her twitch for another minute. "You were right about using this time to work on the case. We can take the 'night owl' out Friday. The rehearsal isn't until Saturday morning anyway, since that's all the time the crew could get off given the mess overseas. Lucky for Cutter, he was already set to rotate out. Meanwhile that gives us two full days to work through reports.''

"You want to work with me."

"Yes."

"Let me help?"

He nodded. As long as he was spotting her if she pulled any lone-ranger stunts, he could live with that, not that Kathleen left him any choice.

She smiled, just a regular smile that shouldn't have the power to rob him of the ability to breathe. But it did.

Her eyes sparkled like a sky full of northern lights right outside his windscreen. Awesome, unexpected and rife with the power to distract him from his job until he crashed and burned.

Tanner pivoted away to refill his coffee. "Why did you want me to wait for you?"

"Oh! Right. I have something for you."

"For me?" he said over his shoulder, replacing the pot.

"Turnabout's fair play. Now close your eyes."

Nothing else left to do, he faced her again. "Gonna hit me with that fence spike?"

"How did you know?" She slipped a hand into her shoulder bag. "Now close 'em and take it like a man."

God, her smart mouth plucked at him as much as those eyes. He shut his before they soaked up any more images of Kathleen.

"Hold out your hand."

Mirroring his presentation from the night before, she inched closer, closer still until the minty fragrance of her shampoo encircled him. The flutter of her shirt across his wrist almost sent him over the edge. Even that whisper of cottony fabric held her warmth, a warmth he'd spent a whole night holding against him. His arms itched to close around her now.

"Ready?"

"Yeah." He pushed the word through his tight throat.

A jingling sounded just before his hand closed around... Keys.

He opened his eyes and stared at the keys peeking from his fist.

"I took care of getting us another car. But I thought you might like to drive for awhile."

Guilt pinched him. Hard. He knew how difficult it had to be for her to pass over the reins, but she'd done it in the interest of peace. She'd made a real effort toward compromise, and he'd been plotting how to maneuver her so the investigation went his way.

Except, he couldn't escape the niggling fear that something would happen to her. He could almost hear her earlier accusations in his brain.

Stuffing down rogue twinges of guilt, he said, "Thanks."

"No problem." Her smile reached her eyes, reached to him.

Neither of them spoke. The switchboard rang at least twice. A parade commentator droned from the television. The coffeepot hissed. And Tanner simply stared, took in every curve of her face, the faint sprinkling of freckles across her nose while she stared back.

Did her redhead complexion spread freckles in other places? He burned to stroke aside the neckline of her shirt and find out.

Pushing away from the cart and heading straight back to his room seemed the smartest move. "See you in the morning then."

One step later she stopped him with a hand on his upper arm. "Why don't we start now?"

Her hand scalded through cotton. With a will of its own, his biceps flexed beneath her touch. "Now?"

"Sure. We could go over to the hangar and check out the plane again."

An odd request since there wouldn't be any other personnel to meet with, but he wasn't risking another battle. He would find Crusty later. "Let's get to it then."

"I thought you might jump all over that idea." With a decided spring to her step, she shoved through the lobby door.

He felt like scum.

Following her to the car, he tried to dodge the guilt dogging him. She could take her protector-syndrome psychobabble and stuff it. So what if he watched out for folks, helped when he could? Big deal. That didn't mean he was a control freak who didn't know how to be a team player.

He'd enjoyed the hell out of building a fence for Tiffani's watchdog. Stepping in to coach Candi's son's T-ball team had been a blast.

Then the relationships fizzled when there wasn't a project to hold them together. No problem to fix.

And when the investigation ended, there would be nothing left to tie him to Kathleen.

His fist closed around the keys. If she knew he was secretly keeping an eye out for her, he suspected she might hang him with the few remaining ties they had left.

Maybe if she tied him up....

Walking into the hangar, she stifled a laugh at the very un-Kathleen thought.

Maybe she could just gag him. The guy wouldn't stop talking about the investigation, planning their time together down to the microsecond.

The Air Force had received enough of her efforts for one day. Tomorrow would bring work soon enough.

Putting off work for some kind of social life made for another un-Kathleen thought. Of course an airplane hangar with halogen lights wasn't the traditional nightlife seduction setting, but their rooms back at the Edwards Inn seemed too cliché.

She stifled her inner voice insisting she'd chosen the hangar as a safer, less intimate location.

No, dammit! They both wanted this. Tanner had made his desire very clear at the adobe mission. And heaven help her, she wanted him too—only him—so very much.

Tanner tucked his hands into his back pockets. ''Where do you want to start?''

God, she didn't know. So much for being in control of her actions. It had been so long since she'd done this. Not since her divorce, and only once before she'd met Andrew.

Kathleen shoved thoughts of her ex firmly away. He had no place in her life, in her decisions, or in this moment. ''Let's sit up front in the cockpit, talk through the case and what we've come up with so far.''

''You're calling the shots tonight.''

Yes, sir, she was. Kathleen charged through the belly of the plane into the narrow stairwell leading up to the cockpit. Climbing the ladder, she was too aware of the view she presented Tanner. If she was this nervous about him just looking at her, the night wasn't going to play out well at all.

Kathleen scurried up the ladder and plopped into the right-hand seat. Dipping his head, Tanner tucked his shoulders sideways as he cleared the bulkhead, but didn't sit. ''That's the copilot's seat. You're in my place.''

''Hmmm, so I am.'' She pointed to the aircraft commander's seat on the left. ''That one will be yours in a few weeks. Might as well break it in.''

Would he think of her, of this night, when he climbed into that seat for real? The thought brought a heady rush

of power. He'd held such sway over her thoughts for so
long. How odd to think she could do the same for him.

Settling into the bucket seat, he exhaled, long and slow.
His hands skimmed over the control panel with reverence.
His fingers wrapped around the stick, muscles in his arm
flexing as he began his pseudo flight ritual she'd come to
recognize.

"Do you know that you go through the motions of flying
even when you're not in the plane? Like when we're in the
car or sitting in a restaurant."

He shot her a smile even as his feet gravitated to the
rudders. "It's called chair flying. Sort of like air guitar."

"Really? I thought it was something you did uncon-
sciously."

"Sometimes. Other times it's deliberate. Before every
flight I sit in a chair, usually at my kitchen table. I spread
the chart out in front of me and fly through every step,
every radio call. Hands and feet. Stick and rudders. I go
through the motions."

"What about lately, when you don't have a flight
scheduled?"

"I relive old ones, think through them and analyze for
ways I could have tightened the mission." Staring straight
ahead, he extended both legs until his feet rested firmly on
the rudders.

What did he see in his mind's eye? He continued to fly,
almost as if in defiance of the forces that grounded him.

"Where are you flying now?"

Stopped midflight, he pulled his hand from the stick,
palm up and studied it as if he'd even caught himself unaware. "Last summer. In Sentavo. The mission to airlift
the war orphans out."

"That was one helluva save. Word has it the whole
crew's been put in for Distinguished Flying Crosses."

"We were lucky." He dismissed the praise with a typical

Tanner shrug. "About halfway through assessing the children and in-processing them, things went to crap outside the hangar. Incoming fire. We had to scramble out. I started the engines while the rest of the crew and rescue team loaded the kids. Mortar rounds tore up the runway. We had to take off on an adjacent field."

"Incredible." And he was—the man even more than the flight.

"Intense. But we airlifted seventy-two children out of Sentavo that day."

As much as she willed thoughts of Andrew away, Kathleen couldn't help but notice the difference in the two men's flyer stories. All aviators had their tales to tell. Some, like Andrew, thrilled listeners with his aerial daring. Why hadn't she realized that others, like Tanner, found their thrill in what the mission accomplished?

Seventy-two orphans saved.

Tanner's hands continued their familiar path along the instruments, each movement executed with a reverent confidence. Like a skilled lover's caress.

His thumb circled over the trim tab button. "Only two weeks on the ground, and I already miss this so damned much."

Kathleen watched that thumb's deliberate circling, her breasts beading in response. She squirmed in her seat.

She forced herself to breathe, swallow, breathe again until she could speak. "Your back's going to be fine as long as you take care of yourself. Become best friends with your chiropractor. Listen to your body." She told herself as much as him. "It's no crime to be human, with a mortal body that has needs no matter how much we wish otherwise."

Kathleen hitched a knee up on the leather seat so she could turn toward him, lean closer, make him understand.

"I know you think I don't grasp how important being

back on flying status is to you.'' She searched for the words to accomplish what all her medical training hadn't. ''Maybe I understand limitations better than you can imagine. No matter what I do, I will always be thirteen inches shorter than you are. Biology dictates I won't have your upper-body strength. I can pit myself against you doing sit-ups until the end of time and it won't change basic genetics. I have done my damnedest to make the most of what I was born with. Do the best you can with what life dealt you. Control what you can. After that, you've got to let it go.''

The muscles in Tanner's jaw worked, although he stayed silent, and Kathleen wondered if she'd just shot herself in the foot. Great way to get him fired up for sex, criticize the guy. Her seduction skills were rustier than she'd thought. Apparently, they were oxidized shut.

Finesse had never been her strong suit. Which left her only one option. A direct approach.

''Hey, hotshot?''

His flying hands stopped as he glanced over at her. ''Yeah, Athena?''

''You can jump me anytime now.''

Chapter 14

You can jump me anytime now. Kathleen's words winged across the cockpit, dive-bombing the last of Tanner's crumbling defenses.

"Run that by me one more time?"

"My head's fine. We're not stuck in a survival situation." She stuffed her hand in her purse, whipped it back out and slapped it down the dash. "And we have birth control."

Her fingers slid away to reveal two square, plastic packets.

His hands fell from the flight controls. The view outside the window not only blurred, he could swear the windows were already fogging.

Those little packets told him she'd planned ahead, no impulsive act, rather a fully thought-out decision. She'd suggested the hangar with just this in mind.

Kathleen O'Connell wanted to have sex with him. In an airplane. Even dreams didn't play out this well. There had to be a catch. But bump on his nose be damned, he would worry about impulsive mistakes and catches later.

Tanner hooked his hands behind his head and said, "Logistically speaking, it would be more comfortable for both of us if you came over here and jumped me, instead." Her eyes widened, and she went so still he wondered if he'd heard her wrong. Disappointment grounded him faster than antiaircraft fire. A gut-clenching realization followed that having her shouldn't be this important to him. But it was.

Then she smiled. "Sounds like a plan to me."

Shooting out of her seat, she reached to cup his face in her hands. Her mouth met his as she fell into his lap, her legs draped to one side.

This was better than having the best Christmas present of his entire childhood handed to him. This was Kathleen, warm, willing and definitely eager, judging by the way she insinuated herself over his thighs. Tanner wasn't sure he could survive much more of Kathleen's determined assault on his senses.

Slanting his mouth over hers he tasted apples, cider, cinnamon—warm honeyed flavors he would never be able to sample again without thinking of her. And he wanted more than a sample now.

Apparently, so did she.

Her tongue tangling, twining with his, she scooted closer. Her hip nudged insistent pressure against him, hot friction that left his jeans uncomfortably tight.

Too much. Too soon.

Grasping her hips, he stilled her restless movements, only to find the feel of her beneath his hands stirred him all the more. How could one woman be so toned and soft all at the same time?

Just like Kathleen. Tough and curiously vulnerable.

His hand tucked under her shirt and found more of that velvety softness as he stroked the small of her back. Kathleen's breathy moan filled his mouth just as she filled his arms, warm, difficult to capture but so incredible when he did.

Suddenly the enclosed airplane became a torture chamber as he yearned to see more of her. Two of her buttons later, his mouth explored her fragile collarbone and discovered those freckles he'd wondered about. A light dusting, but every one begged to be tasted, followed until he reached the gentle curve of her breasts.

Air whispered across his chest, and he couldn't even remember when she'd unbuttoned his shirt. Not that he cared as long as she kept touching him.

And, man, was she touching him. A pleasure he fully intended to reciprocate. Trailing a finger along the waistband of her pants, he gauged her reaction, not wanting to rush her, needing to make this as un-freakin'-believable for her as it was for him.

Her fingers vise-gripped his wrist. She stared straight into eyes. "No more playing around, hotshot."

She urged his hand inside her waistband as she nipped his bottom lip. She kicked her shoes free, each one thudding to the floor.

The lady didn't have to tell him twice.

His hand dipped inside, cupping the warm curve of her bottom, edging aside the stretchy fabric of her pants. With an extra tug from Kathleen, her pants and underwear slipped, rolled, peeled down her legs and off.

Swinging a leg over, she straddled his hips, a bare knee on either side searing through his jeans. For twelve years he'd wanted her, had imagined this moment more than once, yet he'd never even come close to the reality.

His eyes feasted on her, as greedy as his hands. Wild red hair tangled around her face. A lone strand fluttered to rest on her full, damp lips. The vee of her shirt plunged low, white cotton pooling around the tops of her thighs.

Her deft hands popped free the button fly on his jeans. The temperature in the cabin rose at least ten degrees.

Nudging aside his boxers, she clasped him in her soft hand, flicked her thumb over him. His eyes slid closed as his head thudded back against the seat. He inhaled, blinked, scavenged for control as he captured her wrist. "Slow down, hon. No rush on this."

"I want fast. Now. Isn't twelve years long enough to wait?" The pupils of her cat eyes widened, darkened, until only a small ring of blue remained, leaving no doubts about how much she wanted him.

"Yes, ma'am, it is."

He splayed a hand on Kathleen's back as he reached forward, rocking her toward the dash so he could palm one of the packets. Kathleen plucked it from his hand as they sat upright again.

Her fingernail lightly rasped up the length of him before she sheathed him with excruciating precision. "Next time, we'll do it your way."

Next time.

Those two words pleased him as much as the silken glide of her body as she lowered herself onto him. He didn't want to think about why her words were so important. Not at this particular moment.

Slow, torturously so, she slid her way down until she settled chest to chest against him, enclosed him in a moist heat that threatened to end it all.

He thrust up. She gasped, shivered, moaned.

She may have orchestrated this, but damned if he would let her control everything. He tunneled his hands beneath her shirt as his face ducked to nudge aside her collar. His mouth closed around her satin-covered breast, laved attention on the needy peak. Circling her tightening nipple, he mirrored with his hand teasing lower where their bodies joined, finding an answering bead of arousal.

A purr swelled in the back of her throat, vibrating through her chest, under his mouth. She scored her fingers up his chest, beneath his shirt until her fingernails dug into his shoulders, deeper, harder, until with a throaty cry she sagged against him.

Two shuddering breaths later, her head flung back, revealing a perfect stretch of neck for him to explore, while he guided her hips and she demanded a rhythm all her own. Until they both gave up the battle and simply moved. Together.

Tanner's hands crawled all over her skin, needing to touch every inch of that velvet softness, longing to possess all of her if only for a few hours. For once, he could hold her the way he'd always wanted to. For once, Kathleen didn't fight him. Instead, she sighed, moaned and whimpered her pleasure in a running monologue that had him so crazy he didn't know how long he could stave off the building pleasure.

Her throaty purr started again, followed by a hitch in her breath he now recognized. He was so grateful for that sigh of hers, that increasing sweet sound. The need to finish, pour into her until there wasn't anything left, shuddered through him and he wasn't going alone.

Tanner caught her before she collapsed back onto the control panel. She arched against his hands, her hair streaming against his fingers.

He wanted to watch her, tried to fight off his own release. A losing battle. The sky opened up and he fell in, no plane, no chute, just a free-falling surrender.

Cupping the back of Kathleen's head, he anchored her to his chest while his aftershocks rippled through him. Or were they hers? Who knew?...since they both shook, sagging against one another, breathing a monumental task for what could have been minutes or hours.

Kathleen nuzzled beneath his chin with one last purr of contentment. "You were right."

Fingers combing through her hair, he let each strand slither free while he watched the shifting reds. "About what?"

"About us working this out of our systems. I absolutely do not feel like fighting with you right now."

His hand stopped midstroke. Work each other out of their systems? Damned with his own words.

What did he expect? This was Kathleen, after all. He suffered no delusions that she had some great desire to enter into a relationship with him.

Except, somewhere along the way, she'd become his friend, and his every instinct screamed he'd just messed that up. All he would have to show for their friendship was a blown-up car and a night of no-strings sex.

No-strings sex with the hottest, most intriguing woman he'd ever met.

A woman who made it clear she didn't need a damned thing from him.

An hour later Kathleen buried her face in Tanner's neck, knowing too well their pocket of time together in the airplane would have to end soon.

She should peel herself off him and go. But she couldn't find the will to leave. Not yet. Being with Tanner had been…everything. Both times. Her way, followed by his.

Now she sprawled over him, chest to chest, hearts still thudding at a rate that would blast alarms on any EKG machine. Except her heart rate raced from more than great sex.

Okay, awesome sex.

Her pulse answered with an extra surge. Maybe she could hang out awhile longer.

Kathleen listened to Tanner's heartbeat, nuzzled her

cheek against the bristly hair sprinkling his chest and twirled his dog tags around her fingers. A small pewter medal peeked between the dog tags.

"What's this?"

He looked down at her hands, lifted her wrist to press a lingering kiss before replacing her palm on his chest. "A St. Joseph's medal."

Kathleen twirled a finger through the sworls of hair trailing down his stomach. "Oh, yeah. Your lucky charm. Where did it come from?"

"Tara bought it for me...that last Christmas."

Her finger slowed before resuming. "Why St. Joseph?"

"As kids, we dubbed Joseph our patron saint since we didn't have a dad. We figured maybe he would rustle us up a stepfather."

Tears stung her eyes, the sharing turning too intimate as he offered pieces of himself, a gesture she wouldn't be able to reciprocate. She'd always stunk at sharing. What did she have to give him, anyway? Not much came to mind. So she opted to just listen, stroking his chest over where his medal rested.

"Silly, now that I look back, because we didn't really need anything. We had a great family even without a father. The whole no-dad thing was a big part of why Mom pushed us into sports. I had father-figure coaches coming out of my ears."

His mom must have chosen those role models well, because no doubt Tanner would make a great parent someday. Fun, dedicated, a little pushy, but accepting and quick to forgive. No child of his would ever hide out in a tree because she'd disappointed her parents again.

He dropped a kiss on top of her head. "What about you? Your family? You've mentioned sisters."

Restlessly she wriggled to sit up, buttoning her blouse. "Three of them. Two older. One younger. All perfect."

"Come on, O'Connell. Talk." Tanner stilled her hands, then tunneled up the back of her shirt, urging her to his chest.

Strong fingers massaged muscles she hadn't realized were kinked, melting her against him. "We're just the typical upper-middle-class family. Dad's a doctor. Mom's an interior designer."

"And your sisters?"

"Sara's a plastic surgeon like Dad. Bree's a newscaster, a weather girl working her way up. Celia's a fashion consultant." Perfect people with perfect lives. No messy divorces or failed relationships. "They're all married with kids. Real superwomen."

"So's their sister." His fingers continued their never-ending trek up and down her spine.

"Hmmm. Keep doing that." His hands offered a great distraction from disagreeing with his assumption. No need to argue with him, anyway, as it would sound like she was angling for compliments.

Already Tanner had said words she would have once given anything to hear from Andrew. Sure, she'd become accustomed to the fact that she just didn't click with the rest of her family. But she'd expected better in the way of acceptance from Andrew. He should have understood she felt the calling to serve her country as strongly as he did.

Worse yet, he'd doubted her. Her sisters might be able to manage it all, but Andrew hadn't had faith in her ability to do the same. Somewhere along the line, she'd begun to doubt herself. Too bad marriage didn't come with a nice safe treehouse to hide out in when things went bad.

Kathleen let herself accept the comfort of Tanner's arms for a full minute, then shut off the past.

She shifted to safer and more pressing matters. Food. "Enough about me. I'm starved. Let's scout around for someplace that's open and get something to eat. There's a

Quick-Mart not far past the main gate. Maybe if we get there before midnight, we can find something edible.''

"Microwavable sandwiches and supersize sodas while we talk shop. Hmmm. Not much of a first date, but I'll make it up to you later. What do you like, Italian? Greek? I know this great seafood place back in Charleston, right on the water, great view. You pick.''

Date? Is that what they were doing now, and later back home? Dating? He sounded genuine, not like some cornered guy spouting what he thought she wanted to hear just because they'd had sex.

She didn't regret what they'd done together, and she wasn't one to delude herself into believing good sex equaled a relationship. However, while he might not be Mr. Commitment, she should have remembered he wasn't the one-night-stand type, either.

He was a good man, so passionate, an incredibly generous lover and she was...

Scared.

What did she want in the morning? Once they returned to their rooms with those microwavable "date" sandwiches? She honestly didn't know, except that she wasn't ready to discuss any of the options yet.

Kathleen brushed her lips across his before easing herself from him. "I don't know about you, but I'm wasted. Can we talk in the morning? We packed a lot into one day, a walk in the desert, E.R. run, drop in with the police, and now... Well. I'm feeling very mortal at the moment.''

At least that much was honest.

He grabbed her arm and tugged her back into his lap. "Kathleen?''

"What?''

"We're not done yet.''

"I'm out of condoms,'' she lied.

"That's not what I meant." The corner of his eye twitched.

"I know." She smoothed away the tic, pressed a kiss to his twice-broken nose and backed out of his lap. "But later. Please?"

When she wasn't totally brain-dead, lacking in common sense, and incredibly vulnerable to the draw of those sapphire eyes. Blue eyes that looked at her as if expecting something she wasn't ready to give.

He opened his mouth to speak, then paused. His face tipped as he listened.

Birds flapped through the rafters in the silence. Tanner hefted Kathleen into the copilot's seat and tossed her pants into her lap.

"Someone's out there. Get dressed while I check on it," he said, making fast work of buttoning his pants and shirt. "Probably just the security police wondering why our car's in front. I'll show them my line badge and send them on their way. And, Kathleen?"

"Yeah?" She clutched her clothes to her stomach.

"We aren't done yet," he repeated. Tucking in his shirt-tails, he disappeared down the stairwell.

We aren't done yet.

Shivering with the lingering promise of his words, Kathleen slipped on her leggings. He wasn't going to let her get away as easily as she'd hoped.

She'd been selfishly worrying about herself and hadn't given a thought to his feelings. But she'd never considered she might have any effect on him.

Harboring some silly crush on Tanner had been safe for just that reason. She'd never expected it to play out, so the fantasy was risk free.

What they'd done tonight was very real.

At least their unscheduled visitor had granted her a reprieve until she could decide what to do next.

After she found her other shoe stuck beside the rudders, Kathleen descended the narrow stairwell into the cavernous cargo hold. Raised masculine voices echoed, startling her still for a second before she charged down the metal track.

Halogen bulbs spotlighted Tanner's broad back as he slammed Crusty against the hangar wall.

Chapter 15

Fury blasted through Tanner in an afterburner burst. Forearm pinning Crusty to the hangar wall, Tanner stared down his old "pal" Daniel Baker who'd somehow managed to find him and Kathleen. "You set us up."

"Rein it in, Bronco." Coal-black, hard eyes stared back in spite of the easygoing voice. "Let's talk about this."

"Talk?" Anger fired, fresh and full force. A primal need charged through him, a need to pay back whoever had threatened Kathleen—could have killed her in the car explosion.

Crusty seemed the most likely candidate.

Tanner knew his anger was raging out of control, and he couldn't make himself care. No doubt, frustration over Kathleen's brush-off wasn't helping. He wanted to pound that ex of hers into the ground for making her so wary. Wanted to pound a wall because he hadn't been much better himself in Germany two short weeks ago. "I've given you more than one chance to talk, and all you offered was a detour that almost got us killed."

"Hey, the Wing and a Prayer was packed when I told you about that side road. Quinn and that Fitzgerald fellow were even sitting at our table. Do you honestly think I let air out of your tires in some high-school prank?"

Tanner's rage narrowed to the man he'd called friend. "How do you know about the tires?" He notched his arm tighter against Crusty's chest. "Or better yet, you can tell the security police all about it."

"Good. Let's go."

That stopped Tanner faster than any argument. "What?"

"Let's go. At least maybe there you'll listen."

"Okay." He nailed Crusty with a forceful glare to match his bracing arm. "I'm listening. Talk."

"Could you ease up on the arm a little so I can breathe?"

Tanner relaxed his hold but not his guard and kept his arm loosely pinned across Crusty's chest. "I'm listening."

"Black ops."

"Black ops?" The guy actually expected him to believe he participated in covert military missions supporting CIA operations? Daniel Baker a spook? Spiky-haired, rumpled-clothes Crusty a spy?

A gasp sounded from behind them. In the second Tanner twitched to look at Kathleen, Crusty muscled free with a grace and strength Tanner hadn't expected from the slighter, wiry man.

No more lapses, he zoned his attention on Daniel Baker. Tanner didn't need the distraction of Kathleen standing beside him with stitches in her head because of an accident that somehow related to this man. "You're telling me you're an agent?"

"Great disguise, isn't it?" Crusty chuckled, his wrinkled flight suit rippling with each laugh until his face cleared. "I do a little work for the Air Force OSI running Black Programs. I test new flight equipment to be used for Black Ops. Top-secret gizmos. You already knew we were on a test mission, you just weren't told how sensitive that mission was.''

Not ready to relax his guard just yet, Tanner stepped left, putting his body between Crusty and Kathleen. ''Why weren't we told? Did anyone else on the team get a heads-up on this?''

''Nope. Need-to-know basis only, bud. This one is pretty intense. Let's just say we get very frequent polygraph tests. I couldn't risk even hinting anything. Sorry about the erased tape, but I had to slap a magnet on that sucker before anyone else listened in.''

The explanations rang true—except for one dangling thread. ''And the car? How did you know about that?''

''I've had a security police bud keeping an eye out since this mess started. He gave me a heads-up on your accident.'' Crusty's gaze settled on Kathleen's bandage. Brown eyes shifted back to cold black in a heartbeat. ''We need to find the son of a bitch responsible for this. I've been tearing up the base looking for you. Left messages everywhere. Finally hit pay dirt when I checked back at the Edwards Inn and the desk clerk told me you were headed over here.''

It made sense, and Tanner wanted to believe Crusty's anger over the accident was genuine. After all, the guy had once had a few feelings for Kathleen, too. But Tanner wasn't willing to risk her safety on a hunch. ''Do you really expect me to believe this on your say-so?''

''Glad to hear you're not so trusting.'' A sharp gleam sparked, reminiscent of old days when Tanner and Crusty had debated football strategies. ''The 'powers that be' wanted to give the investigation a chance to play through without breaking security. I told them it wasn't working. General Crockett has scheduled a briefing for your team after the holidays because of all those too coincidental snafus lately. Of course, that was planned before this latest incident. My mission and my flying were clean that day. I've got a list of numbers you can call now if it will set your mind at ease and keep you from tackling me again.''

Already Tanner regretted that, not because he was convinced Crusty wasn't responsible, but because the action had been prompted by frustration. Frustration with Kathleen, with himself, with his growing sense that talking wouldn't solve a damned thing. No chat over a couple of Quick-Mart sodas and cheese puffs would even begin to fix their problems. ''Supposing I buy in to your story, then that brings us back to the new pin-pull actuator.''

Crusty nodded. ''Yeah, but didn't the inspector sign off on all the tests? The paperwork is pristine. O'Connell would have spotted a blot on those records in a heartbeat.''

The woman in question cleared her throat, dragging attention back to her. ''Randall told me he had plenty of time to take me on a tour.''

Tanner didn't even bother ignoring the sting of jealousy. ''What has the Randy inspector hitting on you have to do with this?''

Kathleen's mouth pulled tight for a flash before she explained. ''Those reports were almost too clean, the tests too perfect. Randall said his boss was thousands of miles away. He could write his own schedule. Or…'' She gestured for Tanner to finish the obvious.

''Or not clock in at all and just sign off on whatever Quinn wrote up.''

''Exactly.''

Tanner wondered what else Kathleen might have uncovered that night if he hadn't let his libido send him crashing across the bar. Wasted thoughts now, anyway. ''If he didn't check the testing results, were the parts faulty because of overlooked flaws? Or did Quinn take advantage of Randall Fitzgerald's slackness to cut corners?''

Crusty forked his fingers through his haphazard hair. "Whoever it is, they're getting antsy. Otherwise why risk tampering with a car? And the Mexican border is too close for comfort if he's running scared."

Time to test his friend's story. "Okay, Crusty. Which one of your generals would gripe the least about being pulled away from his turkey sandwich leftovers so we can get a search warrant?"

Kathleen's face lit with a smile that left Tanner longing to lock them both in the cockpit for the rest of the night. He wrenched his focus back to the problem at hand rather than the ones that awaited him later with Kathleen. "Any thoughts on this, Athena?"

Her smile hitched even higher, brighter. "Regulations say we don't need a search warrant if the building's on government property—like the testing warehouse."

Damned if he wasn't starting to like that reg book of hers. Too bad it didn't come with instructions on how to understand the woman who carried it.

Kathleen peered through the rental car windshield at the dimly lit warehouse. Tanner sat silently beside her, Crusty lounging in back.

They'd checked out Daniel Baker's story before bringing him along, and apparently their old pal was an intelligence expert on testing the latest aerial surveillance equipment. They all three had their marching orders for a meeting in General Crockett's office first thing in the morning.

Not that they intended to waste the evening when they could be gathering evidence to strengthen their case in front of the general. For now they needed to scour the warehouse for any clues that might point to faulty equipment or a lack of proper testing procedures—and pray no one was slipping over the border.

All perfectly logical, or so she told herself in an attempt

to avoid the obvious. She was scared to be alone with Tanner, so she'd fallen into an old habit of losing herself in work to avoid dealing with relationships. Working through the night provided a tempting diversion. "What do we do now, fellas?"

Tanner draped his arm over the steering wheel, staring at the building as if deciding the best way to tackle it. His fingers drummed the dash.

Crusty leaned from the back, hooking his elbows on the seat between them. "What are the odds that the guard's going to let us inside without calling Quinn first?"

"Nonexistent." Tanner turned to Kathleen. "Are you positive about the search reg?"

She quirked a brow.

"Never mind." His fingers picked up speed on the dash. "So if we conduct our own search, we're covered legally."

"You and I are. It's not so clear-cut for Crusty, since he's not a part of the investigation."

"Okay, then." The drumming stopped. "That leaves Crusty to keep the guard occupied while you and I scope out the office."

You and I. He'd included her, no banishing her to the sidelines. His surprise offer brought a heady rush of pleasure that rivaled even the glide of his hands over her body.

Tanner twisted to face Crusty. "Are you comfortable with distracting the guard for us?"

"You're kidding, right?"

Given the gleam in Crusty's eyes, Kathleen suspected there might be more to his Black Program operations with the OSI than he had shared.

With an abrupt nod, Tanner faced front again. "Which leaves figuring out how to get inside that locked office."

Kathleen's eyes homed in on the third-story window. Quinn's. They'd met him inside for two interviews, and she could envision his desk, filing cabinet, computer. His personal records on the testing process would likely be there. It wouldn't take her more than five minutes to find what she needed if it lived in that office. The window was even vented open two inches.

A length of rope. A grappling hook. And she would be inside.

Tanner followed her line of sight to the window, then back to her. His face tightened. "No. Think of something else."

So much for his including her. "Why? It's the fastest, easiest way. It makes sense."

"You're only hours out of the E.R."

"And cleared."

"I'll do it."

"Yeah, right. Like your shoulders will fit. Not to mention *you* have *not* been cleared by your doctor."

His brows slammed down. "Then we'll find another way."

"Your way, you mean," she snapped.

A whistle sounded from the back. "Time out, you two."

Tanner and Kathleen turned to look at Crusty.

Their old pal shook his head. "Just like old times."

No kidding. There went any hopes that Tanner might change. She didn't expect him to roll over in a complete surrender. Just a compromise. Some sign that he would share control with her.

Kathleen forced herself to think, reminding herself to work with Tanner and Crusty, her team. No lone-ranger strategies. "Do either of you have a better idea? Otherwise we're stuck spending the rest of Christmas in this parking lot."

Tanner's chest expanded, stretching his shirt just before a weary sigh rumbled free, filling the car. "We can get the rope back at base. Then I'll spot you."

That concession, albeit a begrudging one, stirred a hope she hadn't allowed herself to feel in years.

Damn. Who would have thought hope would be more frightening than the prospect of a lifetime alone?

Tanner paced under the window. Checked his watch. Scanned the deserted gravel parking lot. Paced again.

The hazy cover of night could engender a false sense of security, but Tanner refused to let it lull him. Lot lights combined with stars to cast a dim halo over the building, enough for Tanner to scout for the guard and watch for Kathleen. Pray she wasn't pulling some stunt while he wasn't looking.

Ten minutes had passed since she'd glided up the side of the building with catlike grace. That woman wreaked hell on his heart rate. He told himself she wouldn't fall and the worst they were facing was a possible confrontation with the guard.

Not that it helped.

They had to wrap this up. If the Randy inspector hadn't been logging in his hours, how many other projects fell into question? As long as Quinn was on the up-and-up, the fallout could be minimal. If Quinn had been taking advantage of Randall's slackness to cut corners, the ramifications could be mind-blowing, involving multimillion-dollar test programs.

Stakes high enough someone might be willing to kill for them.

Damn it, what was taking her so long? What if Crusty hadn't been able to keep the guard occupied?

Tanner traced and retraced his well-worn path under the window. Why had he ever agreed to this in the first place? His damned impatience had lead him to charge ahead rather than wait until the morning when they could have waltzed straight in with the security police.

If she didn't come out of that window in thirty seconds, he would…

He didn't have to answer his own sure-to-backfire question since Kathleen's white-tennis-shoe-clad foot eased over the ledge, followed by the other as she lowered herself into the night.

Relief kicked through him so intense it almost drove him to his knees. He watched her rappel down the building. The woman was so incredible she sucked the air right out of his lungs. With the fluid grace of a natural athlete, she closed the distance to the ground. Each glide sent her hair rippling, sent his pulse pounding through him with memories of having that body move against him with the same grace.

Her white shirt fluttered with each gust of wind, whipped like a glaring flag of surrender. She was too vulnerable. He wanted to urge her to hurry. Wanted her to take her time. Wanted her off that building.

He braced his feet in case he had to catch her if she fell. Which she wouldn't. Even knowing she wouldn't need him, Tanner waited below. Ready.

She flung away from the building, thudded, pushed away, thudded again—a foot slipping, then steadying.

"Kathleen," he growled low.

"Shhh. Almost there."

Two more and she would land. Except she skipped the last leg and launched herself into the air, landing like a surefooted cat.

He forced himself not to yank her into his arms. Too much emotion. Too raw. He needed time to find his own footing and get them the hell out of there.

Her eyes glimmered with ill-suppressed excitement. "Tanner, you'll never believe—"

"Not now. In the car while we wait for Crusty to come out."

The glint of excitement in her eyes dimmed. He grabbed her arm and tugged her around the corner toward their new rental. Whipping the door open, he urged her inside before circling the hood and sliding behind the wheel.

He slammed the door closed, kicking himself ten times over for ever putting her at risk in the first place. So what if she hadn't been caught? They were damned lucky. Tanner hooked his wrists over the steering wheel and reminded himself not to let his frustration lead him into saying things that would send his lone rangerette running farther away.

Kathleen rested a hand on his arm. "Did something happen while I was inside?"

"Nothing." His muscles bunched beneath her touch. "But it could have."

"Tanner, I spent two years married to a man who couldn't appreciate what I do for a living. This is who I am. This is what I do. If you can't get over that, all the talks in the world aren't going to do a bit of good."

"Damn it, Kathleen, I care what happens to you. Is that so terrible?"

Her gaze softened. She cradled his cheek in her palm, leaned to kiss him.

He tucked her close, alive and safe against him. He kissed her back, once, twice, before resting his forehead against her. "We should have waited until morning."

"No. We shouldn't have." Her hand trailed to his chest. "We did it, Tanner."

The grip of fear twisting round his heart for Kathleen started to ease with each steadying breath, with her light massage along his arm. Maybe she was right. He just needed to trust her. They'd worked together, gotten her in and out of the building without a problem. "What did you find?"

"Nothing."

"Nothing?" He'd gone through hell for nothing?

"A very telling nothing." Kathleen eased back, her hand still on his chest. "Quinn's already cleared out his office. Everything. The files are empty. The shredder is full. His computer is blank. He's probably halfway to Mexico by now. If we had waited until morning, we would have missed out, if we're not already too late to catch him before he leaves the country."

A rustling sounded behind them. In the back seat. Dread socked Tanner right in the gut just before the cold barrel of a gun pressed against his neck. He stared in the rearview mirror at the brown eyes staring back with frantic intensity.

Quinn Marshall's reflection smiled as he pressed the gun deeper into Tanner's neck. "Oh, I would say you're right on time to give me that ride over the border."

Tanner's hands fisted around the steering wheel. He hadn't checked the car before tossing Kathleen inside, and now the nightmares of his past replayed with chilling precision. Except this time there was no question but that he was to blame.

Chapter 16

Kathleen stared at the gun, blinked, stared again, and still her brain refused to process the obvious for at least three horrifying seconds.

The glow from parking lot lights spilled into the car too well for there to be any mistake. Quinn Marshall had a gun pressed to Tanner's neck.

The long barrel of the silencer pressed a hideous threat against Tanner's skin.

Bile burned a path up her throat. Forget calm under fire and combat training. All those hammered reactions fell away as she fought the need to scream.

A flicker of reason feathered through her panic. A scream would startle Quinn. His finger could twitch. Tanner would be—

She shut down that thought before it stole rational thinking altogether. Where was Crusty? She had to stall until Crusty stepped outside.

Quinn nudged the gun up into the underside of Tanner's jaw. "Drive."

A pulse throbbed in his temple. Tendons strained along his neck as he turned on the ignition. "Where? There's not a chance you're going to get out of the country. The security police are already on your trail."

Kathleen struggled for something to contribute. "We checked in with the security police the minute we got out of the desert."

"Damned shame the two of you are so competent." Quinn's gun shifted from one to the other with nervous jerks. "I'd hoped a walk in the desert would buy me more time. Or at least throw out the big guy's back."

She didn't see the need to tell him the investigation had been shut down for the holidays. Quinn had only made things worse with his tire stunt.

Hurry, Crusty. Hurry, hurry, hurry. "Give it up, Quinn. Don't add kidnapping charges to everything else. It's well past midnight and at least six hours to the border. When we don't make our morning meeting, the border's going to close up for you."

"Good point." Quinn's words raced with nervous intensity. "That's why we're not going to drive now. Time to improvise. Go back to base. Since you ruined my road trip plans, we're going to steal a plane. Then, my friend, you're going to fly us out of the country."

Kathleen twisted around. "You've got to be joking. That will never work. What about security?" She scrambled for something, anything. "He can't fly, anyway. He's grounded."

"He looks mighty healthy to me. An old ace like me feels safer in the air than on the ground." Quinn centered the gun on Kathleen's temple. "Quit stalling, Bennett, and drive back to base."

Tanner's biceps flexed and rippled even though his hands stayed on the wheel.

Kathleen stifled a groan. Not because of the gun to her

head, but because of its power over Tanner. No doubt Quinn had chosen his tactics well.

During the twenty-minute drive back to base, Kathleen told herself everything would be fine. Quinn couldn't get away with hijacking a military aircraft. Tanner would undoubtedly do something. Or the base security police would stop them.

But there could be shots.

If only Tanner didn't make such a big target.

God, she hoped Crusty would send up an SOS soon.

She should have kept her mouth shut about search regs. She and Tanner could have been back at the Edwards Inn, tangled in the blankets and each other.

But she'd been too scared to have a more meaningful talk with Tanner after their earlier intimacy, too afraid of launching herself headlong into heartache. Her fear had launched them both headlong into a nightmare, instead.

Like with Andrew, she'd let her personal life interfere with her professional decisions. Except this time the outcome could be so much worse. Her culpability so much more. With Andrew she'd merely turned a blind eye. This time she'd been an active participant, inflicting her will on Tanner.

They neared the front gate, a guard standing vigil beside a tiny hut. Kathleen tensed, readying for a possible confrontation. The gate sign proclaimed the duty guard's name, Airman DuPree from Baton Rouge, Louisiana. The man who could end this nightmare.

He wore BDUs—a battle dress uniform of camo with a blue beret perched on his head. An M-16 slung over his shoulder. A 9 mm strapped to his hip.

And he looked all of twenty years old.

Quinn lowered his gun out of sight. "Take it slow and easy. Flash your ID and drive on through. I've got my jacket slung over this gun, pointed right at Captain

O'Connell's pretty back. Don't even think about signaling Airman DuPree.''

Three guns within reach and she couldn't do a thing. A hail of bullets could tear through all of them. She wouldn't even think about Tanner dying, his mother losing another child.

Tanner dead. Kathleen shivered.

The rental car slowed. Without a base sticker on the bumper, Tanner would have to show his ID. What would he do, and could she protect him from the shower of bullets that could too easily rain down on them?

The gate guard shone his flashlight around the car's interior while Tanner reached for his wallet. He flipped it open to show his ID. "Evening, Airman."

Airman DuPree snapped a smart salute. "Merry Christmas, sir."

"Thanks." Tanner returned the salute and drove.

All her wary expectation evaporated.

Quinn rustled in the back. "Good job, Bennett. Now over to the flight line."

They passed the air park museum, old war planes perched on blocks, continuing through the base until Quinn pointed to a lot behind a hangar. "Here. Park. Clip on your line badges."

As they stepped from the car, Kathleen realized Quinn might actually be able to pull off this insane plan. The guy wasn't going to risk the flight line fence guard and barricades, where they would each have to show IDs again. He would waltz them through the hangar onto the flight line all because Quinn's job allowed him access to a few security codes. A cipher lock on the fence, another into the hangar, then a third lock would lead them out onto the flight line. Three codes in place to keep out all but trusted government employees.

Quinn motioned Tanner forward with the gun before jabbing it back into Kathleen's side. "You first, big guy."

Stepping into the hangar, Kathleen scanned the empty cavern for options and found nothing. She followed Tanner, taking comfort in the steady rhythm of his even steps.

Then she saw the bunching of muscles along his back and she knew.

He planned to make his move soon, a big, bold Tanner-charge that could likely leave him with far worse than a broken nose.

Emotions threatened her control. She struggled for logic and prayed it would be strong enough to convince Quinn and to block six foot five inches of Tanner's steely will. "You know, Quinn, we're talking serious jail time if you're caught."

"I don't have a lot of choice, now that you two have uncovered my little sideline." His agitated voice picked up speed, the tinny echo bouncing through the empty hangar. "I'm not going to prison. How would you feel, Bennett, being grounded for life like that? No way. I'd rather take my chances getting shot down flying away from here and go out in a ball of flames like a real warrior. But I won't crash. I can evade. I can make this work."

Desperation mingled with something else in Quinn's voice, something Kathleen recognized too well.

Ego.

She'd totally discounted the ego factor. Quinn actually thought he could take on Tanner Bennett, the security police, the border patrol, even the entire Air Force—and win. He wasn't giving up.

Kathleen knew, without question, Tanner would make sure she came out alive. He wouldn't hesitate to give his own life in exchange. That scared her worse than the thought of taking a bullet herself.

As much as she might want to believe she was special

to him in some way, she knew he would do the same for anyone. And, heaven help her, that made her respect him all the more.

She wouldn't let him do it.

Kathleen stopped cold in the middle of the hangar. "I'll be your hostage."

"What?" Tanner battled for control through the red haze of rage. The damned crazy woman was trying to barter her life for his. As if he would ever consider leaving her alone with Quinn for even a second. He'd struggled through survivor's guilt after his sister's attack and death, barely. He wouldn't even consider the possibility that Quinn could get his hands on Kathleen. "O'Connell, no—"

"You don't need him." She stepped forward. "Just take me. Leave Tanner tied up and take me with you."

"Kathleen, damn it, no!" Tanner's arm shot forward to block her.

"Cut it out, Doc," Quinn snapped. "I doubt you're interested in my charming ways or my Cayman Accounts. You can stop fluttering the eyelashes."

"Listen up, Quinn." Kathleen's chin tipped defiantly. "I've never been the eyelash-fluttering type, and I don't intend to start now. I'm being practical, just trying to make sure some of us get out of here alive. You're not going to leave me behind, because a woman makes a more sympathetic hostage—and a better bargaining tool."

"Kathleen!" Damned fool woman actually thought he would let her do this. "Shut up."

She plowed ahead, vintage lone ranger in spite of the frenzied panic radiating from Quinn. "You know as well as I do, Tanner's going to cause trouble. You need to tie him up now. Do you really think he'll let you get away with this? Let you keep me as a hostage while he sits on the sideline? First weakness on your part, and he'll take you out and we could all end up—"

"Or I could just shoot him." Quinn's arm swung in a wild arc as he shifted the gun to Tanner.

"No!" Kathleen grabbed Quinn's wrist, turning the 9 mm back to herself.

White-hot panic seared through Tanner. Damn it, if only she would keep her gorgeous mouth shut. He had a plan for tackling Quinn at the door once he got Kathleen past the threshold. Now the guy looked ready to snap, his arm trembling, the gun wavering so damned near Kathleen, the trigger finger flexing—

No. No. And hell, no!

Tanner sprang forward toward his compact target. The woman who would have gladly taken a bullet for him.

Kathleen felt the impact all the way through her teeth. Damn, but Tanner tackled like a pro.

Confusion, frustration, outright fear all rocked her with as much force as Tanner's linebacker body slamming her sideways.

Pop.

A bullet hissed from the silencer through the air just before they smacked the ground.

She waited for the stinging sensation. Some kind of pain beyond the jarring of hitting the floor. Anything to reassure her she'd been hit rather than Tanner.

Nothing. Not a scratch.

"Tanner? Talk to me! Now, damn it!"

"Shut up, Athena," he growled in her ear, raw emotion tempering his unmistakable anger. "I'm pretty pissed at you right now."

Relief melted the tension from her. "You can be as pissed as you want as long as you're alive."

Quinn loomed over them. "That was damned stupid. Brave but stupid. Why does everybody always insist on being a hero?"

Kathleen struggled to breathe, a difficult proposition with

238 pounds of Tanner shielding her and showing no signs of moving anytime soon.

Quinn knelt, gun clutched in two hands between his knees. "Roll off her. Now. We're not wasting anymore time."

Tanner flipped off Kathleen, slowly, easing to his feet. He towered over her, lights at his back casting his face in shadows. He extended an arm down to help her up.

Then she saw it.

Blood.

Streaming down the side of Tanner's face.

A scream built. Begged for release. Professional objectivity went all to hell as she leaped to her feet. "Oh, God, Tanner. Let me look."

"It just nicked me." Tanner shoved aside her hands and wiped away the blood with an impatient swipe of his wrist.

Kathleen peered through the dim glow. It seemed like the scratch he claimed it to be. Not that the knowledge stopped the grinding fear. Quinn was out of control and that made him beyond dangerous.

Tanner grabbed Kathleen's arm and shoved her behind him. "You're not leaving here alone with her, Quinn."

"Touching. A real *Days of Our Lives* episode in the making." Quinn steadied the gun. "Nice try, Doc, but I can handle the big guy here. Two hostages are better than one. Gives me a spare to dispose of. Now move."

Tanner's rage mushroomed within him like an A-bomb as he walked across the tarmac toward a row of C-17s. Not a damned SP in sight on the mammoth runway that sprawled for miles into the desert. No visible activity due to the holiday.

Fears for Kathleen swirled with his grief over what had happened to his sister. He would make the son of a bitch pay for threatening even one strand on Kathleen's head.

Flight line badges flapping as they walked, Quinn urged Tanner across the hundred feet to the nearest C-17. The runway lights did little to brighten the overcast night.

There was nothing to stop them from stealing a plane. The aircraft was even gassed up and ready to go since planes always refueled immediately after landing.

Wind whipped at Kathleen's hair as it had only two weeks ago when they'd stood together on the flight line in Germany. But the fire in her eyes had dimmed. The shooting had rocked her. And while the fear for him lingering in her eyes thumped him right in the chest, it also scared him a helluva lot more than any bullet.

She would toe the line now, and Quinn had to know it. How far would Quinn push her?

Tanner thumbed aside the slow trickle of blood on his pounding temple. If he'd kept his mouth shut back in Germany, listened to her diagnosis and parked his own butt in the infirmary, she would have been safely dispensing diagnoses and prescriptions.

Way to go, hotshot.

A couple of military cops eased into sight in their blue Ford Bronco—too damned far across the shadowy tarmac to be of any help as they drove away.

Tanner kicked aside the chalks and cleared the engine covers. Quinn trailed them inside the plane, up the stairwell, Tanner into the left seat, Kathleen into the copilot's seat.

Quinn chose the instructor's seat behind her. "Make it fast. No more stall tactics."

Tanner snagged the emergency checklist from a hook beside him, a five-step start-up, the fastest way to move the aircraft if an emergency arose. This certainly qualified.

The stars and runway lights illuminated miles of concrete, stretches of empty desert and a dried-up lake bed. He

flipped switches before he gripped the throttle, dumping ga
into the engines.

How damned ironic. He sat in the aircraft commander'
seat, a wide-open runway and endless sky outside his wind
screen. Two weeks ago he would have given anything fo
that crew position, to hold the stick in his hand and fly hi
plane again.

Now he would sell his soul to be anywhere else.

He increased the throttle until the engines caught. Th
C-17 roared to life, rolled down the tarmac toward the ru-
way. He wasn't going down without a fight. With a flic
of the hand, Tanner turned the wing flaps to signal to th
security police the plane was being hijacked, not just stole

Then the standoff would begin.

Tanner taxied as slowly as he dared until the SF
screamed across the runway, squealing to a stop and block
ing the plane. Not out of the woods yet, but he would fin
a way to get himself between Kathleen and that gun aga
when the time came. He eased up on the throttle.

"Go!" Quinn shouted.

"I can't drive over them."

"Don't play dumb with me, Bennett. Take off on th
lake bed."

"Can't do it." A weak lie, but he was playing for time
The plane could do that and a lot more. He had befor
when taking off on a Sentavo field far rougher than the lak
bed beside them.

Apparently Quinn knew, too. "Don't mess with me. R
member that disposable hostage. Now turn!"

Tanner accepted the inevitable for now and guided th
plane into a turn. The engines roared, louder, vibratin
through the plane. He would get Kathleen out of this, n
matter what the cost.

A slight dip of the nose, and they sped off the runwa

Tanner winced. Would another bump twitch Quinn's finger on that trigger?

Focus never more important, never tougher to find, Tanner glided through his smoothest takeoff to date. Fear for Kathleen offered a hefty motivator.

Fighters would probably be on their tail soon, but wouldn't shoot down the C-17 as long as he stayed well clear of the no-fly zones around major cities.

Already a new plan began to form in his mind while the plane gained altitude. If only he could get her off the aircraft. Hell, he would settle for tossing her out…

Out of the plane.

His plan solidified as Tanner leveled the cruising plane.

Quinn exhaled a laugh. "See, I told you I could handle the big guy. Now kick back, ladies and gentlemen, and enjoy your nonstop flight to Central America."

If Tanner had his way, and he damned well intended to, Kathleen would be safely on the ground long before they landed.

Chapter 17

An hour later Tanner scanned his control panel, then the inky night sky outside his windscreen. Luminescent green from the instruments lent an eerie glow. Quinn sat in the seat behind Kathleen with the gun trained unwaveringly on her head as they crossed the Mexican border.

The hour of routine had steadied the throbbing in Tanner's temple. He didn't even want to think about the bullet that had grazed him, that could have been embedded in Kathleen's soft body.

She might be subdued now, but Tanner knew that at the first hint of threat to him, she would start yanking that gun toward herself again.

A trembling started low, too much like the one that had gripped him back at the abode mission after the car explosion.

He forced his focus on flying and hammering out the specifics of his plan. Under the cover of regular flight tasks, he'd managed to flip the setting on the silent transmission of the IFF. The Identification Friend or Foe radio frequency was now indicating a hijacking situation.

So far, Quinn hadn't noticed. Air security had tightened since Quinn's active duty days, and Tanner was counting on the older aviator not knowing that air traffic controllers were undoubtedly tracking them. Likely a DEA jet had vectored in from the border, racing up as U.S. fighters peeled away. Quinn would be apprehended on the ground by federal agents.

That was where things could get tricky.

Thus the need to get Kathleen off the plane. Now. He'd failed to protect his sister years ago, but by God, he wouldn't screw up this time.

Tanner flipped the autopilot switch.

Quinn jolted in his seat. "What are you doing? Keep your hands where I can see them. Don't move."

Kathleen's brow furrowed, her eyes blazing her question across the cockpit. *What the hell are you doing?*

Tanner ignored her for now. She would know soon enough, and she wouldn't like it one bit.

One battle at a time.

Quinn's hands shook. "Fly the plane. Now!"

This guy was too wired. It wouldn't take much for him to lose control of that trigger finger. Tanner's temple ached with an all-too-real reminder of Quinn's unpredictability.

"Chill, Quinn." Tanner held up his hands. "I'm not going anywhere. I just want to talk for a minute."

"Why would I want to talk?"

"Because you don't want anyone to get hurt. You may be a crook, but unless I miss my guess, you're not a murderer."

"I wouldn't bet on it, big guy."

Tanner didn't figure he would, either, still he needed to keep Quinn calm.

But then maybe it would be better to just end it now.

All he needed was one fast jab to Quinn's jaw and it would be over. Sure, Quinn would have time to give Tanner a sucking chest wound, but Kathleen would have the crucial second needed to take out Quinn. No doubt she could do it, too.

Except how would she land? Worse yet, if the bullet went astray and blew a hole in the plane...

In spite of all that steely will firing from her eyes across the control panel, she was far too mortal.

Control. Think. No blasting in, half-cocked.

Tanner eased back. Some of Kathleen's logic would serve him well now. "You're a smart guy, had to be to pull this off for so long. I'll bet you have a cushy retirement planned."

"I just want my money. That's all I've ever wanted. I've had enough of being an underpaid, undervalued government employee."

"You were only in it for the money. You didn't want all this grief."

Quinn kept his gun steady in one hand, his eyes glowing like a jet jock sharing war tales. "I figured the scam was minimal risk for a big payback. How could I pass up the chance when I realized Randall liked to keep loose hours? So I ran half the tests and pocketed the money for running the other half. If half the tests went well, stands to reason the other fifty parts should work, right?"

Not hardly. "Now that you have your money, you're going to want to stay alive and enjoy it." Tanner allowed every ounce of anger to seep into his words. "And I'm telling you, pal, as long as Kathleen's around, there's a damned good chance we're gonna have a shoot-out. I'm feeling edgy. Yeah, I'm trying to control it, but if it looks like you're gonna hurt her, even just a little bit, I'm gonna lose it. Then I'm gonna go after you. Sure, you might get me."

Tanner canted forward. "But I might get you first."

Quinn's gun wavered.

"Are you willing to risk it? Why not just let her go and focus all your attention on me?"

"Let her go?"

"Let me go?" Kathleen's horrified voice ripped his gaze off Quinn and onto her. "Not on your life, you big—"

"Parachute out." Tanner let his eyes linger on Kathleen for one selfish moment. Convincing her would probably be tougher than persuading Quinn. "Do it, Kathleen. Use that awesome brain of yours. I'm not leaving without you. And I stand a helluva better chance at making it out alive if you're not here distracting me. I'll throw you out the hatch if I have to." He fought dirty and fought to win. The stakes were too important. "Doc, it's time to be a team player."

"Damn you," she whispered, just a small, eloquent whisper, but one that said so much coming from his restrained warrior goddess.

He'd won. A hollow victory if Quinn didn't go along. "Well, Quinn?"

Clouds whipped past the windscreen for what seemed like miles before Quinn slid the gun from Kathleen's head. "Okay. We've made it over the border. I can afford to ditch her."

The kick of relief punched the air from Tanner's lungs.

"But..." The silver-haired aviator steadied his gun. "You're gonna follow us to the back. I don't relish the idea of you jerking the plane and knocking me out."

"Fair enough." Tanner leaned to the control panel and opened the load ramp.

The plane glided along on autopilot while they descended the stairwell into the cargo hold. Red lights filled the belly of the plane with a hellish glow. The back of the plane yawned open into the abyss of an opaque night sky broken only by a smattering of stars.

Quinn paused at the base of the stairwell, his gaze darting back and forth from Kathleen to Tanner as if reassessing the situation. Unease prickled over Tanner. Aw, hell. It couldn't go bad now. He almost had Kathleen out of the plane.

Quinn threw back his shoulders, a cocky grin spreading across his face. "You know what, Bennett? This is your lucky day. I'm letting you both go, now that we're over the border."

It sounded too damned good to be true. "Why?"

"Call it residual sentimentality from my active duty days. Or call it common sense because you're both loose cannons who are just lovesick enough to throw yourselves in front of my gun one too many times and get somebody seriously hurt. Like maybe me. Regardless, it'll make for less baggage to deal with on the ground. And I don't really need you anymore."

Quinn's eyes glowed. "I've always wanted to fly one of these beauties, anyway. Low, past radar like the old days. I'll ditch the plane where the Air Force can retrieve it later. This is your chance, big guy. Parachute up and pile out."

Tanner searched for signs that Quinn might be feeding them a line in order to catch them off guard, shoot them and dump their bodies. He found nothing but impatience in Quinn's eyes.

The guy actually planned to let them both out. Tanner sucked in air like water. Kathleen would make it.

And Quinn really thought Tanner would willingly leave his plane while the guy got away clean.

Quinn deserved to pay for putting lives in danger. Only by the grace of God and a good set of flying hands had Crusty and his crew lived.

Who was he kidding? Tanner burned to make Quinn pay for threatening Kathleen. Forget that he intended to let her go. The bastard who'd kidnapped his sister had let her go, but she'd died, anyway.

The bullet may not have hit Kathleen, but it could have, and Tanner intended to make sure Quinn didn't get away with it.

But he wouldn't let Quinn—or Kathleen—know that until she was safely out of the plane. The automatic tracker on her parachute would bring rescuers within a few hours. With her safely out, he could deal with Quinn.

Olive-green parachutes dangled from hooks. Tanner tossed one to Kathleen before selecting another for himself while Quinn stood guard to the side with his gun.

Tanner's own chute felt heavy in his hands. The scent of military-issue equipment wafted up, the familiar mix of must and hydraulic fluid bringing an odd comfort. He strapped into his parachute, knowing full well he wouldn't use it. Going through the motions kept Kathleen moving.

Her slender arms slid through the straps while wind howled through the open back. With brisk efficiency, she hooked the D-ring over her chest, cinched it tight, then repeated the procedure with the leg straps.

Precision. One-hundred-percent-perfectionist Kathleen.

Her methodical attention to detail gave him another dose of comfort as he readied to send her out of the plane. She might be risky, but in a make-sure-her-ass-was-covered kind of way. If they both got out of this alive, he could find a lifetime of comfort in that realization.

Kathleen stopped in front of Tanner, cupping his face in her palms. The hazy glow bathed her skin in a red that was as fiery as her wind-tossed hair, as his determination.

"Hey, hotshot?" Husky and low, her voice trembled with emotion, anger and something else he didn't recognize. "You can't control everything."

He hadn't fooled her for a minute. She knew him too well.

She pressed a fierce, hard kiss to his lips, then tore herself away. In perfect form, not that he expected otherwise, she leaped from the plane.

Quinn flicked his gun to the gaping opening at the end of the load ramp. "Okay, you next."

Tanner turned to Quinn, eyed his opponent, and calculated the odds of wrestling the gun from him now that Kathleen was gone.

Then it hit him. How ironic that by the end of this mission, she had being a team player down pat. He was the one screwing up. Not Kathleen.

He'd missed the big picture. The plane was being tracked. It was almost certain Quinn wouldn't get away. What did it matter if he was taken when he landed or in the air? Or who dispensed the justice?

If anything, Tanner needed to be on the ground with Kathleen. A real team player didn't leave his wingman.

And, damn it, she was even more than that to him. Kathleen was special. He'd known it when he first saw her twelve years ago. He knew it now as well.

Being with Kathleen was like swinging from a chandelier. Unpredictable. Exciting. Hell on his heartrate.

But he loved her and wouldn't have her any other way.

Tanner stepped away from Quinn. "Go easy on the stick. Remember this baby's a newer model. It's a fly-by-wire, not like the C-130."

Arms tucked in tight, Tanner thundered down the belly of the plane toward the open ramp. What the hell. Control had become a thing of the past around Kathleen, anyway.

He flung himself out of the plane into the blanket of stars.

Kathleen whipped her parachute free and stared up into the murky sky, not that she expected to find the big lug, anyway. Damn him. Why hadn't she made him jump first?

Because she knew he wouldn't have.

She strained to see, although not much was visible, with cloud cover muting the moon and stars. She'd landed right back in the desert again, twice in less than forty-eight hours. Except, this time she was alone.

Fear poured over her with each gust of sand-laden wind. Not fear for herself. She could take care of herself until a rescue plane tracked the beacon on her chute.

But she was scared spitless for Tanner. She'd seen the gleam in his eyes, the need for revenge powered by an overwhelming sense that he could make it happen through his will alone.

Ego. That invincibility he'd needed to carry him through combat could be the very thing that brought him down.

Then she heard it. A reverberating thud and grunt about fifty yards away.

Tanner.

Was it her imagination, or had the ground shuddered under her feet when he hit the desert floor? Or maybe it was sheer, earth-shattering relief rocking her from her toes to her teeth.

Kicking free of the pool of parachute nylon, she stumbled toward the sound.

"Tanner? Tanner!" she shouted, running toward him. Medical training marched gory scenarios of shattered bones through her mind. Parachuting was dangerous, especially in the dark. And he'd already been injured protecting her. "Tanner! Answer me, or I'm going to ground your butt until the next millennium!"

A blur took shape in front of her. A big, broad-shouldered shape. Tanner bent over with his hands on his knees, his parachute lying in a pile behind him.

"Hang…on…Athena." He straightened, slowly, wonderfully tall and whole. "Just trying…to catch my… breath."

She sagged with relief. It had to be relief. She was too close to tears to consider it could be anything else without totally losing control.

The final ten yards between them closed in seconds. She slammed against him. He was alive. They both were. In a day that could have ended so differently, they'd made it, worked together, flushed out Quinn and lived to tell about it.

And Tanner had followed her to the ground.

She stroked her fingers over his gunshot wound with expert hands. After finding reassurance, she let her hands rove into his hair, this time with impatient, lover hands. "Kiss me, damn it. Now," Kathleen demanded, even as his face was lowering to hers.

"Already on my way."

Her hands scoured over him, detailing every healthy inch with a need she didn't even try to delude herself into thinking was for medical reassurance.

He hadn't stayed with the plane and thrown his big reckless body into the line of fire. She couldn't think beyond celebrating that. Apparently, neither could he. Tanner's mouth feasted on hers, his embrace strong, solid and so damned exciting.

Like the man.

Kathleen tugged at his clothes, her hands frantic, powered by that relief and something else. She tore his shirt over his head, bemoaning the scarce second when her lips had to slide from his.

Clothes yanked off and flung free fluttered to the desert floor around them until wind whipped over her bare skin. Wild, invigorating gusts of gritty wind scraped at her body, reminding her they were both alive.

In a tangle of arms and legs, they fell backward onto the parachute, Tanner's body cushioning her fall.

God, how far she could fall if she let herself. And she

did, for just a moment, giving herself up totally to sensation as she'd never done before. She kissed him while he kissed her back so thoroughly she couldn't have seen even if her eyes had been open.

From somewhere he pulled out a condom. From his wallet maybe? She didn't care. Why waste a second more even thinking about anything other than him?

Grabbing the edge of the parachute, she rolled, pulled Tanner on top of her, draped the silken folds around them until even the hazy moonlight faded away.

Nothing but silk, Tanner and the glide of his body sliding into hers, filling, stretching her until her thoughts scattered like sand in the breeze.

She locked her legs around his waist, locked him to her. Smooth parachute beneath her, Tanner above her. Bristly hair, hard muscles and callused skin rasped over her while silky nylon whispered under her.

Her body writhed against his, begged for release. She fought it off, not ready to lose this moment, unwilling to return to a world of thoughts, logic, reasonable worries that would steal more moments like this from her.

She scaled the rugged planes of his chest, her fingernails gripping, clinging. Like climbing a sheer cliff, she held on until she had no choice but to let go, to surrender control.

Tingling heat started low, pulsed, spread, burned over her. She set her teeth. Fought it back again.

Tanner's breath flowed hot against her ear. "Come on, honey, let it go. I'll catch you, then take you there all over again."

His words tore through her restraint, shredding it until she became like a parachute ripping open, sending her, screaming, catapulting down. And catch her he did. Right before he lunged into her again and, as promised, sent her right back on a second flight into a total loss of control.

She wasn't flying solo. With a hoarse groan of comple-

tion, Tanner collapsed on top her, a welcome weight
grounding her as aftershocks trembled through her.

Burying her face in Tanner's neck, Kathleen tasted the
warm sweat along his shoulder and wanted to stay wrapped
inside their parachute forever, where she wouldn't have to
face how much her complete loss of control scared her.
Tanner deserved so much better than what she had to offer.
Yet she knew too well those silken walls couldn't protect
her from a risk nearly as frightening as any they'd faced
that day.

The risk of letting herself love Tanner.

Tanner held Kathleen against him and breathed in her
scent. Mint and Kathleen permeated their parachute haven,
surrounded him in silk and Kathleen, just as she'd enclosed
him, holding his body in hers seconds before.

The parachute slithered away as Kathleen slipped from
beneath him. Tanner flipped to his back while she gathered
her clothes, a shadowy, slim outline in the night as she
dressed. Silently.

Of course, he couldn't put together more than a couple
of words himself at the moment so he pulled on his clothes
as well. Stuffing his legs into his pants, he ignored the throb
in his head that had nothing to do with a gunshot wound.

Frustration churned through him, anyway, an increas-
ingly familiar sensation around Kathleen.

There was nothing to do now but wait. A rescue plane
or chopper would arrive soon. Upon landing back in the
States, he and Kathleen would undoubtedly be separated
for debriefing on the incident. He didn't expect there to be
any legal fallout. They'd followed procedure down the line,
resisted when possible, but the whole process could stretch
into days. They would be lucky to make Cutter's wedding.

"Kathleen?" Tanner sat, his back against a tree. He held
out his arms and waited.

Slowly she lowered herself, her back against his chest. He accepted her need for silence. He'd learned that much about her. She needed her space. But he needed to hold her, listen to her heartbeat and remind himself she was alive.

This would be his last chance for days. He refused to think this might be his final opportunity to hold her at all now that their last tie had been cut.

They'd worked together, brought down a crook who'd evaded detection for years, and made the C-17 community safer for their friends. Damn it, they had reason to celebrate.

So why could he feel her pulling away even as she sat in his arms? Just as she'd done after they'd made love in the cockpit.

And, damn it, they had made love. It wasn't just sex. He wanted ties, strong and lasting ones.

With Kathleen.

How could a woman so competent in the work world be so damned wary when it came to relationships?

How much did he really know about her? Kathleen wasn't a woman of many words. She might run that smart, gorgeous mouth of hers plenty around him, but rarely about herself, something he'd never realized before.

Fragments of conversations, pieces of herself she'd unwittingly shared shuffled around inside his mind. Words about her "too perfect," "wonder women sisters." An ex-husband who didn't respect her job any more than he'd respected her, a man who'd been a disloyal scum.

When had she ever found acceptance?

Once again he'd missed the big picture. This woman needed more from him than he'd thought. That proud tilt of her chin hid a pack of very human insecurities.

He'd been so focused on her not needing his protection,

he hadn't realized Kathleen needed something far tougher for him to provide. She needed reassurance.

How was he supposed to fix that for her? Talk about Mars and Venus, men and women—he didn't have a clue how to tackle this one for her. If he blew it, the pain would be just as real as if she'd taken a bullet.

They'd made it through a day he hadn't expected to see end. He would have given his life for her, battled anything to keep her safe. This time there weren't any tangible enemies to conquer, walls to knock down.

Other than the ones she'd built around herself.

Tanner stroked her hair back from her brow as the morning sun rose, officially ending their Christmas together. He spoke, even knowing full well she wouldn't answer. ''I love you, Kathleen O'Connell.''

Chapter 18

"**W**ill you promise to love him," the military chaplain filled the base chapel with his resonant baritone. "Honor him, keep him in sickness and health as long as you both shall live?"

"I will," the bride answered without hesitation.

Kathleen had never considered herself the cry-at-weddings sort, but the Clark, candlelit nuptials were sorely testing her on that one.

I love you, Kathleen O'Connell. Tanner's words from two days prior echoed through her brain, her own silence echoing afterward.

Kathleen sat in the pew of the Charleston Air Force Base Chapel and wondered if her answer, or lack thereof, would be any different, now that the world had returned to normal?

She could still feel his disappointment, but she hadn't been able to make herself speak. Not while her emotions were still so raw, so tender, not unlike her well-loved body. She'd used their rescue as a much needed escape.

As a cop-out.

After two hectic days of questioning by military author-
ities, she'd been cleared and released. Quinn had been captured the minute he'd landed, thanks to the tracking beacon
Tanner had sent up. Quinn was in custody, awaiting de-
portation back to the States. The planes with his faulty part
had been grounded. Even Randall faced charges for his
negligence.

Kathleen had completed her debrief and caught the first
plane back to Charleston with only minutes left to dash to
her town house and slide into her full-dress uniform for
Grayson Clark and Lori Rutledge's wedding. Kathleen
hadn't even known if Tanner had returned in time.

Then she'd seen him stride in during the processional,
watched him now as he stood beside Grayson as best man.

And, Lord have mercy, what a best man Tanner made in
his full-military-dress uniform. Only a slight crease remained on his temple from the gunshot wound. He hadn't
even needed stitches, just a tetanus booster and a butterfly
bandage.

Medals gleamed across miles of chest. His blond hair
glistened as if he'd just stepped from a shower—or had
perspired from making love to her.

Kathleen shifted to safer, more church-worthy thoughts.

Hundreds of ivory candles reflected off the stained-glass
windows, showering multifaceted blessings on the small
grouping gathered round the altar. Lori stood serene and
glowing in a princess-cut satin gown, regal as ever with her
hair swept high, interwoven with tiny white flowers and
velvet ribbons. Wearing his full-dress uniform, Grayson
held her hands, his voice steady and confident as he repeated his vows.

Matron of honor, Julia Sinclair, in midnight velvet held
the hand of flower girl Magda, Lori's adopted daughter
from the Sentavo rescue mission. The little girl's honey-

brown curls danced around her face, a circlet of flowers pinned on her head.

A small wedding party, no doubt, but with their priorities in order. Love and certainty shone from the bride and groom. Not like during the circus of a ceremony Kathleen had let her mother plan. Lori and Grayson's marriage would be blessed with the support of friends wherever the Air Force took them.

And she knew now that's the way it should be.

Kathleen felt lonelier than ever, finally fully aware of what she'd been missing. After a taste of the camaraderie she'd experienced with Tanner over the past few weeks, how could she go back to her solo existence?

Sure, she'd proven her ability to work on a team in the professional world, but what about in a personal realm? Could she cut it as a wife and a mother?

Of course, who said the man even wanted to marry her? Yet how could a woman's thoughts help but travel that petal-strewn path while she watched a wedding so full of promise? The promise of things Kathleen wanted for herself.

When Tanner looked into her eyes, as he was doing even now across the chapel, she saw love shining in those crystal-blue depths.

Love mixed with disappointment.

She'd let him down after they'd made love in the desert. How odd, but she'd never considered herself to be a coward. Yet she'd taken the safer route her whole life, giving what she could within the confines of academia, her own personal comfort zone, all the while respecting rules above all else. It was how she coped in a world that didn't always have a place for her.

Looking at Tanner and remembering his words to her after they'd made love, words she somehow knew he didn't scatter about easily, she wanted to step outside of her safe world and find a place for herself in his. She felt that she had changed, had grown since her mess of a marriage with Andrew.

Since loving Tanner.

And Tanner certainly was more of a man than Andrew had ever tried to be.

Kathleen sat straighter in her pew, eyes trained on those broad shoulders, the strong lines of his face softened by the boyish bump on his nose.

Could she do it? Could she tell Tanner she loved him, that she would give her absolute determined best to a relationship, and take things one day at a time?

Kathleen trained her eyes on the altar. The bride and groom oozed confidence, not a wedding jitter or nervous twitch between them.

Which was fine, because Kathleen's knees were now knocking enough for everyone.

Tanner had never seen a warrior goddess pass out. But he suspected Kathleen wasn't too far from hitting the floor of the base club, smack-dab in the middle of the reception.

Freckles popped out along her pale face. Her hand trembled as she lifted a glass of champagne to her lips. Had she even heard half of what the matron of honor had said to her?

Was she ready to listen to him now?

The reception was drawing to a close as were his duties as best man. The newlyweds had just driven off for their weeklong honeymoon at a secluded bed and breakfast on the barrier islands. Little Magda had left with her new grandparents. He would miss seeing Lori and Magda when they joined Grayson at his new assignment in Washington, but their paths would cross again, a surety of Air Force life.

After all, hadn't the Air Force brought Kathleen and him together again when he least expected it?

Standing near the bar, he only half listened to Lance, Crusty and Lt. Col. Dawson. Tanner found his attention too easily riveted on Kathleen as she stood talking with Julia Sinclair by the half-eaten wedding cake. As sharp as ever, Kathleen mesmerized him—woman and warrior in full-dress uniform. Silver trim and medals along her deep-blue jacket declared her a top-notch officer.

Her hair was swept up in some kind of twist. A stray lock brushed her jaw, declaring her every bit a woman.

Her to-the-floor pencil-thin uniform skirt tantalized him with memories of the slim legs beneath. Hot as hell, even shaking in her low-heeled shoes, she stirred an answering heat within him that never failed to knock Tanner flat.

Lance Sinclair finished off his drink and placed it on a passing waiter's tray. "Time for me to punch out. Congratulations again on nabbing your upgrade slot, bud. We can use more of your kind in the left seat."

Tanner thumped Lance on the shoulder. "Be careful out there."

"Will do." Lance flashed him a perfect-toothed smile. "Meanwhile, I've got forty-eight hours with Julia before I head back out, and I intend to make the most of it. Catch you later, guys."

Tanner watched Lance walk to his wife, then sling an arm around her shoulders as he passed her the keys. Military marriages took a lot of hits, as he'd heard often enough from Lance, but the Sinclairs seemed back on track. Some marriages weren't so lucky, like Lt. Col. Dawson's, but the overall average of the day was damned strong.

Lori and Grayson on their honeymoon. Lance and Julia finally ready to start a family. Loadmaster Tag and his wife, Rena, sending their first kid off to college.

Tanner eyed Kathleen as she smoothed aside her stray strand of hair. Yeah, he liked those averages and intended to do his best to increase the odds once his duties as best man were complete and he could get her alone.

Crusty tossed another stripped-clean chicken wing on his plate and wiped his fingers. "Any other cars you want to blow up or planes to steal before I go back to California? Maybe there's a train out there you'd like to derail? Take another bullet, perhaps?"

Lt. Col. Dawson hooked an elbow on the bar, flashing a thumbs-up. "Nice job figuring out the Edwards accident. But next time, could you work a little more panache into the finale? I mean, really, who hasn't stolen a national asset?"

Crusty scooped a handful of mints from a nearby bowl. "Hey, I did that just last Tuesday before breakfast."

The familiar, good-natured camaraderie wrapped itself around Tanner like a favorite well-worn sweatshirt. Across the room he could see Kathleen was receiving much the same treatment.

Lt. Col. Dawson followed the direction of Tanner's gaze. "All joking aside, you two did a damn fine job in a hellish situation. When it came down to the wire, you and O'Connell pulled together. She's got that promotion recommendation sewn up. You've certainly earned your upgrade. Just promise me that next time you're given pilot-in-command duties, you'll land with your aircraft."

"Sir, that seems to be sound advice." Hearing earlier that he had been returned to flight status and his upgrade slot was secured had been a relief, no doubt, but took a surprising back seat in his mind. Celebrations wouldn't be on his agenda until he settled things with Kathleen.

Lt. Col. Dawson's craggy face broke into an easygoing smile. "Like most flyers, I avoid flight surgeons like the plague, but O'Connell's a 'good troop.'"

A rush of pride knotted in Tanner's chest as he heard the commander voice one of the highest praises—for Kathleen.

He'd told her they all respected her. If only she could hear it, see it, too.

An idea took shape in his mind. He'd wondered what he could do for Kathleen, what he could give the woman who seemed to need nothing. Even if she didn't want him, a thought he damn well didn't want to consider, he could give her this. "Sir, it's been great talking, but I need to find the club manager."

Tanner shoved away from the bar and wound his way through the reception hall toward the kitchen. Doubts dogged him with each step. What if he couldn't get through to her? What if his pattern of failed relationships continued now, when it mattered more than ever that he succeed?

But, if he didn't try, he would definitely lose out on the best thing ever to happen to him.

His feet slowed as realization tackled him. He'd told himself he'd tried with relationships, but he'd been lying to himself. He'd been so afraid of losing again he hadn't let himself get close to any woman he could actually love.

Faced with the possibility of losing Kathleen on the airplane, even now in a different sense, Tanner realized the best way to honor his sister's life was to get on with living his own. Time to let go of the past.

Tanner tapped the Officer's Club manager on the shoulder. "I need to buy a keg."

Kathleen scanned the crowd for Tanner again. If she had to wait much longer to get him alone, she would lose her nerve. Not to mention the four canapés she'd managed to choke down.

Then she saw his head bobbing above the crowd. Close-cropped blond hair glistened in the chandelier's glow. Tanner broke free from the crush of wedding guests as he moved toward the stage with a pony keg on his shoulder.

Well, that would certainly make him the most popular best man around.

Tanner stopped in front of the band and slung the keg down onto the dais with a resounding thump. Vaulting up on the stage, he commandeered the microphone from the band leader.

"Excuse me, my friends, but I have one last speech to make. Given that I'm a man of few words..." Chuckles rumbled from the cluster gathered around the rostrum. "I'll keep it brief."

All eyes trained on him, not that it surprised her. Look for the crowd and Tanner would be in the middle, holding court. He made his minions laugh. People gravitated to Tanner because they felt good about themselves around him. She crossed her arms and leaned back to enjoy the show.

"Continuing in our squadron tradition of Anything, Anywhere, Anytime," Tanner said into the microphone, "since the bride and groom have left the building, we now have squadron business to transact. It has come to my attention, as the senior copilot, that a very important member of our unit has had the unmitigated gall to walk around without a call sign."

Kathleen eyed the keg. Shock glued her feet to the floor.

"No!" the crowd roared. "Say it isn't so!"

Tanner held up a hand. "I realize this is a foul, but it's true. And again, pointing out that I'm the senior copilot in the unit, I have taken it upon myself to remedy this situation before I drop back to the bottom of the food chain as the junior aircraft commander. Would the crew dogs please pass Dr. Kathleen O'Connell to the front?"

Good Lord, she was about to cry like a baby in front of her fellow officers.

Hands reached and hefted her up in a makeshift throne, lifted her high, passing her off to the next set of waiting hands. Kathleen stared down at the sea of faces underneath the bumbling but considerate hands. Cheering her on, familiar crew dogs in their crisp uniforms jostled her forward. All in fun. All including her, not at all on the outskirts. The transfer continued until Lt. Col. Dawson and Crusty lowered her to the stage.

Tanner turned to face her, his eyes intense in spite of his lighthearted tone. ''Kathleen, we're very sorry we haven't given you a nickname up to this point. But usually there's a watershed event that drives the bestowal of the title. The past few days certainly qualify.'' He raised a broad palm and lowered it to the top of her head. ''By the power invested in me by the United States Air Force, as the senior copilot of this unit, I dub thee…Athena. Warrior Goddess.''

Cheers and applause swelled from the crowd as they surged forward. Surrounding her.

Tanner stepped back, leaving Kathleen in the spotlight. Men and women, families she'd come to know, cared for, served with, encircled her, radiating their respect.

Their acceptance.

She should have known Tanner wouldn't be a traditional flowers-and-candy kind of guy. In keeping with the nutcracker necklace and an Athena spike, Tanner had given her something far more valuable, so very special, because his gift had been chosen just for her. And she'd earned it in a way she'd never earned a spot in her family or with Andrew.

For the first time, she fit.

An hour later Kathleen felt Tanner's hand slide into hers. She didn't have to look over her shoulder to know it was him. She recognized his touch well as he stood behind her, supporting her without overshadowing.

Kathleen set aside her plate and broke off her conversation with Crusty. She stepped away from the bubbling champagne fountain toward Tanner. "Yes?"

He ducked his head and whispered in her ear, "Are you ready for that talk now?"

A nervous tremble started in her stomach, milder than earlier, but still there. Two days ago her answer would have been no, but she'd learned a lot about herself lately, about Tanner, about taking risks. She could handle those rogue nervous twinges, had to, because the payoff promised to be awesome.

Tilting her face up to his, Kathleen squeezed his hand. "Yeah, I think I am."

The surprised lift of his brows pinched her with guilt, but she would make it up to him.

"Where do you want to go?" he asked.

Anywhere too private and they wouldn't talk. Sex would offer a too convenient distraction, an easy out she wouldn't take this time. "Let's just walk. See where our feet lead us."

"Fair enough."

Side by side they left the club. Stars and streetlights dappled bricked walkways. The temperate southern winter night carried a light chill, but not enough to pierce their uniform jackets.

Silently they strolled, keeping pace with each other until they came to the flight line. Kathleen wasn't sure who'd lead whom, but there they were, right back where they'd started almost three weeks ago. Standing on a windswept flight line.

An SP cruised by, checked them out, then continued down the flight line.

Kathleen let her hand drift up to finger one of Tanner's medals. "Thank you for what you did back there. That was really…"

She searched for the right word.

Tanner winced. "Sweet?"

"Special." She dropped the aerial achievement medal back in place, smoothed the rows of other medals flat against the broad chest that carried such a big heart.

"I'm glad it made you happy. You deserved it." He eyed her with uncertainty, as if gauging her next move.

And he had good reason, given her track record.

She'd blamed so much of her fear of relationships on her ex. After all, he'd been the one to cheat on her, the one to walk. But hadn't she been running all her life, closing herself off from real emotions rather than risk failing? She'd been attracted to Tanner all those years ago, no doubt had a colossal crush on him.

Then he'd become a real man to her the night his sister had died. Once she'd been forced to see him as more than a sports jock, a safe crush that would never play out, she'd run like crazy from the possibility of facing emotions more substantial than infatuation.

She'd been playing out the same scenario even twelve years later. Forced to see Tanner as more than some jet jock, she had to face her powerful feelings for the man. The real man.

No more hiding, she asked, "Where do we go from here?"

Tanner's chest expanded beneath her hand, then lowered with a hefty exhale. "You told me once you want a man who talks, a man who says what he's thinking, because you're not one for guessing games. So I'm going to lay it all out here for you. I love you, Kathleen O'Connell. Doc. Athena. Cadet or Captain. I love every gorgeous, infuriating, exciting inch of you. I love the way you challenge me. I love the way you make me be a better man when I'm with you. And I want the honor of loving every inch of you for the rest of my life."

He tucked a strand of hair behind her ear, his powerful

hand so gentle against her bandage that her eyes stung. "That's where I stand. Help me out here, Kathleen. I need to hear what you're thinking, too."

"I'm thinking I want to say all the same things to you." She pressed both hands to his solid chest to keep him from lunging forward, and to steal a little comfort and reassurance from the solid wall of muscle and man beneath her hands. "I want to jump in with both feet and say to hell with being careful. But, God, Tanner, I'm so damned scared of messing up again."

"Honey, you go right ahead and jump. I'll spot you every day for the rest of our lives. And I trust you'll do the same for me."

The intensity in those blue eyes swayed her, but she knew she wanted to be convinced. Stepping outside a life-long comfort zone wasn't so easily accomplished. She had one last ghost to banish. "What about kids?"

"What do you mean?"

"If I...try this and I blow it again, what about our children? If you want them."

Without hesitation he answered, "Yes, I want them. With you." His brows pulled together. "And you? What do you want?"

God love him for asking. No one else ever had. She'd always had to fight for what she wanted from life, and she'd fought alone. Not any longer. Andrew had made her fear she was too reserved, too much of a loner to be a good mother. But she knew that wasn't the truth—probably not then and definitely not now.

With faith that this man would accept and nurture all her dreams as his own, Kathleen shared her heartfelt wish. "Yes, I want them." Certainty flowed through her. "With you."

Tanner's eyes closed, his head falling to rest against hers.

His throat moved with a long swallow before he looked down at her.

That sense of déjà vu hit her again. Thoughts of standing on the airfield in Germany flashed through her mind, brash Tanner staggering off the airplane, fighting through the pain. Bravado had glossed over his hurt and a fear that he would lose something important. She saw that same flicker of fear in his eyes now, a fear slowly easing away.

He'd been afraid of losing her.

He really loved her.

Then he smiled, a full-dimpled smile. He threw his head back and laughed, hefted her up and spun her around twice before cruising her to a safe landing on the runway. "You won't be sorry, Kathleen. There's nothing you can't do once you set your mind to it, and now that you've set your mind on us, hon, we're a sure thing. With the combined forces of our not-so-subtle wills, we'll make this work."

The man certainly did have a way with words, and she'd always loved a man who could talk. She'd always loved this man. "Yes."

"Yes what?"

"Yes, I love you. Yes, I'll marry you. And yes, I'll populate the Air Force with our little warrior gods and goddesses."

"That's my Athena. A woman of few words, but when she talks, she says all the right things."

"Kiss me." Kathleen arched up on her toes as he leaned down, their lips meeting. She let her mouth soften under his, cling, just a leisurely sort of kiss, the kind given with ease as if it were her right. And it was.

Finally, after twelve years of longing, she could just kiss, enjoy, savor the feel of Tanner's mouth against hers, confident in the knowledge that she could return for more anytime, anywhere for the rest of her life.

Kathleen ended the kiss with a final nip. Her hands

hooked around his neck, her head on his chest as she eyed the airplane just across the tarmac. Deliciously wicked intent fired inside her.

She stepped out of his embrace and patted along her jacket, then her skirt until Tanner finally asked, "What are you doing?"

"This uniform doesn't have enough pockets. I seem to have forgotten my UCMJ manual."

"And that's a problem because…?"

"I can't look up whether it's against regs for us to climb into that plane over there so you can jump me."

A slow smile kicked that dimple into his face again, a grin guaranteed to flutter her heart for at least another fifty years. "The way I understand that reg, Captain O'Connell, we're in the clear, since we're just taking cover from an imminent rainstorm."

Kathleen stared up into the cloudless night sky, but didn't bother contradicting him. After all, rain was always imminent in Charleston. Tanner had taught her she could bend the rules on occasion without compromising her principles. "Come on, hotshot. I'll race you to the airplane. Winner gets to jump the loser."

Tanner clasped her hand in his. "Athena, the way I read that one, it's a team effort where we're both going to come out winners."

Epilogue

Tanner slung his helmet bag on the counter and opened the refrigerator. Light sliced through the darkened kitchen, adding just enough illumination for him to find a postflight snack. No need to turn on the overhead and risk waking Kathleen.

Sleep was a precious commodity with a newborn in the house.

Rummaging through the shelves, he opted for a soda before bumping the door shut with his hip. Leftover adrenaline had him too pumped for sleep just yet. Even on a routine training mission, he still enjoyed every damn minute in that left seat. Thanks to the tender—and diligent—care of his resident flight surgeon, Tanner's back problems were a thing of the past.

As were any ghosts. Kathleen had laid those to rest for him, as well. He liked to think he'd done the same for her. The birth of their daughter a few weeks ago had solidified an already strong marriage.

Yeah, they made a top-notch team.

Resting a hip against the counter by the nursery monitor, Tanner chugged back his drink and listened for sounds of his daughter breathing. A never-ending thrill.

Low static crackled from the receiver, then the slow creak of a rocking chair eased over the airwaves, followed by Kathleen's voice. "Hey, sweet baby, still not sleepy, huh? That's okay. There's nothing I'd rather do right now than hang out with you."

Her whiskey-warm tones dive-bombed his senses with just as much power as they had thirteen years ago—a predictable, yet undeniably exciting rush, even after a year of marriage. The date marked a year exactly. As well as exactly six weeks after their daughter's birth. Definite cause for celebration.

Anticipation charged through him full throttle.

Tanner pitched his can into the recycling bin, eager to see Kathleen and the baby, but unable to resist eavesdropping just a little while longer.

"We're both gonna nap tomorrow with your daddy, since he has the day off. Deal? Deal." The steady creak of the rocking chair echoed its soothing song. "For now it's just us girls, Tara, baby. So let's talk. There're so many things to dream about, your first words, first day at school, first date."

He quirked a brow at the monitor. Nuns don't date.

"The world's wide open, my girl," Kathleen crooned. "You can be whatever you want. Doctor or circus clown. Your call. Of course, your daddy may have heart failure if you opt for the high-wire acrobat stint. But I have it on good authority he's a mighty fine spotter."

Smiling, Tanner scooped up the nursery monitor and clicked the two-way button to join in the late-night chat with his family.

Holding the monitor up to his mouth, he donned his best

in-flight radio voice as he left the kitchen. "This is COHO two zero requesting a flight surgeon to meet me at the parking area. Do you read me, Athena? Over."

A husky chuckle sounded before she answered. "Affirmative, COHO, but I'm currently engaged in refueling operations with our little copilot. Request you reroute and meet me in the nursery."

"Roger that, Athena." Tanner rounded the corner, making tracks for the slim band of light peeking from the baby's room. "Changing course to join formation."

He closed the last ten steps in seconds, nudging the door with his toe. The open door framed Kathleen sitting in a white rocker. Her red hair fluffed, sleep-ruffled around her face, her green satin nightshirt unbuttoned. A tiny pink fist rested against the curve of her breast as Kathleen nursed their daughter. Contentment shone from her, warming the room, warming him.

How could she have ever doubted herself? Kathleen had tackled motherhood with all the study and perfection she did everything else. Those maternal instincts had kicked in the minute the stick turned blue. The woman was unconquerable.

Tara was one lucky little girl. And he was one lucky husband. "Happy Anniversary."

"It certainly is." Kathleen smiled, as at home in a nursery as she was on a flight line or in the operating room. No stereotyping for her daughter, Kathleen had insisted on pale-blue walls with puffy clouds. Tiny angels wearing pink ribbons grinned from those clouds, one looking remarkably like his sister.

An answering grin tugged at his face. Tanner pushed away from the door and crossed to Kathleen. Leaning, he dropped a kiss on Kathleen's mouth, then on Tara's tufts of red hair. "Hey, princess."

Tara turned to the sound of his voice. What an incredible

rush, that sweet recognition. Better than outrunning a MIG fighter jet. He loved the way she knew him. He loved her. And her mama.

Sinking to the floor beside Kathleen, Tanner let his head fall to rest on her knee. Best seat in the house.

Kathleen feathered gentle fingers over his brow. "Good flight?"

"Routine. But, yeah, good. Breaking in a new copilot. You know how they are."

"That I do." She squeezed his shoulder. "Love you."

He returned the words with as much ease as she'd delivered them. "Love you, too."

Kathleen draped a rag over Tanner's shoulder and transferred Tara into his waiting hands. "Your turn, hotshot. Do you have the jet?"

"Yes, ma'am, I've got the jet." Tanner cradled Tara in his hands with a newly acquired confidence. He brought Tara to his shoulder and patted her tiny back until she burped. "Oh, yeah, a new little crew dog in the making."

Both hands securing his daughter, Tanner rose to set her down for the night. Side by side he and Kathleen watched their daughter, Tanner smoothing a hand along her back until her lashes fluttered, opened, then settled closed. For countless minutes longer they stood still and watched.

"Tanner," Kathleen whispered.

"Yeah, Kathleen?"

"Race you to the bedroom."

Excitement kicked right back into overdrive within him. "Winner gets to be jumped."

"Ready, set…" She sprinted ahead, making it all the way to the hall before he caught her, scooping her up.

"Hey, Athena, that was cheating."

"Just bending the rules in my favor to keep you on your toes, hotshot. Wouldn't want to become too predictable."

"Not a chance of that."

Clothes flew, landing in haphazard piles. His flight suit made one hell of a great resting place for mint-green panties.

He lowered her to the bed before sliding across the mattress beside her. ''Have I told you lately how much I love every unpredictable inch of you—just the way you are?''

''As a matter of fact you have, but I could always use a reminder.''

Kathleen snagged the rumpled bedspread and whipped it over them. Tanner tucked his wife to his chest and kissed her until sighs and moans swirled in their tented darkness. Along with contentment, heat and love. And, oh yeah, more heat....

There was nothing he enjoyed more than taking cover for an uninterrupted hour with Major Kathleen O'Connell-Bennett.

*   *   *   *   *

Don't miss Zach's story,
coming in January 2003,
as Catherine Mann's
WINGMEN WARRIORS
series continues
in Silhouette Intimate Moments.

INTIMATE MOMENTS™

presents:

Romancing the Crown

With the help of their powerful allies, the royal family of Montebello is determined to restore their heir to the throne. But their quest is not without danger—or passion!

Available in December 2002, the exciting conclusion to this year of royal romance: THE PRINCE'S WEDDING by Justine Davis (IM #1190)

When Prince Lucas Sebastiani discovered he was a father, he was determined to reunite his royal family. But would new mother Jessica Chambers accept the prince's proposal without a word of love?

This exciting series continues throughout the year with these fabulous titles:

Available only from Silhouette Intimate Moments at your favorite retail outlet.

Where love comes alive™

Visit Silhouette at www.eHarlequin.com

SIMRC12

eHARLEQUIN.com

community | membership

buy books | authors | online reads | magazine | learn to write

buy books

Your one-stop shop for great reads at great prices. We have all your favorite Harlequin, Silhouette, MIRA and Steeple Hill books, as well as a host of other bestsellers in Other Romances. Discover a wide array of new releases, bargains and hard-to-find books today!

learn to write

Become the writer you always knew you could be: get tips and tools on how to craft the perfect romance novel and have your work critiqued by professional experts in romance fiction. Follow your dream now!

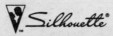

V *Silhouette*®

Where love comes alive™—online...

SINTLTW

If you enjoyed what you just read,
then we've got an offer you can't resist!

Take 2 bestselling love stories FREE!

Plus get a FREE surprise gift!

Clip this page and mail it to Silhouette Reader Service™

IN U.S.A.	IN CANADA
3010 Walden Ave.	P.O. Box 609
P.O. Box 1867	Fort Erie, Ontario
Buffalo, N.Y. 14240-1867	L2A 5X3

YES! Please send me 2 free Silhouette Intimate Moments® novels and my free surprise gift. After receiving them, if I don't wish to receive anymore, I can return the shipping statement marked cancel. If I don't cancel, I will receive 6 brand-new novels every month, before they're available in stores! In the U.S.A., bill me at the bargain price of $3.99 plus 25¢ shipping and handling per book and applicable sales tax, if any*. In Canada, bill me at the bargain price of $4.74 plus 25¢ shipping and handling per book and applicable taxes**. That's the complete price and a savings of at least 10% off the cover prices—what a great deal! I understand that accepting the 2 free books and gift places me under no obligation ever to buy any books. I can always return a shipment and cancel at any time. Even if I never buy another book from Silhouette, the 2 free books and gift are mine to keep forever.

245 SDN DNUV
345 SDN DNUW

Name	(PLEASE PRINT)	
Address	Apt.#	
City	State/Prov.	Zip/Postal Code

* Terms and prices subject to change without notice. Sales tax applicable in N.Y.
** Canadian residents will be charged applicable provincial taxes and GST.
   All orders subject to approval. Offer limited to one per household and not valid to
   current Silhouette Intimate Moments® subscribers.
® are registered trademarks of Harlequin Books S.A., used under license.

INMOM02   ©1998 Harlequin Enterprises Limited

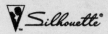

COMING NEXT MONTH

SIMCNM1102